# Trained

# By

# Vampires

## Joy Mosby

Trained by Vampires

2nd Edition

Editor: Leah Aldrich

Ruby Gulch Enterprises LLC

P.O. Box 64

Craig, CO 81626

This is a work of fiction. Names, characters, places, and incidents either are the product of the author's imaginations or are used fictitiously.
Any resemblance to actual persons, living or dead, business establishments, events or locales is entirely coincidental.

*For Mikey,*
*"All that I am*
*All that I ever was*
*Is here in your perfect eyes"*
*- Snow Patrol*

# CHAPTER 1

I waited outside the arrivals terminal at Ben Epps Airport in Athens, Greece, for the shuttle to the hotel I had booked a few minutes after getting off the plane. I fingered the phone in my pocket, willing it to ring and wishing I knew where Vince was. There was no way the 'evil ones' beat me here, even if they had known where I was going. But Vince knew. He could have found a way to meet me here or be arriving shortly, unless the 'evil ones' had done something horrible to him. I shivered and rubbed my arms, just thinking about them made my skin crawl.

The shuttle stopped in front of me a minute later, it was early in the morning, and it was empty except for the driver. "Kalimera," he said, after opening the door and coming down the stairs looking for my luggage.

"Good morning," I said, thinking I was responding in kind to his salutation.

"Where is your luggage?" he asked, switching to broken English.

Fumbling for an excuse. "It was lost." This man did not need to know I had been forced to leave everything I owned at the 'evil ones" villa in order to escape from them.

"I am sorry," he said, going back up the steps and taking his seat. "You look tired; let's get you to your hotel."

"Thank you." I climbed the stairs and took the seat behind the driver. I let out a long breath and looked out the window. It was still dark, and even though the past twenty-four hours had been hell, a little jolt of excitement passed through me when I thought about where I was. My life had changed so much in the past week it was hard to believe I was alive, let alone in Greece.

Who would have thought leaving my boyfriend would lead me down a road I could never imagine? After leaving Mark, I began to hear voices in my head. They were not a figment of my imagination either. They were vampire voices. I had been manipulated by one, mortally wounded by another, and saved by a different one. I found out I am the prophesized savior of the vampire race, 'The One', though what they needed saving from is beyond me. I knew next to nothing about what it meant, but I had a flash drive in my wallet and it contained all of the information Vince, the vampire who saved me from slavery, had. I was exhausted, but the first thing I wanted to do was see what was on the drive and find out what being 'The One' meant.

"Here we are," the driver said as he pulled up to the hotel entrance and stopped the shuttle.

I got up and went to the head of the stairs. "Thank you," I said before going down the stairs and off the bus.

"Paracalo."

I went through the door of the hotel to the front desk where a tired-looking older man sat in a crumpled suit that looked like it had been slept in.

"Hi, my name is Mary Sims. I just made a reservation for a room." I tried to speak slowly, praying the man understood English. My name is not really Mary Sims it is Katie Hunter. Mary is the identity Vince set up for me to keep the 'evil ones' from finding me.

"Yes, you talked to me. I just need your passport and credit card." He looked down at a monitor and started clicking a computer mouse. "How long will you be staying with us?"

I hesitated at the question. I wanted to stay in Athens and wait for Vince, but every day I stayed increased the risk of the 'evil ones' finding me. Vince would be able to track my movements by the credit card he gave me. He would know how to find me. "Just tonight," I said, digging in my wallet and giving him my passport and credit card.

"Very good," the man said, entering my information into the computer. "Where are you going from here?"

"I'm not sure yet." Even if I had known, there was no way I going to tell this guy. It would be too easy for the 'evil ones' to track me. "Do you have a computer I could use?"

"We have a guest computer," he said, pulling out a floorplan and showing me how to get there. "You will need to use your room key to access the room."

"Thank you," I said, signing the credit card slip and taking the key he gave me.

"Sleep well Ms. Sims."

When I reached the locked door outside the computer room, I slid my key into the door, went inside and sat down at the computer. Letting out a deep breath I plugged the flash drive into the USB port and waited for the computer to read the content of the drive. My leg bounced up and down impatiently as the old machine whirled and spun. Finally, a window popped up with a document icon on it. I clicked on it and got an error message in Greek. I could not read it, but based on the operating system, I guessed the computer could not

3

open the document with the software on the machine.

Frustrated I opened the internet browser and tried to open the document with a program online but the internet was so slow it kept timing out. After twenty minutes of failure, I gave up, blinking back tears. I needed sleep. I would find a computer the next day.

I went up to my room and opened the door. It was a standard room with a queen size bed. Everything about the room was typical with pastel color tones of tan, pink and blue. There was a desk in the corner with a chair, and a television sat on top of a dresser.

I checked the closet, bathroom, and under the bed to ensure no one was in the room with me. I stripped off my clothes and went into the bathroom. Since I did not have any other clothes, I washed my panties in the sink with the hand soap provided by the hotel and hung them out to dry on the towel rack.

Looking in the mirror, I pulled back the gauze on my neck, where one of the 'evil ones' had taken a chunk out of me two nights ago. The wound was gone. I touched the angry looking, red puckered skin where the stitches had been the night before. How had I healed so quickly? I had stitches before, when I shut a car door on my hand and it took weeks to heal. My hand was better too. I bruised it when I punched first my cheating ex-boyfriend, then one of the 'evil ones' in self-defense. When had that happened? I tried to think back to the last time it hurt. It was before we left Vince's house in San Sebastian.

Was this one of my new powers? Was I able to heal quicker than I used to? It had to have something to do with my mom and being 'The One'. As much as I thought this business with the prophecy was a myth, things kept happening to me that made me want to believe it might be true. I shook myself. Why would I be 'The One'? It still did not add up for me. Without any answers, I shrugged and got into the shower.

I took a long hot shower and cried the whole time. I cried for the loss of my former life. I cried for the pain my disappearing would cause my parents and friends. I cried at the pain I had suffered in the past forty-eight hours. I cried for Vince, wanting him to be alright. Would he find me soon? Would he change me into a vampire even though I was not sure what I wanted? Did I have a choice? He thought I was 'The One' after all, and my destiny was to become a vampire.

After I cried myself out, and left with more questions than answers, I went to bed hoping I would be able to leave all the bad thoughts behind and get some sleep. The drapes were pulled, the do-not-disturb sign was on the door, and the deadbolt and the chain were engaged. I made sure the ringer on my cell phone was on and the volume was turned all the way up in case Vince tried to call me. I set my alarm clock for nine in the morning and I went to sleep, thinking I was as safe as I could be for the night.

# CHAPTER 2

Miguel paced around his office. How could he have let this happen? She was gone, and he had no way of knowing where she went. He tried to track down the people at the airport who helped her, but by the time his episode, as he liked to call it, was over they were gone. He could not even find out her assumed name. He tried to hack into the security video at the airport but it was too good. He even tried to bribe the security guards to let him look. It was annoying that he could not buy the airport as he could the rest of the city. The airport was property of the state, and he could not use his influence to get what he needed from them.

He was not really sure what happened while he was trying to get to Katie at the security checkpoint. He had been trying to stop her with the pain from the slave bond, but it backfired. If he was honest with himself, it was almost as if she had thrown the pain back at him. Vampires did not have seizures; they were never afflicted with pain, unless, it was inflicted by brute force. She must have removed the slave bond, but how? He had never heard of a human being able to remove one before, unless, she had been changed from his slave to another's. She was 'The One' though; maybe being able to remove it was one of her powers. He would probably never know.

Why were Vince and Katie at the airport at the same time?

Was she with Vince the entire time? Were they traveling together? Antonio said he only took Vince to the airport, but it seemed like something had changed with the boy. He looked nervous and flighty. Almost like Antonio was no longer his slave. Miguel was too upset to worry about it when he gave his report. He sent Antonio on his way before he thought about what was going on.

Miguel beat his hand against the wall. Why had he banished Vince? His best friend was gone, all because of jealousy. He still could not believe Vince took Katie to the hospital and did not change her, but she was not at the hospital. She had to have help from someone. It could not have been Vince. Miguel had gone to his house and there was no trace of Katie there. Lolita had walked the halls and had not detected anything. Did Vince somehow hide Katie's amazing scent? With Vince gone he could check for himself.

Without another thought, he left his office and went to the garage. Normally he would have Theodore drive him where he wanted to go, but tonight he wanted to be by himself. He needed to think, he needed a plan to find Katie. He did not know what he would do when he found her, but he would take one step at a time.

The feel of the Aston Martin's engine growling in front him brought a smile to his lips that he had not had in the past forty-eight hours. He tore out of the garage barely slowing down as he came to the gate. It had been too long since he had been behind the wheel. He missed controlling the beast, as its tires squealed, trying to find purchase around the switchbacks leading down the hill. He slowed when he got to town, he did not want to deal with the humans and their driving, but causing an accident would be even worse.

The gate to Vince's villa was closed as he approached it, but he no longer cared what his onetime friend would think of him as he rammed his car through. As much as he loved the high gloss silver paint of the car, he wanted to look around Vince's home more.

Parking his car at the front door, he got out to see if the house was locked. Of course it was, but he would not let the lock stop him. He kicked the door until it splintered away from its frame. As soon as he stepped inside he smelled it. Lilac and woman, Katie had been here. How had they missed her smell? Infuriated, Miguel raced down the hall following the aroma. He stopped outside a bedroom before moving inside. The room was saturated with the smell of Katie.

It was all Vince's fault, Miguel thought. If Vince had come clean with him from the start, he would not be in this situation. If he had told him about the tattoo marking her side, he would not have tried to make her his slave. He would have seduced her and treated her like the queen she was meant to be.

He had to do something. Had to get back at Vince for what he had done. But how? Vince was gone with a new name and identity. Knowing his longtime friend, it would take years to track them down. What had he said a few days ago? He was moving his money around because of a 'tip'. Vince must have been planning to escape with Katie for days. How could he have been blind to Vince's true allegiance? Now that he thought about it, Vince only stayed in San Sebastian as long as he did to be there when 'The One' showed up, not because of his friendship with Miguel. Vince had been planning to take 'The One' from the beginning. Miguel cursed himself for blindly believing in the friendship Vince offered so many years before.

He went to the bar in Vince's living room, found a towel and tore it into strips before taking the lids off the bottles of liquor. He shoved the strips of towel down the mouths of the bottles. Starting at the back of the house, he lit the strips on fire and threw the bottles at the walls. He slowly, methodically walked through the house making sure nothing would be left of the home Vince loved.

With the house engulfed in flames he got back into his car and pulled away to watch the flames consume the home of his newfound enemy from a safe distance. When the sirens from the firetrucks grew near he drove home feeling better. At least he was able to destroy something of Vince's, no matter how small.

He pulled into the garage at the villa just before the sun came over the horizon. He wanted to feel happy about destroying something of Vince's, but he was still lost to the rage of losing Katie. He walked toward his office to begin searching for them on his computer when Lolita cornered him outside the office door.

"What have you done little brother?"

"What needed to be done. Vince betrayed me; I had to make a statement for everyone else." He moved around her and entered his office with her on his heels.

"What do you mean? Did he leave with Katie?"

"I had to check. I know we checked his house earlier and found no trace of her, but something was not sitting right with me so I went back. As soon as I walked in the front door, I could smell her. Vince stole her from us." He went to the chair behind the desk and sat down. "I had to hurt him, and lighting his house on fire was the only thing I could think of."

"I'm sorry Vince betrayed you, but we have more immediate concerns to worry about." Lolita gracefully sat down in the chair opposite of Miguel's. "You didn't wait for the fire department to put out the fire?"

"No, it was too close to dawn. Why?"

"The wind changed direction, our city is on fire."

Lolita took her phone out of her pocket and pulled up the footage of the fire now engulfing most of San Sebastian.

Miguel put his head in his hands. "She was sent here to save me," he murmured, rubbing his eyes but not looking up. "She failed. Look what I have done."

"Miguelito, we all make mistakes." Lolita rested her hand on his shoulder. "Now is the time to plan. We need to find her and destroy her before she controls us all."

"Why would I want to kill her, Lolita?" Miguel looked up from his hands and met her eyes. "She is to be our savior. It's my fault she's not here, not hers."

"What do we need to be saved from?" Lolita asked, throwing her hands up in the air. "We have everything we could ever want." She waved her hands around to indicate their lavish lifestyle.

"I don't know, but I know she's going to find a way to save us from it. I have to find her and make her understand that I didn't want any of this to happen." Miguel turned to his monitor.

"Not all prophecies come true," Lolita purred, trying to sound calm and loving. She would do anything to change the obsession Miguel had with this girl. "Imagine the power we could have if we made her our slave. We could buy Versailles, we could live like Henry and Marie, do you remember how much fun we had when we called on them? We could rule Europe and eventually the world. We could have everything our hearts desire; bring the world to its knees for us."

Miguel looked away from his computer and rolled his eyes at her. She understood nothing. "Don't you see Lolita? If Katie doesn't save us we are all going to die and spend the afterlife being tortured in Tartarus. I don't want to die. With what we have already done to her, I can only beg her for leniency. I'm sure she wants both of us dead."

"I never understood Father's obsession with a cult that no longer applied to the world we live in. I expected your interest in it would fade when he met the sun." She crossed one leg over the other realizing she would never turn him to her side. "I was wrong, but at least I only have to listen to one of you yammering on about it. I should have gotten rid of you the same way I got rid of him."

Miguel jumped to his feet, flew over the desk, and grabbed the front of Lolita's blouse pulling her toward him until only a thin piece of paper could slide between their noses. "What did you do to Father?" he bellowed at her.

Lolita wrapped her hands around Miguel's arms and squeezed. "I couldn't take listening to him anymore. After you two got back from Delos all he did was talk about the prophecy, and how she would come here, to our home and save us all." She pried Miguel's hand off her and pushed her chair back to give herself room to stand up. She walked toward the door trying to smooth the wrinkles out of her blouse. "I drugged him then tied him to a tree facing east. It was too bad the drugs wore off before he died. His screams interrupted my dinner." She turned and inspected her manicure. "I am the strongest female vampire, Miguel. I will not let some little bitch take that from me."

"I will let you live for now Lolita." Miguel walked back to his chair. "But know it is only because I would have died shortly after you found me. If you know what is good for you, disappear. Leave Katie alone, and never speak to me again or you will join Father in the afterlife."

Lolita's mouth dropped open in astonishment for a second before she started speaking. "I will do as I will, brother. You should know better than anyone not to get on my bad side. I'm going to give you some time to calm down. I will leave at dusk. When you have outgrown this fantasy and are ready to see her as the threat she is, you know how to get in touch with me." She stomped to the door and slammed it on her way out.

# CHAPTER 3

Vince watched the plane take off into the night heading toward Greece. He slammed his hand against the wall he was leaning against. He only missed the plane by minutes. He hoped Katie would be alright on her own. He made his way to the ticket booth in the Madrid airport to see if there was another flight to Athens he could take before the sun came up.

"I need to be in Athens by four in the morning their time," Vince said to the agent, giving her his ticket for his missed flight. "Is there anything you can do?"

"Let me see, Señor," she said, clicking away on her computer. Vince pulled his phone out of his pocket. He wanted to call Katie and tell her he was trying to get to her, but her phone was off and there was no voicemail service attached to the phone. He could text her but, knowing her, she would think Miguel had found her and was looking for her. He did not program his number into her phone on purpose. If one of them ended up with Miguel or Lolita, he did not want Katie tied to him in any way. He would try to call her after her flight landed.

"I'm sorry, Señor, the next flight for Athens does not leave until eight fifteen tomorrow morning."

"That will not work." He cringed inwardly. Katie was going to be on her own for over twenty-four hours. Could she keep herself

15

safe in a town where she knew no one and did not speak the language? "When does the first flight leave tomorrow evening? My business requires me to be available by phone from five am to seven pm," Vince said, giving his standard response as to why he could not travel during daylight hours.

"There is one leaving at seven-oh-five, will that work?"

# CHAPTER 4

Lolita shut the blind on the window as soon as the plane took off from San Sebastian. She could hardly believe Miguel banished her. The city was hers long before it had ever been his, and it was only his because she gave it to him after she took care of Phillip. She was so tired of hearing about the prophecy and, 'The One' who would show up in their little town and change the world. All vampires would bow down to this human. Lolita bowed to no women and few men. Some prophesied girl was not going to change her status in the world.

She had spent years ensuring she was the strongest female vampire in Europe. A hundred years ago, vampires did not make strong female vampires on purpose. A female needed to be seen not heard; protected and cherished. The feminist movement changed everything; strong female vampires began to pop up all over Europe. She hated it. They were the reason why she traveled so much. When she heard of a female vampire taking over a city she would take care of the problem. She liked to end their lives herself, but if they were blatant with their power she would hire a human to kill them. If a mere human could take down a vampire, they were not as strong as they claimed. Death by a human made an example for any vampire who thought they were stronger than she was. It helped keep the vampires of Europe in their place.

With 'The One' finally making an appearance it was time to get her house in order. Over the years, she had come up with many plans to take care of 'The One' if she ever arrived, but as time went by it seemed less and less likely she would ever make an appearance. It was time to dust off the plans she had made.

She would always have Miguel's ear and if he had control of Katie . . . Lolita had been so close to having them both. Her first plan failed, but she never expected it to work. Making her Miguel's slave then turning her would have worked out nicely, but Katie was smarter than Lolita thought.

It was time to find her and kill her. She regretted making Miguel so mad, now she would not have his knowledge of the prophecy. She should have paid better attention when her father and Miguel talked about it. Miguel was trying to track Katie down and he would not tell her where he was looking. If he did find Katie, she would be stupid to take him back. He raped her after all. Lolita smiled to herself, it had been so easy to plant the thought in Miguel's head.

"Katie's headstrong; she needs to be taken down a few rungs. She needs to know who she belongs to."

"How? If I hurt her with the bond she will know everything has been a lie."

"How have men made women come to heel for centuries? Force her to do your will."

He did not like the idea, but he was losing Katie and he could not bear the thought of letting her go. Raping her let her know who she belonged to.

Well, Lolita thought to herself, the best laid plans

18

and all. She was on her own once again. She liked not having to depend on anyone else for help. She always took care of herself anyway.

She knew how to please men. Born by a whore and growing up in a whorehouse, she learned early on how to keep a man coming back for more. She spent many nights being abused by them, but as they pounded into her for the small amount of money she made she learned and dreamed. She was meant to be more than a cheap whore in a soldier's town. Philip had been the best seduction of her life.

She shook herself out of her thoughts of long ago and made herself think of the present. How was she going to find Katie? She had copies of everything Miguel had found on her. Her parents would be an easy way to lure her out, but they were in America and she hated Americans. The girl was dumb, but not dumb enough to go home. There would be little purpose of traveling all the way there, but Lolita would keep the idea in the back of her mind just in case she could not find another way to get to her.

She needed to find Katie and figure out how to get to her without Vince getting in the way. Vince had always been a thorn in her side. He never trusted her. She tried to seduce him once, but he would have none of it and from what Miguel told her, Katie was with Vince. If anyone knew how to disappear, it was him.

The easiest thing for Lolita to do would be to take a hit out on Katie, but if word got around that she could not take care of a human on her own, she would lose credibility. What she really needed to do was find out where Katie was, then she could take care of the little bitch herself.

She would put out an information only bulletin. Anyone who had information on where Katie was could claim a reward of sorts. There were always young, greedy vampires trying to get a jump start on their fortune. They wanted to live like the old ones, but they did not understand how much time and patience it took to build up that kind of wealth.

Before Lolita left the city, she searched high and low for Antonio. He would be able to tell her where Vince went. Unfortunately, she could not find him. The manager of the hotel where he worked told her, that he moved out of the city and no one knew where he had gone. She began an internet search to try to track him down. Very few people could avoid the internet nowadays. It made tracking people down so much easier. He had not touched his social media accounts in weeks, but she found his résumé and it told her everything she needed to know. He was working the day shift at a hotel in Madrid. It appeared he was avoiding vampires. She would have to call on him and see what she could find out.

At least she had better luck finding Antonio then she did trying to trace Katie. She hacked Katie's accounts before she left Miguel's, only to find she had not been online for the past three days. She placed trackers on her email and social media pages just in case Katie logged in to them.

Lolita reclined her seat and closed her eyes. She needed to rest while she could. She would be busy when she landed in Madrid.

# CHAPTER 5

I woke up to the alarm clock, covered in sweat with my heart racing. The nightmare had been brutal, I was in the shower and the 'evil one' was behind me forcing me again. I tried to get away from him, but there was nothing I could do.

"Bastard," I yelled at the empty room. I had gotten away from Miguel, one of the 'evil ones', but the memories he left me with were going to haunt me for who knew how long. I had to shake it off; I had too much to do. I could not spend the day drowning in misery over what I let happen.

I got up and checked my phone to see if there was any word from Vince. I slouched when I saw there were no missed calls. I looked longingly at the bed. Four hours was not enough sleep but I had to get moving. I took another shower, used the disposable toothbrush and comb the hotel offered, and I got dressed wearing the dirty clothes Vince gave me the day before. He had to cut off the clothes I had been wearing after Lolita, the other 'evil one', took a chunk out of my neck. I stuck my phone in the front pocket of my jeans, and made sure I had my travel wallet before I left the room.

In the lobby, I sat down at the hotel's complimentary breakfast and tried to come up with a plan. Vince told me he wanted me to see my mother's temple. I needed to figure out who she was before I found out where I needed to go. The flash drive was my biggest problem. I needed a computer with a program to open the file. I thought about finding a cyber café, it might work on one of their computers, but there were always so many people milling around and I wanted privacy. I needed clean clothes too. I looked at the black credit card sticking out of my wallet. I could buy a computer and clothes, but I did not know how I would ever repay Vince. Unfortunately, I did not see another way to figure out where I needed to go and stay safe at the same time. Decision made, I finished my breakfast and went to hail a cab to take me to a shopping center.

Shopping for electronics in a country like Greece is a very confusing experience. While the salesman who helped me spoke a little bit of English it took much longer then it needed to. I bought the cheapest computer with the program I needed included. It was still more money than I wanted to spend, but I did not have much of a choice. I would find some way to pay Vince back.

I found a quiet corner near the food court and spent what felt like an hour resetting the language on the computer to English. With a deep breath, I plugged the flash drive in and crossed my fingers praying I would be able to view the document this time. It opened quickly and I blew out a breath.

I pushed the play button and realized right away that I was going to need earbuds. Vince had recorded a commentary to go with the presentation and I did not want anyone to overhear it. I packed everything up, went back to the electronics store and bought a pair of earbuds. I returned to my corner, thankful it was still unoccupied, set the laptop on the table, and plugged in my new earbuds.

After pushing play, a screen popped up saying: "The Origin Myth of the Vampire," Vince's voice began to narrate while screens with ancient paintings and tombs began to scroll by.

"During the War of the Titans, after Zeus and his siblings overthrew Kronos, Zeus chased down the rest of the Titans. Asteria, the Titan of the stars, prophecy, and dreams, turned into a quail and flew into the ocean to escape Zeus's advances. Needing a place to hide, she asked Poseidon for permission to become an island in order to hide from Zeus. He granted her request, and she became the island now known as Delos.

"Asteria's sister, Leto, begged Asteria to allow her to give birth to her children, Apollo and Artemis, on Delos. She promised Asteria temples would be built on the land and their worshippers would keep her company. Over time Asteria allowed many gods and goddesses to erect temples on her ground and many Greeks made a pilgrimage to the island to pay homage to the Gods whose temples were located there.

"Even though she turned herself into an island she still sent her essence out into the world. It saddened her to see the wars men fought over land because of a birthright or where they were buried. There was a lack of sanctity of life. She did not want her island to become covered in the blood of man for the right to claim her. She sent a proclamation to her oracle demanding no one should die, nor woman give birth on the island and demanded that all of the dead who were buried there be removed. Her goal was to keep herself safe from the wars and death.

"Everyone abided by this sanction until one night during a Dionysus festival. One of the pilgrims, Tadeas, drunk with wine climbed onto the roof of Dionysus's temple to look at the stars. He lost his balance and fell to his death.

"Asteria was furious at Dionysus for allowing the man to die on her soil. She went to him demanding reparations for violating her law. Dionysus was too drunk to care and dismissed her.

"She decided to punish Dionysus for allowing Tadeas to die in her realm by bringing him back to life. Enlisting help from her daughter, Hecate, the goddess of witchcraft. They brought Tadeas back to life, but not as a human, as an animal who could only survive by drinking the blood of humans.

"It took three days to complete the ritual, and Tadeas awoke mad with bloodlust. He went back to the Dionysus festival, and massacred everyone in attendance. Asteria found him in the middle of the bodies now empty of blood and explained his new life.

"He could eat all the food he wanted and drink all of the wine he longed for, but he would never feel satisfaction or gain nourishment from them. He would wither and grow weak, but he would never die. The blood of man was the only nourishment Tadeas would be able to survive on. He would crave blood until the day he killed all those he loved. Cursed to live out his existence in the dark of night, with only the stars to keep him company.

"Not believing he would have to spend his existence in the dark of night he took a boat to the closest island, Mykonos, and drank from humans until the sun rose. As the rays of the sun landed on his skin, Tadeas started to smoke and burn. He did the only thing he could think of to protect himself; he dug a hole in the ground and covered himself with dirt. He longed for death to ease his pain, but he could not bring himself to suffer more of the sun's rays.

"Tadeas did not return to Delos for many years. It is

said he went from island to island trying to quench his need for blood. In sane moments, he tried to find an honorable way to die, but no matter how many times he was stabbed, beaten, or drowned he would always come back.

"Wanting nothing more than to die an honorable death, he went back to Delos to try to persuade Asteria to help him. He devoted himself completely to the Goddess. He built a temple and kept it free from wear and tear thinking she would look kindly on his piety and grant him a favor. After years of devotion, she came to him to see what boon he would ask.

"Tadeas explained he was lonely, he only wished for more of his kind and a way to die honorably. When his time came, he wanted to take the boat over the River Stix to Hades, and not end up in Tartarus.

"Asteria thought about his request and came back with an idea. She would show him her necromancy then he would be free to create others like him with one condition: All of his kind must worship her for all time. Tadeas promised this, and Asteria showed him how to create vampires. They would be sterile, unable to beget their own brood the way humans do, but he would no longer be alone. Then she changed the magic to allow her creations to have an honorable death. If they were decapitated or were stabbed in the heart during battle, they would be allowed to cross the River Stix and enter Hades.

"Tadeas went on to create many vampires. He was our leader, or so I have been told, for many centuries. He made the laws we live by and taught us the way of the Goddess. He disappeared long before my time and no one has seen or heard from him in a millennium. His stories are still told and his necromancy is still passed down from vampire to vampire."

The next slide on the screen said, "Asteria's Prophecy."

"The prophecy was made by Asteria's Oracle on the island of Delos when Christianity started gaining ground," Vince's voice went on. "One of Tadeas's vampires, who had a fetish for young girls, found a girl around ten years old who had the gift of prophecy. She prophesized that he would die soon and spend the afterlife in Tartarus for the sins he committed against her. This enraged him. He beat her severely then changed her into a vampire. Unfortunately, the change was unable to heal the damage he did to her mind.

"When she was found her maker was tied to a stake and left for the sun. Tadeas took the girl in and made her the Oracle. The brain damage made it impossible to teach her anything new and she was only partly literate to start with. Which is why translating the prophecy has been difficult since its inception. The Oracle was in a trance when she wrote it down and created the tapestry. When she was asked about it later, she could not remember or read what she wrote.

"The best translation I have found reads:

"Those of my begotten who have forgotten me will be made to heal by a woman bearing my mark.
She will be found on the east shores of the great ocean beyond the Pillars of Hercules, in a protected bay.
None will be able to deceive her, as she will be able to listen to what is in the hearts of my creation.
Her powers will manifest as her knowledge of her kind grows.
Those who try to enslave her will reap the recompense of her exasperation.

26

The one who mentors her will be endowed with an accolade from the chosen one.

The one who changes her will be her consort and reign at her side.

She will bring my creation back into the fold."

"Others of our kind have translated it differently over the ages; I think mostly to suit their own desires. The one Miguel believes in is similar to this translation except for the line, 'Those that try to enslave her will reap the recompense of her exasperation,' was translated, as 'The one who enslaves her will bend her to his will.' This is why he tried to turn you into a slave.

"If we are separated either by force or by your choice, go to Delos and seek out the disciples of Asteria. Show them your tattoo and they will show you everything they have about The Prophecy," he said as his face came up on the screen. "They will try and keep you safe but do not trust them too much. They will see you as 'The One', but they might treat you as an object and not a human. Good luck Katie, wherever I am I will think of you and pray for your safety," Vince said and I watched him hit a button on the keyboard ending the video.

I closed the laptop and looked around. Vince's program and voice had sucked me in. I forgot I was sitting in a shopping center in the middle of Athens. I was amazed Vince had given me the information not knowing if I would want his help or not. The fact that he gave it to me without any assurance that I wanted his help made me believe he wanted me safe. He did not care how it happened or if he would be at my side. I also wondered if he had not changed his mind about helping me. It could be the reason why he had not caught up with me yet. I was going to drive myself crazy wondering what happened to Vince. I wish he would have given me his phone number, then I could check on him. I just needed to know what was going on.

My stomach growled. I needed to eat. I put my laptop back in the bag and went to get something to eat. I felt more myself after food and caffeine. I was still scared to be on my own, but this was something I had to do. I wanted to stay away from vampires, but if I did not go to Delos, I would spend the rest of my life wondering what I would have found there. I also wanted to be prepared in case another vampire found me. I wanted to make sure I could feel them before they noticed me. I wanted time to run in the other direction.

I pulled the computer back out and started looking for the fastest way to Delos. It looked like it was a small, mostly deserted, island right next to Mykonos. Most people stayed on Mykonos and took the ferry to Delos to see the sights.

I pulled up a search engine to see what it would take to get to Mykonos. I could fly and get there quickly, but it looked like the next flight was not until the following morning. There was a ferry leaving in the afternoon, it was a long ride, but I would get there sooner than I could fly there. It would work. I closed the laptop and looked down at my clothes. Definitely not something I would consider island wear in the middle of June. With a few hours to spare, I bought a small wardrobe to get by with before leaving for the port.

In the cab on the way to the port, I looked out the window as we passed the Acropolis. I wished I had time to explore it, but I was on a tight schedule. If the 'evil ones' figured out where I was, I needed to get as far away as possible as quickly as possible. I promised myself I would make time as soon as things calmed down.

# CHAPTER 6

Once Vince had his travel set up for the next night he pulled his phone out and called an old friend. "Who is this?" asked the voice on the other end of the phone.

"Maria, it is Vince." He smiled, heading for an exit.

"Vince? I have not heard from you in ages," Maria purred. "What can I do for you?"

"I am spending the day in Madrid before my flight leaves tomorrow evening, and I thought I would see what you were up to." Vince pushed through the doors leading to a taxi stand and joined the line.

"Same as any night, your company would be a nice change."

"I am getting a taxi right now, where should I meet you?" Vince asked, feeling guilty. He was looking forward to seeing Maria while Katie was out there on her own.

"Come to the house. I spend most of my time here these days."

"Very well. I will see you soon."

He told the cab driver where to go and looked at his watch. It would still be pointless to call Katie; her flight would not land for two more hours. He sat back in his seat and hoped she would be alright on her own. She could take care of herself, but with everything she had gone through in the past week she was functioning in a semi-shocked state. He was going to have to do something to help her relax once he caught up with her.

When he arrived at the house, he paid for the cab, got out with his bag and walked to Maria's front door. It opened before he had a chance to ring the doorbell.

Maria stood there in all of her Goth glory. Her curly red hair was up in a clip making it shoot out in a million different directions. She had on a skintight black dress with slits running up each side. The neckline shot down to the bottom of her cleavage, leaving little to the imagination.

"Vince," she called, stepping up to him and wrapping him in a bear hug. "How long has it been? Fifty or sixty years? What are you doing away from San Sebastian?" She took his hand and pulled him into her home.

"I believe it was after the civil war," Vince said, trying to keep his balance as she pulled him down the hall and into the parlor. "Miguel and I had a falling out. I do not think it can be mended."

"You and Miguel?" Maria said, indicating Vince should sit down. "The last time I saw you two, you were thick as thieves. What changed?"

Not wanting to get into the prophecy, Maria did not believe in it like many vampires of this day and age. He went for the truth. "A woman. What else could force two men such as us to part company?"

"A woman." She sat down across from him. "Why am I not surprised? Who won the girl?"

"Right now, neither of us." He crossed one leg over the other and folded his hands together.

"So he kicked you out, or are you following the girl?"

She clapped her hands together to summon a servant.

"Both actually. He is not taking her rejection well. I think Lolita messed everything up for him."

"Lolita came back to San Sebastian?" Maria asked, taking the wine from the servant. "She hasn't been back since the loss of their maker. Must be some woman."

"Yes, the woman is very special and you know how jealous Lolita can be." Vince took his glass and held it up in salute. "To old friends."

"To old lovers," Maria purred before taking a sip. "How special is this girl?"

"I left my home of a hundred years to go after her, which should tell you enough."

"So you think you have found 'The One', after all this time. How can you be sure?" Vince was surprised she made the connection.

"You will meet her someday soon, then you will understand." Vince thought it would be great to watch Katie read Maria's mind. Her smell alone would draw vampires in from miles away. The thought gave him some trepidation. The vampires in Athens were not as civilized as the ones she had met in San Sebastian. He prayed she would be smart and get a hotel room as soon as she landed. She was not dumb; she knew he would be able to find her wherever she went if she used the credit cards he gave her and there was always the flash drive.

Hell, he expected her to use his credit card to buy a computer and watch the presentation he put together. If she did, she would figure out how to get to Mykonos. Vampires were not allowed to stay more than a night on the island, and there was nowhere for her to stay on Delos. He wanted to pull out his laptop and track her by the flash drive, but he did not want to be a rude guest.

"I can't agree with you, but I am your hostess so I will play along. What else can I help you with this day? Do you need rest? Something to eat? Everything I have is at your disposal."

"Thank you Maria. Right now, I just need to escape from the sun until dark. My flight leaves shortly after sundown. I will not be here long."

"Very well, let me show you to your room." Maria got up and put her empty wine glass on a side table.

Vince rose with her, placed his glass next to hers and followed her out of the room. "I appreciate your help. Miguel forced me to miss the last flight out."

"Where are you going?" she asked as they made their way down the hall side by side.

"I would prefer not to say for the time being." Vince hesitated a step. "It will be safer for everyone if no one knows where I am going."

"Are you afraid of Miguel?"

"No, I am worried about Lolita." He caught up the step he lost. "Miguel tried to enslave her, and when the bond was broken, Lolita tried to kill her. She will be dealt with in time."

"You are going to try and train this girl who you think is 'The One'? The poor girl has no idea what's in store for her." Maria stopped in front of the door and opened it. "I trust this will be satisfactory."

"Yes, I am going to train her. She is not completely unschooled and she is brave. She broke Isabelle's finger and did her best to break Lolita's jaw." He stepped into the room and looked around. It was a lavish bedroom done in forest greens and browns. There was a four-poster bed, a wardrobe and a writing desk. "This will be perfect."

34

"She punched Lolita and survived?"

"From what I understand. I wish I could have been there to watch." Vince smiled to himself at the thought.

"Maybe she is special after all." Maria moved to the bed and sat down. "If you are going to train her it means you will not take her or her blood. Can I help tide you over?"

Vince stood frozen for a moment. Maria had been a convenient lover the last time they were together. Slaking his lust sounded like a nice way to pass time. He turned to look at her. Maria was the same beauty she had always been, but somehow, he felt he would be betraying Katie if he slept with her. There was no reason why he should not take advantage of the situation, but he could not bring himself to. "As much as I would like to Maria, I cannot. However, if you have a donor available I would appreciate a snack."

"You have gone down the rabbit hole for this girl if I cannot tempt you." She moved from the bed and went to the door.

"You tempt me plenty, but I must refrain at this time." He went to her, took her hands in his and kissed her lightly on the cheek.

"Always so smooth." She pulled away. "I will send a donor to you shortly. Please let me know before you leave."

"I will. Thank you again. You are truly one of the Goddess's best."

"Now you are just kissing ass." She giggled and closed the door, leaving him alone.

Vince blew out a breath and went to his laptop case sitting by the desk. He pulled it out, and set it on the table. He sat down, opened the screen and powered up the machine. He entered his password, turned on the internet, and opened the tracking program linked to the flash drive he gave Katie.

It looked like she was just about to land in Athens. He would give her an hour or two then call her. He wanted her to be safe on her own. She was capable, but now that he had found her, the last thing he wanted to do was lose her.

His thoughts were interrupted by a knock at the door. "Just a minute," he said, closing the tracking program and the lid on the computer, effectively locking it.

He got up, went to the door, and opened it to find a young blond woman waiting for him. "My mistress said you needed to eat," she said in a soft high-pitched voice.

He let the door open all the way in invitation. "Come in." He was not happy with the choice Maria sent him. This was payback; he was sure, for not wanting to be intimate with her. He did not like young fragile donors. He was always afraid he was going to hurt them more than necessary. He liked his donors as he liked his bed partners. Meaty, tough, curvy with a mind of their own. This waif of a girl was exactly the opposite.

After he closed the door, he turned around to see her sprawled on the bed waiting for him. He walked over to the bed and looked down at the skinny girl. "What is your name?"

"Angel," she replied, running her hands down the side of her nightgown clad body as if she could not wait for him to sink his teeth into her flesh.

Vince climbed onto the bed next to her. He wanted to send her away, there was something off about her, but he needed to eat. The last forty-eight hours had been hell, and the next forty-eight were going to be just as taxing. Despite the girl not being his type she smelled lovely; sweet and tangy. It reminded him of someone from long ago, but he could not put his finger on who. "Do you know why you are here?"

"Yes, you need to eat and I'm your meal. Please bite me; it's been so long since anyone has bitten me."

"Why has it been so long?" Vince asked, moving her blond hair to the far side of her neck.

"Last time they took too much, and Mistress said I had to recover before anyone had more." She withered beneath his touch. "You can have sex with me too if you would like. It's always better when sex is involved."

"There will be no sex, but thank you for the offer. When was the last time you were bitten?" He wanted to make sure a sufficient amount of time had passed. He did not want to be responsible for accidently killing one of Maria's donors.

"It has been months, please . . ." She trailed off. Vince had not seen a donor addict in a long time. He preferred to feed only from humans once. He did not want to be responsible for anyone becoming addicted to the erotic pain of being bitten, or the euphoria of blood loss. "Please bite me."

Without waiting, he leaned down and sank his teeth into her throat being careful not to hit the vein. Her blood was hot, hotter than most humans. It had a distinct taste to it, sweet like honey only sweeter, he remembered then what her smell had reminded him of. He pulled away, but it was too late. The girl was on drugs. He was not sure what, but likely heroin or some other variation of the poppy.

# CHAPTER 7

After boarding the ferry, I found a bathroom and discovered how hard it was to travel on my own. I stuffed my rolling suitcase and laptop case into the small stall with me. I hung up my laptop case on the hook and left my suitcase at my feet with one end sticking out.

As soon as I sat down, the outside door opened and two women's voices filled the room with Greek chatter. I listened to their footsteps approach the outside of my stall. I watched in horror as hands came down to my suitcase, grabbed the end of it and pulled it to the other side of the door.

"What are you doing?" I yelled, trying to stop myself in mid-stream to confront them.

They laughed, and I heard them run out of the bathroom with my luggage rolling behind them. I finished up as quickly as I could. I zipped up my shorts; I threw my laptop bag cross-ways over my torso, and took off after them. My first thought was to go to the ferry workers, but after everything I had been through in the past week, I paused. I was traveling with a fake passport in a foreign country. Finding the women on my own might be a better way of handling the situation. At least I still had my wallet and laptop.

I tried to be calm as I walked around looking for my pink floral suitcase. Glad I did buy a black one, it would have been a lost cause. The ferry was big. There were three levels of seating, plus a garage allowing people to bring their car with them.

I began on the level I was on, thinking they could not have gotten too far. I walked around looking at the ground and at people's feet thinking my suitcase would be easy to see. After finding nothing, I decided to go to the garage level. It would make sense, they would want to hide the evidence, and it would be harder for me to find them.

As soon as I opened the door to the garage level, I heard the voices from the bathroom. I ducked behind the closest car and walked in a crouch as quietly as I could toward their voices. I looked down at my new soft-soled running shoes; they were a lot quieter than my flip-flops. When I thought I was close enough, I pulled my head up by the rear window of the car I was crouched in front of. My thighs were screaming at me from crouching, but I was going to have to use stealth to get my bag back.

I looked around and saw the women one car over and one car up. They had the trunk popped on the car, and I saw my bag sitting open in it. They were going through it with their backs to me. What was I going to do? How was I going to get it back?

I carefully pulled my laptop case around my body trying not to make any noise, and dug around until I found the new multi-tool I had bought earlier in the day. I pulled the biggest knife out and closed the tool making a handle. I was not sure what I planned on doing with it, but it was the only weapon I had. I did not want to hurt them; I just wanted my stuff back.

I stayed crouched behind the car trying to decide what to do. Time was running out. What if they shut the trunk when they saw me? It would be nearly impossible to get the keys away from them if they did. I would have to go with my gut.

I stood up and walked over to them, trying to act friendly with my knife hand behind my back. "Hi, I was wondering if you could help me . . ." I trailed off as they turned to look at me.

The one closest to me was about my height with long bleached yellow hair. She was paper thin like she never ate enough. The other one was short, with a brown bob, and at least twenty pounds overweight. I could take the smaller one, but the bigger one would be harder. She looked like a fighter.

"What do you want?" the yellow haired one asked in a zippy accent. She turned to face me, planted her feet shoulder width apart and put her hands on her hips trying to hide the contents of the trunk. The other woman turned to the side of the car blocking the view as well.

"Funny thing happened to me in the bathroom," I said, continuing to make my way to them. "Two women came in while I was in the stall and took my suitcase from under the door. I thought they were just watching it for me, but when I came out I couldn't find them." I stopped less than two feet from the blond one. "Can I please have my stuff back?"

"What are you talking about? I do not understand you." She folded her arms in front of her chest. "Go away."

"You," I said, slowly pointing at her. "Took. My. Suitcase. Give. It. Back."

"Why? You are rich American; you can buy more stuff."

"Yeah," the other one chimed in, folding her arms to match her partner.

I looked back and forth between them. I did not want to threaten them, but I had to do something. It was my stuff, and I was tired of losing my stuff. I pulled my hand from behind my back and showed them the knife. "I don't want to have to use this, but I will if I have too." I brought the blade to eyelevel and made a show of inspecting it.

They both tried to take a step back, but they were against the car with nowhere to go. The yellow haired one stood up straight and put her hands back on her hips. "You're not going to do anything. You will go to jail."

"You know; I've had a long week. I broke up with my boyfriend, lived out of a tent, suffered from horrible headaches, and broke someone's finger, nose and jaw. Don't worry they were all different people. I was betrayed, hunted, and saved. Now you bitches stole from me. I'm so tired of people telling me what I can and can't do. The last thing I'm going to do is walk away like nothing happened." I took a half step closer to them. "This is your last chance. Put all my stuff back in my bag and give it back or this is going to get messy." I put the tip of the knife in my mouth pretending I was thinking about which one I would cut first.

"You won't do anything," the fighter said and moved to punch me in the face. I ducked, and with my hand around the base of the multi-tool, I slammed my fist into her gut. I moved to the side as she gasped for air and hit the ground face first.

The yellow haired woman was slowly moving toward the front of the car with her hands up. "You killed her," she cried. Tears started running down her cheeks.

"I did not." I rolled my eyes, showing her the blood free knife. "I punched her. Now I'm going to take my stuff back, and if I ever see you again I'm going to call the police. Do you understand?"

"You didn't knife her?" She looked at her friend who

was starting to wiggle around on the ground.

"No, I didn't see the need." I went to the trunk and shoved all of my stuff back into the suitcase. It looked like everything was there. Even if a few things did not make it, I did not care. I just wanted to take what I could and get away from them.

"I suggest you come up with a better way to make a living." I lifted my suitcase out of the trunk, set it on the ground, pulled up the handle and made my way to the stairwell.

I made it up one flight of stairs before I stopped, bent over, put my head between my knees and completely freaked out. I could not believe I had just taken on two criminals and won. I was proud of myself. A few weeks ago, I would have gone to the authorities, reported my suitcase missing, and hoped for the best. My trip would have been ruined. I was not going to let anyone take advantage of me ever again. It was still scary as hell, but it was worth the adrenaline rush.

After I found a seat on the top deck, I used my suitcase as a footstool, and tried to sleep with my laptop bag on my lap. Traveling on your own was hard.

# CHAPTER 8

Vince tried to get up and go in the bathroom to purge himself of the tainted blood he ingested, but his balance was off and he fell to the floor in a dizzying haze. Finding himself spread eagle on the floor he forced himself to sit up and lean his back against the bed. The room spun around him. He did not ingest much blood, but it was enough to keep him drugged for a week and he could not leave Katie on her own for a week.

No longer caring if he made mess of Maria's room or himself he brought his hand up and forced a finger down his throat. He vomited the blood all over himself. He wiped his hand sloppily across his face trying to clean the blood off, then he blurrily watched the girl get off the bed, walk over to the desk, and sit down at his computer. She opened the lid and powered it on. When the password page popped up, she turned and looked at him.

"What's the password?" she asked in a mocking voice. A coldhearted bitch had replaced the waif of a girl who had first entered the room.

"Why would I tell you?" Vince slurred, concentrating on staying conscious. He would not let anyone know where Katie was. "Did Maria put you up to this?"

"If Maria knew I was a heroin addict I would be back out on

45

the streets. I have been very careful to cover any traces of the drug in me. I serve another." She turned back to the computer and typed in a series of commands.

"Lolita?" Vince was trying to find the strength to get up and kill the woman.

"Yes. She told me to be on the lookout for you and a human. I guess she was wrong about the human. She commanded me to kill you, break into your computer and send her all the information on it."

If she were able to hack the computer she would not find anything linking him to Katie. The only thing she might be able to find was his fake itinerary. His real itinerary was in a locker at the airport. He felt guilty not trusting Maria, but the stakes were too high for him to take a chance. He prayed Maria was not on Lolita's side in all of this.

"Tell me your password." Angel pulled a knife from under her dress. "Or I will cut you and I love to cut bad boys."

Vince staggered to his feet, and placed his hands on the bed in an attempt to stop the world from spinning around him. It was not the first time he had ingested drugged blood. He had spent years in the orient learning martial arts and enjoying opium dens, but it had been hundreds of years since he indulged, and it seemed to be more debilitating than he remembered.

He found his balance after a minute and began to walk toward the girl. He wanted to twist her head off, but it would infuriate Maria. He needed to clear his head and deal with her, but he could not think straight. "Here I will do it for you," Vince said when he finally made it to the desk.

The girl put the knife to his throat. "No, you will not. Just tell me what the password is and all this will be a bad dream."

He might have been slow but the girl was human and doped up on the same stuff he was. He grabbed her knife hand, wrapped his hand around it, and snapped the girl's hand backward, breaking her wrist. The girl dropped the knife, let out a scream, and fell to the floor whimpering.

Turning he made the slow trek across the room to the door. When he reached it, he had to pause to rest. His strength was gone, but he needed Maria to see to the girl before he blacked out entirely. He turned the handle and opened the door. "Maria!" He bellowed down the hallway then slumped to the floor no longer strong enough to hold up his own weight.

He heard footsteps coming down the hall and found the strength to look up when red, silk, embroidered slippers came into view. "Vince what is it? What's wrong? Why are you covered in blood?" Maria asked in a concerned voice.

"The girl is on drugs. She drugged me, and tried to break into my laptop." He swung his head toward the girl who was sobbing on the floor with her broken wrist cradled in her good hand.

"Are you well?" She crouched down, pulling his chin up to look at his eyes.

"I will be. Once I realized she was on drugs I made myself vomit, but it is still in my system. I need a safe place to sleep it off."

"Why would she do this? She knows I do not tolerate drugs in my home." Maria got up and walked over to the girl.

"She is Lolita's." Vince tried to stand up, but his strength was gone.

Maria picked the girls head up by the hair ignoring her cries of pain. "Is this true Angel? Have you been spying on me for Lolita?"

The girl looked up at Maria with a tear-stained face and smiled. "Yes, I have been reporting back to Lolita since I came into your house. She knows all your dirty little secrets. She is going to kill you, but first I need the password for his computer."

Without a thought, Maria took the girls face in her hands and yanked her head hard to the side. There was a loud snap, and the girl fell dead at Maria's feet. "Vince, I'm so sorry. I had no idea I had a spy in my home. How can I make this up to you?"

"Just help me to bed. I need to sleep it off."

Maria helped Vince get back to the bed where she stripped him of his bloody clothes and called a servant to wash them. She tucked him into bed and sat down in a nearby chair to watch over him. She could not afford for anything else to happen to her former lover. He was not hers, had never been hers, but if she kept him safe, he would do the same for her if she ever needed it.

Vince awoke to find himself standing on a rocky shoreline in the moonlight. He must be asleep since he did not remember Madrid having an ocean. He still felt groggy from the drugged blood. He blinked trying to focus on the world around him but his head still swam.

"Vince, where is my daughter?" A voice asked from behind him.

He turned to find his Goddess, Asteria, facing him and she did not look happy. He fell to his knees, partly out of respect and partly because he could not stand. "I believe she is on her way to your temple Goddess."

"Why are you not with her? You are her protector. How are you protecting her right now?" Anger and worry flared in her eyes.

"Miguel forced me to miss my flight. I am trying to catch up with her, but I cannot travel during the daylight as she can."

"How are you going to catch up with her?"

"I am tracking her movements with technology. I will be able to meet her in either Athens or Mykonos. One of Lolita's slaves drugged me. I have to sleep off the drug before I can go to her. I am sorry Goddess; there was no other way to keep her safe."

"She is in distress, and I do not know why." She laid her hand on his head and closed her eyes.

Before Vince could absorb the Goddess's words his body exploded with pain. He screamed as fire shot through his body, it felt like his blood was boiling. Was Asteria punishing him for losing Katie? He wanted to ask her, but screams of agony were all he could manage. As much as the pain had him wanting to rip the skin from his body, he felt his mind begin to clear, and his strength come back.

Finally, she let go of him and he fell face first in the sand. "Find her and take care of her or you will know my displeasure."

Vince rolled over and looked around. He was alone on the beach. The waves were crashing on top of each other and the wind picked up creating an angry sea. He wanted to tell the Goddess he was doing the best he could, but now he was worried. Why was Katie in distress?

# CHAPTER 9

The horn on the ferry blew, startling me awake. I made a grab for my suitcase and my laptop bag. I blew out a breath as my hands found both bags where I left them. I blinked and looked out the window; it was dark out except for the lights ahead of us. We were pulling into port. I got up and stretched. I had a kink in my neck and the palm of my hand hurt from using my multi-tool as brass knuckles. It was nothing major but it gave me something to think about.

The horn blew again, and I gathered my bags, ready to disembark the ferry. I hoped the hotel I booked remembered I needed a ride and would send someone to pick me up.

Finally, off the ferry, I headed for the group of people waiting for the passengers to disembark. I began looking for a sign with my new name on it. The hotel said there would be one, but I found none. Maybe they were late, I pulled out a map of town and began to hike to the hotel with a sigh, it was not the first time I had to walk.

Mykonos, I came to find out while hoofing it to my hotel, was a party town. Bars lined the narrow streets and every type of music I knew, and some I did not recognize, pounded out of doorways. Groups of people walked down the cobblestone streets laughing and smiling. It made me miss my friends, and made me realize how alone I felt for the first time since I left Mark. I pulled my chin up. I was fine. I could be by myself and have a good time.

I just needed some rest. Tomorrow I would visit Delos and see the temple Vince talked about in his video. Hopefully I would find the answers I was looking for. I came to the end of the street and pulled my map out again. The hotel had to be around here somewhere, I thought. I turned in a circle looking at the buildings around me. I must have been tired; the hotel was right across the street.

I crossed the street, walked through the doors and went to the front desk.

"Kalispera," the woman behind the counter said.

"Hi, do you speak English?" I asked, pulling my wallet out of my laptop bag.

"Yes, how may I help you?"

"I have a reservation for tonight, someone was supposed to meet me at the dock but no one was there." I gave her my passport and drummed my fingers on the counter.

"Ms. Sims, I am sorry but your reservation was canceled."

"What?" I was not going down this no hotel room business again. "Who canceled it? I've been on the ferry out of cell phone service since I made the reservation."

"It doesn't tell me who canceled it. I'm sorry."

"Do you have a room?"

"How long will you be staying with us?" she asked and clicked a few things on the computer.

"A few days but if you only have a room for the night I will take it, and find somewhere else tomorrow."

"Give me a moment; let me see what I can do."

"Thank you." I turned around wondering who would

have known to cancel my reservation. No one knew where I was going or who I was except for Vince. Was he captured by the 'evil ones' and forced to spill his guts about my new identity? No, I thought. Vince would rather die than let them know what name I was traveling under.

I felt something vibrating in my pocket and remembered my phone. I pulled it out and looked at the number. It had to be Vince; no one else knew the number.

"Hello?"

"Katie, where are you?" Vince asked.

"Safe, where are you?"

"Looking for you at the dock. Did you get my message?"

"Where did you leave it?" There had been nothing on my phone. "Are you alright?"

"Yes, I am fine. I canceled your reservation at the hotel because I have a place for us."

"You canceled my reservation?" I let out a breath. "I'm at the hotel. I'm in the process of getting another room do you want to meet me here?"

"Yes, I will be there shortly," he said and the phone went dead.

I turned back to the woman behind the desk. "It looks like I don't need the room after all. My friend just called, he already has something for me."

She rolled her eyes at me. "I found this while you were on the phone," she said, handing a note to me.

"I am sorry about the confusion." I took the note from her. "Thank you for your help. Can I wait for my friend in here?"

"Yes, make yourself at home." She turned to the desk behind her and looked at some paperwork.

I moved my stuff over to a chair facing the door and sat down.

53

I looked at the envelope with my new name on it. I turned it over and slid my finger under the flap to pry it open. I pulled the letter out and read:

*Mary, if I miss you at the dock call me at:* *012.555.45782. I am here. I will see you soon.*

*V*

I folded the letter, put it in the case with my laptop, and waited for Vince to arrive.

"Katie," Vince said as he breezed into the lobby. He looked the same if only slightly paler then he had the last time I saw him. His normally bronze complexion was tinged with green, like copper with just a touch of tarnish. He was still the tall, hulking vampire with shoulder length, chestnut hair, a sharp featured face and bulging muscles. He opened his arms, to embrace me, I think.

"Vince." I got up slowly and moved toward him. I was not ready to hug him yet. I was happy to see him, but I did not want a vampire close to my neck. Thoughts of the 'evil ones' were too fresh. "I'm glad you found me." I extended my hand in invitation to shake it.

He put his arms down and extended his hand. "I am glad you are alright. We should go, you look tired." He let go of my hand stiffly and took the handle on my bag.

"You have no idea." I followed him out the door and down the street. "I bought some stuff with your credit card, I hope you don't mind."

"That is why I gave it to you," Vince said as I struggled to keep up with his long stride. "I am pleased you used it."

"Thanks." We came to the end of the pedestrians

only street and stopped.

Vince looked up, then down the street and whistled. "Here comes our ride." He looked toward a black sedan coming toward us. It stopped; the driver got out, and took my bag from Vince. Vince opened the door and gestured for me to get in. I got in taking my laptop bag from my shoulder and sitting in the seat furthest away from the open door. I heard Vince speaking to the driver before he sat down next to me.

"Are you up for another boat ride?"

"Not really. The last one kind of kicked my butt."

"I would like to get out to Delos and back tonight. Then we can leave for Crete tomorrow night. I do not know how long it will take Miguel and Lolita to figure out where we have gone, but it is very important for you to see your mother's temple."

"Do you think they'll try and follow us?" Fear raced through me as soon as he mentioned the 'evil ones'. I wanted to stay as far away from them as I could, at least until I could kill them on my own.

"Yes, they are going to want to find you and take you for themselves. Never doubt that."

"Then let's get this over with. Do they know you're with me?"

"No," he said and then said something in Greek to the driver. "They made me help them try and find you at the airport, or so they thought. Unfortunately, I missed my flight because of them. They could not figure out what name you were traveling under. Then you beat them to the security checkpoint. What did you do to Miguel? I saw Lolita trying to keep the humans away while he was laid out on the floor."

"Oh, well he tried to use the bond to hurt me. I guess I somehow turned it around on him and sent the pain back to him." I smiled thinking back to him shaking and falling to the floor of the airport.

55

Vince laughed and tried to cover his mouth with his hands. "Good job. By the time Miguel was back to himself, and they got rid of the crowd, who wanted to send him to the hospital, you were long gone. There did not seem to be much more to do and they gave up. I made it to Madrid right as your plane to Athens took off. I could not get another flight until tonight. I am sorry you were on your own today."

"I was worried when you never called. I thought they took you and were torturing you to find out where I went."

"By the time I had a chance to call you, you were on the plane to Athens, and I was busy today . . ." He trailed off. There was more to his story than he was letting on, but there was no point pushing him. I was proud I took care of myself, but it was nice to have a big strong vampire with me. "The voicemail on your phone was not set up. I could not leave you a message, and I did not want to text you because you would have no idea if it was me or them."

"No kidding. I wouldn't have believed any text message." I looked out the window as the car came to a stop. We were at a marina filled with boats.

The driver did not say a thing as he parked the car in a loading and unloading zone. He got out, opened the door for me and waited while I got out. Vince got out on the other side, said something in Greek, and walked toward the dock.

I hurried to catch up with him. "Will my stuff be here when we get back?" Thinking of the women on the ferry.

"It will be fine," he said when I caught up to him. "Why are you so worried about it?"

"I left everything I owned at Miguel's, then I bought new stuff only to have it stolen on the ferry. I got everything back, but I'm tired of not having the bare necessities." I folded my arms in front of my chest.

He stopped and looked at me as if he already knew what happened. "What happened on the ferry?"

"It was nothing." I tried to play it off. Vince raised one eyebrow at me and waited for more. "Fine, I was in the bathroom with my suitcase when these two women pulled it out from under the stall and took off with it. I tracked them down and got it back."

"What are you leaving out? Your mother told me you were in distress. She was upset I was not there to protect you."

"When did you see my mom?"

"While I was sleeping."

There was a lot of information in his words, but I was too agitated to think about them. "I had to rough them up before they would give it back to me."

"You roughed them up? I am dying to hear what happened. Will you please stop beating around the bush?" He was trying hard not to laugh.

I let out a long breath and told him the story. He smiled in a, my girlfriend kicked your girlfriend's ass, kind of way. "I am glad you were able to recover your belongings on your own, but you are lucky the police did not get involved."

"I know, but I needed to do it on my own, in my own way. I wasn't going to go cry to the police and then be stuck with nothing again."

"I am sorry you lost everything. There was no other choice; your new things will be at the hotel when we get back I promise."

"Don't make promises to me." His words made me think of Miguel, and all of the promises he made with no intention of keeping. I was tired of people making promises they would not or could not keep. Pissed, I stormed down the dock suddenly super mad.

"Why not?" he asked, catching up to me.

"I've had more promises broken in the past week then I've had in my entire life. They mean nothing to me now."

"Miguel and Mark really mind fucked you," Vince said more to himself than to me. "I am sorry. I will not make any promises to you. Your bags will be at the hotel when we get back."

I stopped and turned to him. The vampire was trying, I thought to myself. "Fine, which boat are we taking?"

"The one back there." He nodded to a yacht near the beginning of the dock.

"Let's go then," I walked back down the dock toward our yacht.


It was an amazing yacht. Forty-feet long with a sun deck, and a swim deck, neither I would get to use, but the main cabin had a nice sofa and dinner had been laid out for me.

Vince got us under way while I ate. It felt like the food at the shopping center had been days ago as I cleared the steak and octopus from my plate. When I was done, I went up to the bridge to see how far out we were.

"How was dinner?" Vince asked with his eyes on the sea in front us.

"It was really good." I sat in the chair next to him. "Thanks for setting all of this up."

"I am just glad I was able to catch up with you." He looked over at me. "I take it you were able to get a computer and watch the presentation on the flash drive."

"Yes, I tried to use the computer at the hotel I stayed at last night, but it wouldn't work. I had to buy a computer and headphones today in order watch it."

"Good, I am glad you did. You do not need to justify your purchases to me Katie. If you need something buy it."

"I feel bad. I don't like spending other people's money." I looked down at my shirt and fiddled with the hem.

"Well stop. I have plenty of money. You will not blow through it all."

"Everything you have done for me is amazing, especially after what I went through with Miguel. He never even mentioned the prophecy to me. He thought I was a dumb American girl he could control." I stopped speaking and thought back to my time with him. "I guess he was right in a lot of ways. I have learned more about the world in the past week then I have in my entire life. I'm glad you want to help me. I trust you won't let anything bad happen to me if it's within your power. What I'm not sure about are your intentions. You said you want to help me, guide me, and teach me, but there is no way you don't have some ulterior motives." I turned to look out the windshield at the endless darkness. I did not want to offend him but I needed to be honest with him.

"I have told you everything I know." He started to dodge my question, but then he continued. "I do not have any ulterior motives. I understand you will not trust me until I can prove myself to you. I plan to work every day until you can." I could feel the candor in what he said, but I was not ready to trust those feelings yet.

"Did you have bloodlust until you killed everyone you loved after you were changed?" I asked, unable to think of a follow-up question to his statement. Changing the subject seemed the best course of action and I had questions about his presentation.

"No, not everything the myth says is true." He laughed at me. "I think it means you are more likely to kill the ones you love because you want to see them and let them know you are alive. Unless you

59

have someone to guide you when you are turned it takes years, and for some decades to gain control over the bloodlust."

"What about the ways you can die?" Thinking about how satisfying it would be to rip Lolita's head off with my bare hands.

"That is true." He gave me a sideway glance. "Are you going to try one of them on me?"

"Not right now. You have way too much information, and too many contacts I want to take advantage of first. I was thinking of Lolita. I would love to sever her head from her body."

"You and me both." I felt his need to reach out and touch me but he kept his hands to himself. "It is going to be a few more hours. You should go below and get some sleep."

I did as he suggested since there was nothing to look at as we skimmed over the dark waters of the sea. There was a stateroom I could have used, but the confined space and the rocking of the boat was messing with my full stomach. Instead, I laid on the sofa with a porthole open and let the salty air put me to sleep.

# CHAPTER 10

I dreamed I was going home. But not the home I knew in Colorado, the home I never knew was home. An island with many temples and places of worship. It was a sacred place, and it was my home, it was where I came from. I walked through the gleaming temples and shrines. They were not mine, I did not worship any of those deities, but they were part of me, part of the land on which they sat.

I found myself in an older temple. It was clean and well maintained, but in comparison to the others on the island, it was smaller, and plain. I went inside and found a black altar made of onyx on the dais, worn with age but clean and well-oiled showing off the lack of imperfections in the stone. I mounted the steps and turned to take in the room from a higher viewpoint.

She was standing at the other end of the room. "Mom?" She looked the same as she did in my dreams in San Sebastian. She was on the shorter side, lean but with full breasts and matronly hips. Her long black hair was hanging over her shoulders and there was a smile playing on her lips. She was wearing an off-white toga with a gold pendant that matched my tattoo. She opened her arms to me and without a second thought, I ran into them.

She hugged me long and hard murmuring. "Oh, my girl," over and over again. She pulled back and put her hands on my shoulders. I flinched where the bite had been but there was no pain.

I looked at her angelic face. "Are you upset with me?"

"Why would I be upset?" She looked at me confused.

"Because I didn't save Miguel or San Sebastian." I held my hand up in a pleading motion.

"My dear, saving San Sebastian was one of many outcomes." She smiled, took my hand, and began to walk around the room. "I am quite happy you chose Vince; he will take better care of you than Miguel."

"Can we back up a minute? Are you really a goddess and if you are, why did you die?"

She stopped walking and turned to face me. "Everything Vince told you was true, my love. I created the vampires, and set the wheels in motion to bring you to life. You have to understand; Gods are only as real as the people who follow them. When people stop following us, we lose power. If everyone forgets us, we cease to be. Many of the gods and goddesses became powerless when Christianity began. I had to do something to save myself. Sending the prophecy to my oracle rallied enough of my followers to give me the power I needed to transform into a human. It took a long time though, thousands of years and it took all the power I had. By the time the transformation was complete, many more of my followers had gone to Christianity or they stopped believing in any higher power.

"I was as mortal as you are now. I met your father in Athens at the Acropolis. We fell madly in love, married, and moved to America. I did not want to die but Zeus was furious at me for coming up with a way to bring my powers back when he had lost so much of his. He crashed the truck into the car we were in trying to kill us all. I held on as long as I could. I wanted to watch you grow up, help you manifest your powers, but there was nothing I could do. I came back here and resumed my post, waiting for you to come close enough for me to reach you."

"Why did it take so long?"

"You were too far away. I spent what little power I had when I visited you as a child, but I had to see you and comfort you. You are not only my blood, but the only person who can save me from disappearing."

Satisfied I moved on to my next question. "Why did you say I've chosen Vince? I haven't chosen him Mom."

"He read you the prophecy, you need a protector and you have chosen Vince, have you not?"

"He is helping me learn about what I am and what I need to do. He's going to help me fight Lolita. I guess, yes, he's my protector."

"You will need to defeat her before you are going to be able to rule." She started to walk us around the room again. "Vince is a good choice to teach you, and mentor you in your training."

"I hope so." I looked around the room for the first time. The walls were bare except for a stand encased with glass. "Is that the prophecy?" I asked as we walked by it. I tried to stop to look at it, but she forced me to continue.

"Yes, but I do not want you to look at it now. I want it to be a surprise."

"Did you come to warn me about something?" Normally she had some cryptic warning or advice I did not understand.

"No, you are finally on your way home." Stopping, she turned to face me. "I wanted to tell you how happy I am that you are here."

"I'm glad I'm here too." I smiled, happy finally knowing the

63

truth. "I feel like I'm home for the first time in my life. I feel like this is where I need to be."

"I am glad you think so."

"Where is Hecate?" It was surreal, I had a sister and she was a goddess. It was hard to wrap my head around.

"We had a falling out many years ago." She stopped to look at me. "Some vampires have chosen to worship her over me, others chose Christ, or Allah, still others believe in nothing. Many vampires do not know I am their creator, nor do they care." She sounded annoyed. "That is why you are here though. You are tasked with bringing my creations back to me."

"How am I going to do that?" I had no idea how to revive a religion.

She leaned in and kissed me on the cheek. "In time you will know," she said as I closed my eyes.

# CHAPTER 11

A hand gently caressed my cheek, where my mother had kissed me, and I jerked awake thinking it was one of the 'evil ones'. I opened my eyes and found a wounded expression on Vince's face.

"I am sorry. I was trying to wake you up. We're here." He got up angrily and went out the hatch leading onto the deck.

I groaned inwardly. He thinks I am afraid for him to touch me, I thought. I got up quickly and followed him. Vince was holding the yacht close to the dock allowing me to get down easier when I came out. I jumped down and started walking toward the temples. "I'm sorry. I thought you were Miguel for a second," I said softly as he walked behind me.

I lead the way down the path passing the ruins of temples that were shiny and new in my dream. When we came to the temple of Asteria, I stopped and caught my breath. Without ever being there before or knowing this was where Vince wanted me to go, I lead us to the temple.

Vince stopped next to me and let out a breath. "How did you know where to go?"

"I had a dream on the way here." I looked at the small building; it was the only temple not in ruins. Someone had taken care of it even as the others crumbled. It was stone, possibly marble, but I could not tell in the darkness. There was an etching of a bird on the front of the building; it had to be a quail. "Everything looked different in the dream, new and clean, not the ruins we passed," I said in a far-off voice, remembering how beautiful it had been. "This temple looks the same though. This is where we are going right?"

"This is the temple of Asteria. The prophecy is kept here." Vince took my arm and led the way to the entrance.

As we moved closer to the front doors, they opened and two disciples came out. They wore black robes with the hoods covering their heads. They each carried a staff.

Vince greeted the disciples in Greek and made a motion to me. I waved at them politely. "Show them the tattoo," Vince said after one of them said something in a rough voice.

I turned and pulled up the side of my shirt allowing them to look at the tattoo. They gasped and one of them took off at a run into the temple. The other one bowed from the waist and motioned us forward.

I looked at Vince. "I guess they liked the tattoo?" I took a step toward the entrance.

"I think they did." Vince smiled, matching my steps, even though he did not feel surprised by their reaction.

We followed the disciple, who went in ahead of us through an alcove then into the main room where I had talked with my mother in my dream. It looked almost the same. It was clean, lit by lights instead of torches, with the black altar at the far end of the room. The walls were no longer bare though. They must have turned the temple into a museum. There were unlit glass cases along the walls and in the center of the room.

A vampire came out of a side door before we could move further into the room and inspect the items on display. He was dressed the same as the other disciples, but looking at him I realized they had been human and not vampire. This guy was a vampire. He approached us stopping a little more than three feet away.

He said something to Vince in Greek and Vince answered in an affirmative. "He wants you to take off your shirt to see the mark without hiding anything else that may be present. You do not have to do this."

"It's fine." The vampire was very excited but he was also cautious, I could be an imposter. He must have been through this before.

I pulled my new shirt over my head, handed it to Vince and reached for the clasp on my bra. I unhooked it, and took it off. I felt Vince stiffen beside me. I smiled at his reaction, but I then remembered all men suck. I turned my right side into the light and held my arm over my head allowing the priest to inspect it.

After careful inspection, he dropped to his knees before me and kissed my tennis shoe covered foot. He began to chant and sway back and forth, his head hovering over my feet.

I looked to Vince who rolled his eyes, and thought to me. *The priest is praying to Asteria, thanking her for bringing you to them. He means you no harm.*

I stood there motionless until the priest finished, then I placed my right hand on top of his head. "Bless you my mother's most dedicated priest." I put my bra and shirt back on while the priest stood up.

The priest looked at me and smiled. He stood up, took my hand, and led me to the only case with a light on. *I did not know you spoke Greek,* Vince thought to me. I looked behind me where he was following behind and raised my eyebrows. *We will talk about it later.*

67

Inside the case was an ancient scroll with writing on it. I looked at it then at the tapestry next to it. This had to be the prophecy, I thought. I leaned over to read it:

Εκείνοι των γεννημένων μου που με έχουν ξεχάσει θα γίνουν για να θεραπεύσουν μια γυναίκα που φέρει το σημάδι μου.

Θα βρεθεί στις ανατολικές ακτές του μεγάλου ωκεανού πέρα από τους Στύλους του Ηρακλή, σε προστατευμένο κόλπο.

Κανείς δεν θα μπορέσει να την εξαπατήσει, καθώς θα μπορέσει να ακούσει τι βρίσκεται στις καρδιές της δημιουργίας μου.

Οι δυνάμεις της θα εκδηλωθούν καθώς η γνώση της για το είδος της μεγαλώνει.

Εκείνοι που προσπαθούν να την υποδουλώσουν θα αποκομίσουν την ανταμοιβή της εξημέρωσής της.

Εκείνος που την καθοδηγεί θα είναι προικισμένος με ένα βραβείο από τον επιλεγμένο.

Αυτός που την αλλάζει θα είναι σύζυγός της και βασιλεύει από την πλευρά της.

Θα φέρει τη δημιουργία μου πίσω στην πτυχή.

The prophecy was almost the same as what Vince told me with one major difference. It was not the time to talk to him about it though. I looked up at the tapestry hanging on the wall in a vacuum case above the scroll. It looked just like my tattoo: a quail, in mid-flight turned, with his head cocked allowing for the detail on the side of his head, wings and back to be visible. I held my fingers up to the glass and traced the outlines like I did to my side. "Mother," I whispered as tears began to stream down my cheeks. They were tears of closure, of finally understanding where I came from and all of the crazy things happening to me.

Vince put his arms around me, pulled me into a hug and I let him. "Everything is going to be alright, Katie. There is no need to cry."

"I know. I'm not crying because I'm upset. I'm crying because I get it now. It's all as clear as a bell." I smiled and kissed Vince on the cheek. I swear he blushed. Realizing what I was doing I pulled away. "Can you translate for me please?"

*Of course.*

"Priest," I said, turning to him. "My mother is proud of how you have taken such care of her temple and her island. This is a home I never thought I would find. Thank you for showing this to me." I paused allowing Vince to translate. "I can't stay here now, but I will return. When I do, I will bring the vampires back to Asteria."

Vince paused for a moment to look at me then translated what I said to the priest. He said something in return and Vince answered without consulting me. *He wants you to stay. I told him you are not yet safe, and cannot stay until the threats against you have been eliminated.* I nodded then turned to walk around the rest of the room. It made me sad to see my mother's temple was more of a museum than a place of worship. It was probably the only way they could keep it maintained and a low profile.

I smiled to myself; I was actually seeing something I wanted to see on this trip for the first time since London. I walked around and peered into the cases lining the walls admiring the little chunks of antiquity saved and preserved.

Vince joined me after a while. "We need to go if we do not want to spend the day here."

I did not want to go, but the thought of a hotel room and sleep was too good to pass up. "Give me just a minute." I went to the base of the dais and knelt. *Mother, thank you for giving me the strength*

69

*to make it here to see you and our home. I know you'll come to me when I need you. Thank you. Until we meet again, I love you.* I prayed to my mother, the island, the quail, and the goddess.

I said goodbye to the priest, promising to return, and we hurried back to the boat. I sat up on top with Vince on the way back to Mykonos having a better opinion of the night. As much as I loved the sun, I was part of the stars in the sky and night. I wondered if I loved the sun so much because it was something my mother could not enjoy or if it came from my father. Either way I would pay homage to them both now.

"I did not know you spoke Greek," Vince said, keeping his eyes on the water ahead of us as we skipped across the surface of the Aegean.

"I didn't either." Remembering the unfamiliar words leaving my mouth when I spoke to the priest. "I have no idea where it came from; it was almost like it was not even me saying them."

Vince said something in Greek I did not understand and looked over at me.

"What did you say?" I glared at him. I could feel the smugness coming off him.

"Learn Greek and I will say it again." He smiled, looking back at the night in front of us.

"I think I need to learn anyway."

"Why?"

"Well, all of the priests speak it, you do, and my mother does." As soon as the words left my mouth, it dawned on me. Every time I spoke to my mother, we conversed in Greek.

We spent the rest of ride back lost in our own

thoughts. I relaxed for the first time in a week; I was not on my own anymore.

We docked the boat and walked back to the parking lot at the marina where we found the same stoic driver waiting for us. He held my door open for me. Vince got in on the other side, and once the driver was in, we drove to our hotel.

As we drove, I could not help but think about sharing a hotel room with Vince. Every time I closed my eyes all I could see was Lolita coming at me and taking a chunk out of my neck or Miguel in the shower. I trusted Vince, but he was still a bloodsucker, and thanks to recent events, I had no reason to trust any of them. My mother said I could trust him but she also told me to save Miguel.

Exhaustion was rolling off Vince. He was feeling relaxed and safe, but tired. He thought we had gotten rid of the 'evil ones' at least for a little while. It made me feel better, I needed to use my vampire feeling detector more. I thought I was getting better at reading them or, Vince at least. Why could I read him better than I could the 'evil ones'? Was it because he was not hiding anything from me, or was he better at hiding his feelings than they were?

"I tried to get adjoining rooms for tonight. I know you need your privacy." Vince looked over at me. "Unfortunately the hotel did not have any available."

I turned my head away from the window to look at him. "That's okay." It would be nice to have my own room; it would not hurt me to share a room with Vince. "I think we can survive."

"Good," he said and I felt his relief. "We could have gotten separate rooms, but they would not have been close to each other, and it would be hard for me to guard you from such a distance."

"I agree. I would much rather share a room with you than be too far away if the 'evil ones' show up. I wouldn't have a chance if they caught me on my own."

71

"I am glad we are on the same page. As soon as we get settled in Crete we will begin training." Vince turned his head to look out the window. "Theron, the only vampire I have made, rules the island and the mafia there. No vampires are allowed on the island without his permission and it is all but impossible for one of us to sneak onto it." He sounded excited to see his child again.

"How long are we going to stay there?" I was ready to settle down and stop traveling for a while.

"For the summer at least. It is the safest place I know of," he said as we pulled into the entrance of the hotel.

"Vince." I needed to tell him what the prophecy really said, but he was already out of the car paying the driver. I got out and looked up at the tiered hotel built into a hillside. It was just like the pictures I had seen of the Greek islands. It was white, with soft edges, and arches everywhere. It looked as if every room had a private balcony with a view of the sea.

We walked into the lobby and Vince spoke to the front desk clerk. I was too tired to look around much; it had been a long day, and longer night. I needed to shower and sleep.

"Shall we?" Vince asked, getting my attention.

"Please, I'm exhausted." We walked to the elevator. "Where's our luggage?" I asked as we stepped into the car. I will say, arriving at a hotel in the early hours of the morning was nice. You never had to share your elevator ride.

"It was taken to our room while we were on Delos." He stood straight with his hands behind his back.

"I hope you're right." Was I always going to be paranoid about my belongings? I rolled my head around to

72

relive the stiffness that crept in from the boat ride.

The elevator came to a stop, and the doors slid open to a short hallway with only three doors. Vince led the way to the very last door and unlocked it. He opened the door and let me go in first.

I walked in, flipping the light switches as I went. It was a suite. I smiled. There was a living room, and two bedrooms with attached bathrooms. I would still have my privacy, I thought smiling. There was a long bank of windows along the far wall with heavy drapes. They had not been pulled for the night yet. I thought there was a balcony as well. Maybe if I got up early enough I would be able to get some sun before we had to leave.

I heard Vince close and lock the door. "This is really nice, Vince." I turned in a circle around the room. "You didn't have to spend this kind of money for one night. I would've been happy to share a regular room with you."

"I know, but you are going to want to go outside in the morning. If we shared a room, I would not let you leave and you would not be able to open the drapes to see outside. It would not be fair to you. This way you can go out on the terrace, and I will not worry about you." He sat on the couch and pulled his phone out. "Your room is over there." He pointed to the door on the left side of the room. "Your things should be in there. I have some calls to make before the sun comes up. Go and get some sleep, I will see you tomorrow."

"Goodnight." I turned and walked into my room hearing his phone ring as I closed the door.

The windows continued into my room and there was a door leading out to the terrace. This was going to be a nice place to stay. The king size bed, with a white down comforter on it, seemed luxurious after all the hostels I stayed in during the past few months. The walls were classic Greek whitewash, the floors were a dark dyed concrete and the wood trim was a dark mahogany. There was a dresser with a small television on it. My suitcase was on the luggage stand and my laptop case was sitting on the bed.

I opened my bags, dug out my toiletries and a clean pair of underwear before going into the bathroom. It was nice but nothing special. I turned the shower on, and took off my dirty clothes. I studied the spot where Lolita had taken a chunk out of my neck. It was gone. There was not even a hint of a scar. I smiled; I would not have a reminder of that night marring my skin for the rest of my life.

I jumped in the shower and let the hot water roll over me. It had been a very interesting night. I felt much more confident than I had before. Knowing who my mother was and why my life had taken such a big turn made me ready to face it head on. It was nice to have Vince to help me and protect me. He had his own agenda, and while I was not sure it was going to match up with mine, I was beginning to trust him. As much as I felt like I did not have a choice in trusting him, he was the only vampire who had not tried to kill me or enslave me. He knew who I was, what I could do, what I could do for his race and yet he did not want to take advantage of me.

After my shower, I put on clean underwear and climbed into bed. I looked at the clock; it read 4:45 a.m. I set the alarm for one in the afternoon; there was no way I was going to miss out on some sunshine. I shut the light off and was asleep in minutes.

# CHAPTER 12

The blaring of the alarm had me shooting off the bed wondering what was going on. Standing in just my panties, I looked cautiously around the room before I remembered it was the alarm. I dove across the bed and turned it off before throwing my arm over my eyes. *What in the hell was that?* Vince asked with his mind.

"Sorry, I didn't mean to wake you." I got up and went to the door. "I set an alarm. I wanted to wake up in time to enjoy the sun."

*It is fine. I was not asleep. I just did not know what the sound was.* He thought laughing to himself.

I turned without replying and went into the bathroom. When I was done, I put on my new bikini and a thin cover-up. I want to go straight out to the terrace, but I needed food before I did anything. I walked into the living room in search of the room service menu and found Vince watching the news on the television.

"What's going on in the world?" I found the menu on the coffee table and opened it.

"There was a huge fire in San Sebastian yesterday." He glanced at me looking concerned.

My stomach dropped and I put the menu down with shaky hands. "What?"

"It looks like someone set my house on fire and it spread to half the city." He looked at me, watching my hands shake. "Why are you so upset? I already dismissed my staff. The house was mostly empty. Everything I wanted to save was moved days before. I was leaving one way or another."

"In my dream, Lolita said it was my fault. She said I made her brother crazy, and he burned the city down because of me. She wanted me to pay for what I had done." I buried my face in my hands.

Vince put a hand on my back and rubbed lightly. "This is not your fault. Look at what they tried to do to you. No one was hurt in the fire; the city will rebuild. Do not let this ruin your day." He patted me hard on the back. "What happened to the bite?" he asked, noticing my unblemished neck.

"It healed, I guess." I ran my hand along the spot where the bite had been.

"Do you normally heal this quickly?" He was still looking at my neck, as if I had somehow hidden the mark.

"No," I said in a small voice. "What does it mean?"

"I do not know." He drew his eyebrows together. "I think you should ask your mother next time she visits your dreams. Do not worry; it is probably your mother's magic. What do you want for breakfast? I will order it for you."

"I don't know if I can eat." My dream had come true, I could not save Miguel and a city burned because of it.

"I will order you something." Vince took the menu from my hands. "Go outside and get some fresh air. I will let you know when the food gets here."

I got up mechanically and went through my room to the door leading to the terrace.

It was more like a roof top garden then a terrace.

There was a table and chairs for outdoor dining, a small lawn, and a plunge pool with lounge chairs around it. I looked over the railing; I had a view of most of the city and the Aegean beyond, it was amazing.

I tried to be excited to spend the day in such a great space, but the fire. It had been just like the dream I had with the 'evil one'. I wished I could find a way for her to leave me alone without killing her.

I went to the pool and dipped my foot in. It was cold, unheated, my favorite when it was hot and humid outside. I took my cover-up off, threw it on a chair and dove into the icy water. I surfaced gasping for air at the shock of the cold. I laid on my back and began to float. There was nothing I could do about what happened in San Sebastian. I had no way of knowing my dreams would come true. I needed to stop worrying about it, but it was crazy, my dreams were coming true.

Vince said no one had been hurt and they would rebuild. Was it my fault Miguel went crazy? I think he was crazy way before he met me, but Lolita was crazier than Miguel would ever be. I stiffened and shivered when I thought about Miguel, what he had done to me. I was starting to wonder if life would ever go back to normal.

*Your food is here. Please come eat, we are going to have a long night.*

"I'm coming." I shook off all thoughts of the 'evil ones' and got out of the pool. I used one of the towels left there to dry myself off before putting my cover-up back on. The gauzy material stuck to me and I was not sure how much of a cover up it was, but I had to try. Sometimes the way Vince reacted to me made me think he wanted to take me somewhere to ravage me. The idea did not bother me, but I needed a break from romance. Between Miguel and Mark, I was striking out with the male persuasion, and I wanted Vince to help me. Getting romantically involved with him might mess up what he could teach me.

I went inside bringing a towel with me and saw the spread he ordered. "Is there anything on the menu you didn't order?"

"I ordered a variety since I was not sure what you were in the mood for." He opened his laptop. "Please eat."

Looking at the food on the table, I was starving. I sat down and dug in. Everything was good. After a few mouthfuls I asked, "Have you gotten any sleep?"

He looked over his shoulder at me for a moment before looking back at the screen. "No, I do not need much. Your safety is more important than sleep right now."

"How can you protect me if you're tired?" I bit into a pastry and almost moaned when it melted in my mouth.

He looked at me again and smiled. "I will sleep when we are settled in Crete. Then I should be able to relax for a while."

"Good." I took a sip of the Greek coffee; it was sweet, strong, and good. "What are you working on now?"

"Tracking Lolita." He did not look up from the computer this time.

"Is she still in San Sebastian?" I picked up a piece of toast with feta cheese and olive oil on it.

"It looks like it. I would not be surprised if one of them started the fire because they realized you were at my house when they came over looking. You were in their grasp, but they did not find you. In their minds I stole you from them."

"I'm sorry they burned your house down Vince." I pushed away from the table full for the moment. "Is there anything I can do?"

He turned and met my eyes. "Yes, you can train and become strong enough to kill her."

"Do you think I will ever be strong enough to beat her?" I was not sure I would ever be.

"You have a lot to learn but I am confident you will be able to. It might not be until after you have been turned, but you will beat her."

His words reminded me of what the prophecy said about the one who changed me. I was just about to tell Vince what I read when his phone rang. He looked at the caller ID and then back to me.

"I have to take this call. Go and enjoy your time off, you will be hating life before too long." He laughed to himself.

"Okay," I said, dragging it out. I had no idea what he was talking about, but I grabbed one of the new books I had picked up at the store when I bought my clothes and went out to the lounge chair.

After rolling over a few times and jumping in the pool to cool off I was restless. I did not think it was possible to be bored after the past week of my life, but I could not seem to relax. I should have been relieved I had nothing to do until sunset, but I could not be still.

"Vince?" I asked. "Can you hear me out here?"

*Yes, I can*, he thought to me. *What is on your mind?*

"I'm bored. Is there anything I can do to start my training now?"

*If I were you, I would be enjoying the time off you have. You are going to be very busy for the next couple of months.* I heard him laugh through the glass on the windows.

"Is it going to be boot camp hard?" What was I getting myself into?

*What is boot camp?*

"It's what new military recruits go through when they join the military in the States."

79

*I know what you are talking about now, basic training. Hum, yes, I would say it will be very demanding.*

"I thought we were just going to work on some self-defense stuff." I cringed, I was going to have to be strong and fast to beat Lolita, but I did not know I was signing up for hell.

*It is in a way, but there will be a lot more to it. Let me tell you a story.*

"Okay." I put my head down on the lounge chair and closed my eyes to listen to him.

*I do not remember where I was born, but I remember being captured by Roman soldiers when I was about eight or nine years old, I think. They came into our village, killed all the men and took all of the women and children for slaves.*

*They sold me to a gladiator school because I was already big for my age and had some skill at fighting. The trainer took a liking to me. They thought I would be a good fighter one day. He trained me and taught me to fight as soon as I was strong enough to hold a weapon. I was the best fighter my school had ever had. Since I never knew any other life, I was content there. I was ready to put my life on the line in the ring to bring honor to my school and patriarch.*

*I was around twenty-five, when tragedy hit my school. I had just won a major fight; it brought a lot of recognition and money to my school.*

*You would think a gladiator school with fifty gladiators would be able to take out one vampire easily, but one man decimated us within an hour. I fought with my brothers and tried to save the women and the house slaves,* but there was nothing I could do.

When he reached me, I was tired. I had already fought in the ring that day, but I was determined. I was not going to give up my life for this man who sought to kill the only people I called family without a fight.

He told me I had killed his prizefighter in the ring and because of that, I could not live. I told him it had been the hardest fight of my life and he trained him well. I told him it would be an honor to die fighting the man who trained such a glorious fighter.

I was sure I was going to die, but when I looked into the vampire's eyes I saw a softness that was not there the moment before. Something I said changed his mind about killing me.

He told me to gather what things I would have and to come with him if I wanted to live. I asked him if he was going to kill me, he said, "not today." When I asked him what I should call him, he said Livius.

I did as Livius said and fetched the few things of worth I had. He took me to his school and instead of making me fight in the ring; he turned me into a trainer and his personal bodyguard.

Livius's school was very different from mine. He trained his men at night and let them rest during the day. He said the heat was harder to train in. I know now we trained at night only because he was a vampire and could not supervise during the day. Of course I had no idea he was a vampire until after he changed me.

We sent many gladiators into the ring and they won. More than they ever had before. Livius showered me with gifts and women for my help. He was proud of me. This was in 475 AD.

Later that year, we were getting ready to sleep for the day after a long night of training when a German tribe attacked our school. I did my duty to protect Livius, but during the fight I was stabbed in the gut, it was a deathblow. There was no chance I would

81

recover from the wound, and it would be a slow painful death. I was in the middle of the training yard and had no strength to pull myself to the house. I did not know if Livius lived or not, but I prayed I gave him enough time to get away. Eventually, I passed out from the pain wishing death would take me soon.

Death never came, although I wished it had when I returned to consciousness. Livius was sitting on the ground where with my head in his lap. He was holding his wrist over my mouth, and a slow steady stream of blood flowed from it into my mouth. I had lost most of my blood from my wound, I found out later, and Livius drank the rest of it before forcing his blood into my mouth to begin the change. I do not remember much of what happened after I woke up with his blood filling my mouth. Since I have created my own vampire, I can tell you there is a lot of pain and agony. You must endure it but the memory of it fades quickly. Your mind buries it from you because it does not want to relive the pain again.

Livius made me a vampire because he had always wanted a son like me, and I saved him even though I could have escaped and lived as a free man.

"Is Livius still alive?" I asked, flipping back over onto my back.

He has not adapted well to modern times. The past century changed the world in such vast ways; he could not handle it and became a hermit. The last time I saw him he was living near Mount Vesuvius.

"Thank you for sharing your story with me." I got back into the pool and tread water. "It was hard for you."

I do not enjoy thinking back to those times, but you

*had a right to know since I will be training you.* Something about the story had made him sad, almost depressed.

"Do you miss being human?" I asked, dunking my head in the water to cool off.

*I miss the sun sometimes, but it has been so long since I have seen it that I no longer miss it, except for times like these. If I were human, we would already be in Crete and you would be safe. I do not like thinking of those times because I was nothing but a brainwashed slave. I could do nothing but honor the masters who owned me. I think I was weak minded for not doing what Spartacus did and escaping when I had the chance.*

"I get it." I climbed out of the pool and stretched back out on the lounger. "Once you learned what freedom was it made you sick to think about how much you didn't mind being a slave. We spend our entire lives changing, yours has been a lot longer than most, cut yourself some slack. I bet if your human self saw what you have become he would be proud of you."

*You never cease to surprise me Katie. We will be leaving here as soon as the sun goes down, please be ready.*

I looked at my watch. I could have stayed out there until the sun went down, but I wanted to start my night clean for a change. I gathered my stuff and went inside to grab a shower.

Later at the airport, we were sitting in the always uncomfortable airport chairs waiting for our flight to begin boarding when the question hit me. "How often do you need to eat?" I leaned in close. I did not want anyone nearby to hear us.

*Why would you ask me that?* He raised an eyebrow to me.

"I would like to know when I should keep my distance from you. I don't want you going into bloodlust if I get a paper cut or something." I wondered if vampires got moody when they were hungry like men do.

*I do not have to eat every day or even every week, normally I eat at least once a week though. I had something the night before last, but it did not sit well with me. I will likely grab a bite when we get to Crete.*

I laughed. I could not help it, it seemed to grow from within me and I could not stop.

"What are you laughing at?" Vince asked in an irritated voice. "People are starting to stare."

"You made a joke. I'm so proud of you . . ." I trailed off trying to take deep breaths and holding my side.

"What did I say?" He sounded even more irritated than before.

"That you are going to grab a *bite* when we get there." My hysterical laughter even worse.

"I was merely using a typical American euphemism to explain that I will eat when we get there," he said quietly. "Please get ahold of yourself, you are causing a scene."

"You've got to admit, it's funny given the circumstances." I took a deep breath and was able to stop laughing but I could not help smiling. It felt like it had been a long time since I had really laughed.

"I would call it lowbrow humor at someone else's expense but yes, I see the humor in it." He finally chuckled a few times.

"We are going to have to work on your sense of humor, but we have somewhere to start," I said as the PA announced that our plane was beginning to board.

Sitting in our seats on the plane waiting to leave, I remembered what Vince said about eating something that did not agree with him. "What did you *eat* in Madrid that didn't agree with you?"

He turned his head and looked at me. His feelings were telling me he did not want to answer because he felt stupid for letting it happen. "A spy infiltrated a very old friend's family. My friend did not know the woman was on drugs and the woman did a good job of masking her scent. When I drank from her, the drug-tainted blood affected me as it did her. I pulled away once I recognized the taste, and I forced myself to vomit the blood, but it was too late. I ingested enough for it to addle my mind; I had to sleep it off. That is why you did not hear from me yesterday."

"I'm so sorry. You're better now, right?"

"Yes, thanks to your mother or I would still be sleeping it off."

"What did Mom do?" I looked at him quizzically.

"When she came to my dream wondering where you were, and why you were in distress, she burned the drug out me. If she had not, it would have been a week before I would have been able to travel."

"What happened to the spy?" I did not care what happened to her, but I wanted to know. I was just relieved Mom had help Vince get better.

"Maria took care of her. She was spying for Lolita, trying to get information out of me about your whereabouts."

My stomach fell, Vince was drugged because of me. He could have been forced to give away my location and then what. "This is all my fault. I'm sorry Vince. Is there anything I can do?"

"Do not say it is your fault. It is Lolita's fault and Maria's for not keeping a shorter leash on her donors. I offered to help you get away, you did not force me."

"Still if I had never come to San Sebastián none of this would've happened."

"Did you learn nothing from our trip to Delos? You were destined to go to San Sebastian; you cannot outrun your destiny. You might be able to put it off for a while, but it will ways catch up with you. Thinking about what you should have done is not going to solve anything. Learn from the experience and do not let yourself fall back on what you let happen. You cannot move forward if you are constantly looking behind you."

What he said was true, but it did not make the guilt I felt go away. "I will try and look forward from now on."

"You know what Yoda said, 'there is no try, only do or do not.' You will learn from what you have been through, and take away opportunities to grow from it." Vince settled back in his seat and closed his eyes. "Now rest, it is going to be another long night."

"Thank you for everything Vince." I leaned my head back and looked out at the night sky for a minute before I let my eyes close and sleep take me.

# CHAPTER 13

When we landed on Crete, we were met in the baggage area by a vampire who could have passed for human if I had not felt him. He had black curly hair with an olive complexion and a wide nose. His short frame was dressed in a tailored off-white suit. I thought he must be newly turned. He held a sign with our real first names written on it. We retrieved our luggage and walked over to him. Vince greeted him in Greek and introduced me to him. He nodded without introducing himself and turned expecting us to follow him.

We pulled our bags behind us, struggling to keep up with the vampire. He could have offered to take at least one bag, I thought to myself.

*I will be talking to Theron about this*, Vince thought to me. *This guy has no respect for his elders.*

"No kidding," I said quietly as we made our way to a dark Mercedes sedan with tinted windows.

The vampire popped the trunk and got behind the wheel waiting for us to load our own luggage. There was something odd going on. Vince looked upset as he first put his bag in the trunk then mine. He slammed the lid closed leaving two dents from the impact.

As soon as we sat down on the backseat, the driver took off almost before we had the doors closed. I looked at Vince with my eyebrows raised wondering, what this guy's problem was.

Vince tried to engage him in conversation and the vampire replied in one or two word responses. I started wondering if we were walking into a trap. Since I could not think to Vince without starting a slave bond, I had to resort to technology to have a private word with him. I pulled my phone out and sent a text message to him since I had his number:

Do you think this is a trap?

He looked at his phone when it buzzed and then looked at me. *I do not think so. This guy thinks he is too high up in the chain of command to be relegated to picking up people from the airport.*

I picked up my phone again and typed:

I hope you're right.

*Me too,* he thought and then turned to look out the window. I turned and did the same. There was not much to see as we left the city, but I could see the silhouettes of the mountains and buildings as we passed. Crete was pretty under the light of the moon; I could not wait to see what it looked like with the Mediterranean sun beating down on it.

We slowed down at a guard shack in the middle of nowhere. The driver stopped and spit something out in rapid Greek.

*He said to let him through already. He has a hot date he does not want to be late for,* Vince thought. *We will see if he makes it to his date or not.*

When the gate lifted, the driver hit the gas pedal causing the tires to squeal and took off down the private lane. He slowed the tiniest bit before turning off the lane onto a driveway that wound its way up to a Greek-style mansion. When we arrived at the house he slammed on the brakes hard enough they screeched, I was flung forward in my seat, and Vince put his arm out to stop me from flying through the front seat and into the windshield.

The driver popped the trunk and jumped out. I could feel anger pouring off Vince. It was the first time I had seen him really mad, but instead of kicking the guy's ass like I wanted to, he calmly got out of the car. He went around to the trunk where the driver was throwing, literally throwing, our bags onto the ground behind the car.

I got out of the car quickly; I did not want to miss seeing what Vince was going to do to the vampire. I moved to stand on the walkway leading to the front door, while Vince took the driver by the scruff of the neck and spoke quietly into his ear. The driver struggled and tried to escape, but Vince was not going to let him go anywhere.

*Katie, be a dear and ring the doorbell please,* he thought to me. I hurried up four steps to the front door and pushed the button for the doorbell. Vince came up beside me with the driver in tow. The door opened almost immediately and a tall vampire with dark buzzed hair and a perfectly trimmed goatee stood in the doorway smiling until he saw Vince holding our driver.

"Vince, can you please explain why you have my third in command by the scruff of his neck?" The vampire asked.

*Tell him please, I am too angry to speak.*

"Well, sir this guy picked us up from the airport barely said two words to us, made us carry all our luggage and load it into the trunk. He drove like the world was going to end. Then he tried his hardest to send me through the windshield when we pulled up here. When he got out of the car, instead of helping us with our luggage, he opened the trunk and threw everything out without any care as you can see." I waved my hand toward the bags all over the driveway. "Vince is pissed."

The vampire, who must have been Theron, looked disgusted with his third in command. "Vince, what would you like me to do with him?"

If the driver could have pissed himself, I think he would have. From the feelings I was getting from him, he had no idea how important we were. He was told to go to the airport to pick up some guests. It never occurred to him that he was sent because we were guests of importance.

Vince looked at him for a second. "Get him out of my sight before I send him to Hades, although I doubt they would have him now." He let go and pushed him away.

The driver bowed to Theron while speaking rapid Greek, he was apologizing profusely by the look of it. Theron replied gruffly and the driver ran off.

With the driver gone, Theron opened his arms. "Vince, it's good to see you. I'm so sorry for the way you were treated on your way to my home. I'll punish Ben for his transgression."

Vince shook himself as if he was trying to brush his anger away. He smiled while approaching Theron and took him in his arms. "I am sure you will make a punishment that fits the crime." He pulled back from the hug after a moment. "Let me introduce you to Katie." He held his arm out toward me.

"Katie," Theron said, offering me his hand. "It's a pleasure to meet you. Vince has told me much about you. I look forward to spending some time with you. But come, leave your bags I will have someone come and get them, let's go inside." He shook my hand politely.

I followed the vampires into the house while trying to get a read on Theron. His feelings were complicated. Like Miguel's, but they were not deceitful toward me. He was jealous of Vince for some reason.

We followed him through an ornate ground level until we reached the back of the house. We went out the doors to a terrace where there was a table set up with food and wine. He took a seat at the head of the table and Vince pulled out a chair for me. I sat down and whispered a thank you as he went over to the other side of the table to take his seat.

"Welcome to Crete," Theron said, pouring wine into the glasses in front of him. "I would ask how you liked it so far, but I don't think I would like the answer. I will ask you again after you have settled in." He finished handing me my wine glass then added a few drops of blood to his and Vince's glass. He passed Vince his glass and held his up in salute. "To the prophecy finally coming to fruition. May you reign as long as you are worthy of being the vampire queen." Theron held up his glass for a second then took a sip of wine.

I was a little shocked by his toast, but there was not much I could do about it. "Thank you for your hospitality," was all I could say before taking a sip of my wine.

"Yes, thank you, Theron, this may not be easy on you as we have enemies trying to find us, but this is the safest place I know. We needed a place where we can train and get Katie ready to change." Vince took a sip of his wine.

"When you say enemies, you mean Miguel and Lolita?" Theron asked, taking a sip of his wine, and setting it down on the table. "Katie, please help yourself to the food. You're the only one here at the moment to eat it."

"Thanks." I took a plate and filled it with roasted chicken, spinach, and rice.

"Yes, I believe they have already figured out I helped Katie escape."

"How can you be sure?" Theron set his wine glass down, rested his elbows on the table and smoothed his perfect goatee with his thumb and pointer finger.

"My home in San Sebastian was burned to the ground last night." Vince gulped his wine. He was more upset than he let on about losing his home. Guilt clawed at me again, it was my fault.

"You already cleared everything out though, right?"

"Yes, everything that matters was moved to Pompeii. I never told Miguel about my home there."

"That was wise; you don't think he knows you're here?" Theron picked up his wine again.

"Not yet, but he knows about you. Every vampire over ten years old knows about Crete. He will figure out where we are before long. I am worried about Lolita. If she figures out we are here, I think she will napalm the whole island to get rid of Katie."

"Won't Miguel tell her when he figures it out?" I asked in between bites of food.

"I am betting they had a falling out after losing you. In Miguel's mind the only reason he lost you was because of Lolita." Vince finished his wine and stood up to pace. "You said Lolita wants to kill you. Do you think Miguel would let her?"

I thought about it for a second. "No, he totally believes in the prophecy, he would likely rather die than allow me to be killed."

"Even if he suspected where we went he would not

tell Lolita about it. You are too important to our race." Vince sat back down and poured another glass of wine.

"There's a reason why I have the rules I do about vampires on my island. Miguel is aware of them, as is Lolita. We are in lockdown. No vampires are allowed on the island or to leave without my permission." Theron moved his chair back and rested an ankle on his knee. He picked up his glass and swirled the liquid around. "That should help keep you on the down low."

"Can you trust your vampires?" I asked, taking a sip from my wine. "All they would have to do is pick up a phone and tell Lolita we're here. I don't want you to go to war over me."

"They all know what will happen if they turn on me. I'm not worried about it and you shouldn't either."

He believed what he said. I was going to have to trust him. There was no other choice unless I wanted to leave and risk going out on my own. I was not ready to be on my own yet. "Okay, I will give you the benefit of the doubt for now." I looked over at Vince who was staring at me with a small smile. "Thank you for the food; it was wonderful." I placed my napkin on the table and let a yawn sneak out.

"I'm glad you enjoyed it. We have a cook come in when we entertain humans, but it is not very often."

"Whoever it was did a good job." I looked over to Vince who had gone quiet. I reached out to him to try to get a sense of his mood. All I could feel was hunger. "Vince, why don't you go get something to eat?"

Vince looked at me with a menacing gaze. *That was a rude thing to say.*

"I don't care if it was rude; your hunger is making you cranky." I looked to Theron. "Theron, I'm sorry if I was rude, but Vince needs to eat soon. He had a rough day yesterday."

Theron let out a full bellied laugh looking from Vince to me then back at Vince. "She already knows you too well, Vince. He was the same way when we were together. He would wait until he was starving to eat. Come, let me show you your house then I'll take Vince to get some dinner. Tomorrow night we can talk about how we are going to beat Lolita and Miguel."

We rose as one and followed Theron down the stairs of the terrace to a gravel path where a four-person golf cart waited for us. Theron got in on the driver's side, Vince went to the front passenger and I sat behind Theron. "Modern technology is so nice, this makes it much easier to get around the grounds," Theron said as we took off down the road. "You'll have the use of one while you are here as well."

"That'll be fun." I grabbed the edges of the seat as we went around a sharp corner.

"You will not be driving these very often," Vince said from the front seat.

"Why not? I have a car back at home."

"Because you will be running everywhere you want to go. Your training begins the day after tomorrow." He sounded a little too excited. "Did you buy any workout clothes when you went shopping?"

"I bought a few things, running shoes, shorts and a sports bra. Sorry, I didn't know I would need it." At the time, I had no idea if I would ever see him again.

"Tomorrow you will go shopping for more. I will give you a list of things you will need."

"Why am I going to be running everywhere? I'm in good shape now. I just need to learn how to fight."

"And in order to fight you need to build up your stamina."

"You're going to torture me, aren't you?" I felt grim satisfaction rolling off him.

"I will not cause any long-term damage." I could feel him smile. "But yes, I am sure you will think of much of it as torture."

Theron laughed. "I've been where you are, he is going to make you hurt more than you have ever hurt in your life. I'm glad I passed my training, I never want to go through anything like that again."

"There's a test?" I felt out of my element now. I was an athletic person but I was not good at tests.

"Yes, and, Vince, I would like to talk to you about the test. I have an epic plan." Theron looked at me through the rearview mirror and winked.

"Do not worry about the test now. You can worry about it when you are ready," Vince said.

"Where are we going?" I asked, trying to get my bearings, but we had twisted and turned so much I had no idea where we were now.

"Almost to your new home." Theron pointed to a small house, at least compared to his mansion, with a light on. "I had one of my servants take your things over. If anything is damaged, let me know and I'll be happy to add them to Ben's punishment."

"I will go over everything meticulously and let you know." Vince was still pissed about how Ben had treated us. "He will have to sign up for a sparring session with Katie in a few weeks. Once she has the basics down, it will be very entertaining for us and painful for him."

"Vince, he's been through my training program," Theron said as he parked the cart at the front entrance of the house. "You may need to push sparring back a few months."

Vince laughed. "Is that a challenge?" He turned and looked at Theron.

"Do you want to make a bet?" Theron looked smug. "A gentleman's bet of course."

"So be it." Vince agreed getting out of the cart. "Shall we say two weeks from tomorrow?" He offered Theron his hand.

"Done, to help you out I'll start his punishment tomorrow night. It will give him something to think about for the next two weeks." Theron shook Vince's hand. "Now, let me show Katie around her new home."

I got out of the cart thinking men had such odd ways of having fun. If Vince thought I was going to be able to kick a vampire's ass, even a young one, in just two weeks he had another think coming. I had never been in a real fight. Well, I did break Isabelle's finger, punched Mark and Lolita, and then there were the girls on the ferry, but those were not fights, they were acts of violence I needed to partake in to survive.

Theron lead us through the front door into the foyer. It looked small from the outside, but any house that has a foyer is a pretty big house. It was homier than the mansion. There was soft pink marble on the floor with white washed walls. The artwork hanging on the walls were mostly of Greek villages and the islands. I found them soothing.

Theron took us through a small formal living room, a basic kitchen, a dining room, and a den. Then he led us upstairs. At the top, the walls were covered in Japanese rice paper. He stood in front of the wall and slid the door back allowing me to see inside the room. It was a dojo, with hardwood floors. One wall was covered with mirrors, another had a variety of weapons I had seen before in ninja movies, but I did not know their names. The other wall was all glass, it looked like the glass could slide open allowing fresh air to come in.

We did not enter, only looked through the doorway. "You will not enter this room until we talk about what is expected of you in here. This is a sacred place where you will come to learn martial arts." Vince's voice was as serious as I had ever heard. It made me take a step back. "Theron will you show Katie to her room? I need a moment."

"Of course, Katie, if you will follow me." He turned and led the way back down the stairs.

I followed him as quietly as I could. Had I upset Vince in some way? I could feel tears start to burn the back of my eyes. There was nothing to cry about, but I felt like I had let him down somehow.

Noticing my mood Theron turned toward me at the bottom of the stairs. "He's not mad at you. He takes his martial arts very seriously. He'll explain it all to you when he is ready to start your training."

"Thanks." I wiped the tears from my eyes. I trusted Theron for some reason, he seemed honest, and I thought he was someone who would always speak his mind no matter who heard him.

"Your room is over here," he said, going down the hall and stopping at a closed door off the den. He opened the door and motioned for me to go in first.

A small bedside lamp was already turned on providing a dim glow. I reached out for a light switch and turned it on. The room was a good size. There was a queen size bed with a black metal frame and a light quilt on top of it. There was an armchair with a matching ottoman in one corner positioned to look out the window. There were two other doors in the room.

"Your closet is through that door." Theron pointed to the door closest to the hallway. "Your bags should be in there. The other door leads to the bathroom."

"This is perfect." I smiled at Theron. "I can't wait to see the view from here during the day."

"I think you will enjoy it. The view is why I gave this room to you and not Vince. He has spent enough time here in the past to enjoy the view." Theron stepped back out into the hall.

"Where is Vince's room?"

"It's the next door down." Theron indicated down the hallway. "He told me you would need separate rooms, is that okay?"

I felt a blush hit my cheeks and I looked down. "Yes, Vince and I aren't romantically involved."

"Good," Theron said, sounding pleased.

"What is so good?" Vince asked, stepping out of his room.

"I was correct that you two were not sharing a room." Theron did not bother to lie about what we were talking about. "Shall we go and get something to eat?"

"Yes, but can you please give me a private moment with Katie first?"

"Yes, of course. I will meet you outside." Theron turned and left the room.

"Tell me what you thought of Theron," Vince asked, taking a seat on the sofa.

"He is genuine, dominant, and honest." I sat down across from him. "And I think he finds me very attractive."

"What?" Vince shot to his feet as if he already claimed me as his. "How do you know?"

"He thought to me," I lied. I was not ready to let Vince know I could do more than hear their thoughts.

"Do you want to sleep with Theron?" Vince sat back

98

down and folded his fingers together under his chin.

"Two things, Vince." I got up and paced back and forth. "Number one, I have zero interest in men or vampires right now. Look at what I just went through with Miguel and Mark. Number two, it would be none of your business if I did want to fuck Theron." I was yelling by the time I was done. How could Vince make me so mad so quickly?

"I am sorry I brought it up," was all he said before getting up and walking toward the front door where Theron waited.

# CHAPTER 14

Outside Theron put his hand on Vince's shoulder. "Are you in love with her?"

Vince looked up to meet Theron's eyes. "How could I not be? She is amazing, but I do not think I am meant for her."

"Why do you say that? Not everything the prophecy says is going to come true. You must know that."

"Yes, things can change and with her they probably will, but I am her protector. I should not even try to get involved with her. You know my rules." They got back into the golf cart and Theron drove toward the donor house.

"Bodyguards cannot be romantically involved with their body. You drilled it into my head hundreds of times," Theron said, making a sharp turn and Vince grabbed the chicken bar to keep from flying out. "Is that why you are going to train her?"

"No, if she is to be queen, she will have bodyguards, but she will need to be able to take care of herself." Vince thought about how she had taken down both Isabelle and Lolita. He chuckled thinking how she got her suitcase back the day before. "I think she is a warrior at heart."

"It is probably half the reason you are falling for her. The other half being that she is to be queen."

"At first, I was interested because she was 'The One', but as I get to know her, she is amazing. She has a huge heart. She will not put up with anyone's crap she learned her lesson there. She is not the slut I initially thought she was. Miguel and Lolita really fucked with her head. With a little bit of work, she will be an amazing leader of our kind."

"She's going to have to prove herself to a lot of vampires before she gets too powerful. Most of the vampires around today do not follow the old ways if they follow a religion at all. She might be a hard sell." Thereon stopped the golf cart and got out of the driver's seat.

"Wait until you see what she can already do," Vince said, getting out and joining Theron at the door.

"What are you talking about?" Theron asked, before opening the door and holding it open for Vince.

"She knows you want to fuck her." Vince walked into the house heading for the living room, where the donors would be waiting for them. He was looking forward to a good meal, he might even take two.

"How could she know that? She doesn't even know me." Theron followed Vince into the living room.

"We will talk about it tomorrow." Vince picked up the hands of two females and led them toward one of the more private donor rooms. If he ate with Theron, he would likely go into a frenzy and he did not want to kill all of Theron's donors tonight. He was going to be here for a while.

# CHAPTER 15

Miguel pulled the throttle back from max; the boat's engine could not take the abuse of red lining the RPMs for long. He maintained a slightly slower, steady speed and thought of finding his Katie at the temple. Where she should be. He had a lot to atone for, and he was ready to do anything she asked only to be forgiven and bask in her glory. If not at her side, then close by.

Part of him hated that she had been able to break the bond, the other part of him was happy, maybe he could have another chance with her. Then he remembered how he took her in the shower, she said no and fought him. No, she would never give him another chance to rule at her side. Now he prayed she would forgive him and let him keep his life. After what happened in the shower, she probably wanted to kill him. If she did not, then she was not worthy of being the vampire queen.

He tied the boat up to the dock and ran as fast as he could to the temple. He had been there once many decades before with his father. They examined the text and the tapestry for many nights trying to find all the secrets buried there. They did not find anything more than what they already knew, but to be in the temple of Asteria, the maker of vampires, it was a life affirming thing. Not long after they returned, Lolita killed their father. The thought of his father being tied to a tree as the sun's rays burned him until there was nothing left, made his heart hurt. How could Lolita do such a thing to her maker? The one who saved her from her life as a cheap whore? Miguel would never forgive her for what she had done.

As he approached the steps of the temple the disciples guarding the door recognized him as a vampire and did not delay his entry. He burst through the door and ran into the altar room. He looked around frantically trying to find the woman he wronged, ready to fall to his knees and beg her for forgiveness, but the only person in the room was a lone priest bent over the altar. He looked up at the ruckus Miguel caused when he slammed through the doors.

The priest bowed to the altar and rose to meet Miguel in the middle of the room. "How can I help you child?" the priest asked, folding his hands in front of his robe, then hiding his hands in the sleeves.

"Where is she?" Miguel bellowed at the vampire across from him.

"Where is who?" the priest asked, not liking the feeling he was getting from this vampire.

"Katie, 'The One.'" Miguel turned looking for a door to the back. "Are you hiding her? I screwed up. I need to tell her I'm sorry. I need to make her understand, I would do anything for her."

"She is no longer here," the priest said in an annoyingly calm voice, making Miguel want to backhand him and send him through the thick wall. "She did not feel it was safe to stay here because others were looking for her. Are you one of the others?"

"I was." Miguel fell to his knees letting red tears roll

down his cheeks. "I was wrong. I was so wrong. I must find her and surrender myself to her. I need her forgiveness."

The priest looked down at him with hard eyes. How could this vampire do anything requiring forgiveness from 'The One'? Blowing out a frustrated breath, he said the only thing he could think of. "You must pray to the Goddess for forgiveness."

"I will, but what about Katie?" He staggered to his feet. "I need her forgiveness too."

"I do not know where she went. Her protector would not tell me for her own safety."

"Vince?" he asked, confirming what he had smelled in Vince's home.

"Yes, come pray for forgiveness from the mother and she will show you the way." The priest gestured toward the altar.

Miguel staggered a step before finding his feet and made his way to the altar. He sank to his knees again and bent his head in reflection.

*Goddess, creator of the vampires I humbly ask you for forgiveness for the sins I committed against your daughter.* He prayed to himself thinking of how he took advantage of Katie and used her. All because he could not let a human have power over him. *Please tell me what I need to do to gain your forgiveness and allow me the opportunity beg it from your most incredible daughter.*

There was no response. He did not believe he would get one. He had to find a way to make this up to both of them. He must put everything else aside and do whatever he could to be there for Katie.

He rose from his knees and turned to find the priest watching him. "Do you wish to stay with us here?" the priest asked, opening his arms. "Become a disciple of Asteria and pledge your life to her cause?"

Miguel thought about leaving everything behind, and

becoming a disciple. It would be one way to gain the Goddess' forgiveness, but it was not only her forgiveness he needed. He had to find Katie. "After I have gained Katie's forgiveness I will come back and join you. At this time, I will not be able to give my whole self to the Goddess knowing her daughter hates me."

"We will be here when you are ready, my brother." The priest turned toward the door to the backroom. "If you do not wish to spend the day here you must leave soon."

"Thank you, Priest for your counsel. I will be back." He looked at his watch agreeing with the priest; it was time to head back to Mykonos.

# CHAPTER 16

I slept like the dead. I felt safe for the first time in what felt like weeks. No dreams of my mother, no one was in my room when I woke up. I was not hooked up to an IV, and I was in a house not a hotel room. I felt Vince close by making sure no one bothered me. I wished I could stay in this safe cocoon forever, but I had a job to do. Vince had said shopping? Was a vampire actually going to let me out without an escort to make sure no harm came to me? I found it hard to believe.

I got up, showered, and dressed in comfortable shorts and a t-shirt. I slid my feet into flip-flops and went into the kitchen to find something to eat.

Vince was sitting in a chair in the dining room when I passed. "Good morning," I said as I walked by.

"Did you sleep well?" Vince asked, suddenly right behind me.

Startled, I jumped and spun around. "Please don't sneak up on me." I turned and went to the cabinets to start looking for coffee. I opened the cabinet above the coffeepot and sure enough, pulled out a bag of coffee.

"You need to be more aware of your surroundings. I will sneak up on you until you pay more attention, and I am unable to sneak up on you anymore." His voice told me he was serious.

"That's not fair, I don't have vampire hearing." I turned on the sink to fill the decanter with water then turned to put coffee grounds into the filter.

"Do you think Lolita cares what is fair?" Vince countered, sounding annoyed.

I turned off the sink and poured the water into the coffeemaker. "You're right. She'll take advantage of every weakness I have." I blew out a breath, put the decanter on the hot plate and flipped the power switch.

"Good, everything we do from here on out will prepare you for the day you meet Lolita in battle. I expect you to take your training seriously." Vince leaned against the counter folding his arms across his chest.

I turned, got a mug out of the cabinet, and set it next to the coffeepot. I went to the refrigerator and opened the door. It was stocked with all kinds of food. Most of it would need to be cooked, and I had no idea what to do with it. I shrugged. I was going to have to learn to cook.

"Are you looking for cream?" Vince sounded worried.

"No, I drink my coffee black. I was just deciding what to make for breakfast." I pulled eggs and cheese out of the fridge and closed the door.

"I already made you breakfast. It is in the dining room waiting for you."

"Wow, thanks. You didn't have to." I put the eggs and cheese back into the refrigerator, smiled at Vince, filled up my coffee cup, and went into the dining room.

"I am your sensei; it is my job to make sure all of your needs are met." He followed me into the dining room and I took the seat in front of a plate covered with a lid.

"That's a new one for me." I sat down, pulled the lid off the plate, and dug into the scrambled eggs with one hand while picking up a slice of bacon with the other. "Can we talk about this whole training program?"

"Very well, what would you like to know?"

"Can I get an overview of what you are planning for me?"

"During the day we will work on increasing your stamina. There will be long runs and swims, at night we will practice martial arts. We will also be working on honing your special skills. Theron and his second in command, Helen, will be giving you Greek lessons. I think you will pick it up quickly since you seem to unknowingly speak it already." Vince leaned back in his chair and folded his arms across his chest. "You are going to be very busy."

I chewed the food in my mouth and set my fork down. "I realized something on Delos, every time I dream of my mother we converse in Greek. I wish I knew where it was coming from."

"It is likely a gift from your mother. It is latent so you never realized you were doing it before. If you try and speak it you cannot, but if we teach you the basics you should be able to pick the rest up pretty quick."

"I hope you're right. I think learning Greek is going to be important down the road." Finished eating, I pushed my plate back and swallowed the last of my coffee. "What now?"

"Shopping, then when you get back we will talk in more detail about your training program. Theron and Helen are going to come over to talk to you about your Greek lessons as well."

"Helen is Theron's second in command?"

"Yes, I think you will like her. She is tough but not a bitch like Lolita," Vince said getting up. "You need to hit the road so you can get your shopping done."

"How am I getting to the store?" I got up and followed Vince down the hall.

"Theron is letting you borrow one of his cars." Vince walked to the basement door. "You can drive a manual transmission, right?"

I gulped. "I can, but I'm not very good at it." We made our way down the basement stairs. Theron had not included this on his tour and I wondered why.

"You will need to be careful. Theron's cars are his baby's. He will notice if anything is damaged." Vince hit a light switch at the bottom of the stairs. The room was unfinished with concrete walls and the ceiling was lined with ductwork, pipes and floor joists. Crates lined the walls stacked two and three high. No wonder he did not include it on the tour, it was pretty boring.

"What's in the crates?" I asked as we moved to the far corner. Vince pulled one of the stacks of three back from the wall like they were filled with pillows to open an entrance to a tunnel.

"Sometimes it is better not to ask," Vince replied and headed down the tunnel. "There are no lights in here. If you need to, put your hand on my shoulder."

"Thanks." At first, the backlight from the basement light gave me enough to see by, but as soon as we made the first turn I could not see anything. I reached out to Vince but he was not there. "Vince?"

I heard him stop and I ran into his back. "Sorry, I thought you were further away."

"You need to be less dependent on your eyes. Use your other senses; they will guide you better than your eyes most of the time." I listened to his feet begin to move and I reached my hand out to find his shoulder.

I closed my eyes and listened as we moved through the tunnel. There were no sounds other than our breathing and the quiet shush of fabric and shoes on the dirt floor. Vince was silent compared to me. I felt like I was stomping through the tunnel while Vince glided above it without touching the ground. He could see what was in front of him though while I was blind.

"Watch your step we are heading up into the garage," Vince moved up the steps pausing so I could find the treads. When we reached the top, he stopped and opened the door. A dim light came through the door allowing me to let go of Vince and find my own way. I had to blink my eyes to adjust to the light. The tunnel was so dark even the muted light hurt my eyes.

"How can you see down there?" Eyes need to have some kind of light to reflect the surroundings; there was no light to reflect in the tunnel.

"My eyes are trained to see in the darkest night. I cannot explain how. I cannot see very well down there but it's enough to get from point A to point B." He walked over to a BMW sedan and opened the door for me.

"A BMW?" I looked at it for a moment before sitting down in the driver's seat. It was the nicest car I had ever been in and now I got to drive it? It was going to be a good day. The creamy leather hugged my body as I put my hands on the steering wheel and looked around. There was an LCD display in the center, and a manual transmission. At least the gears were printed in normal lettering, and not in the Greek alphabet. "Is the GPS programmed for English or Greek?"

"I am not sure let's find out." He walked over to the passenger door, opened it and sat down. "Turn the key on I need power to see how it is programmed."

I turned the key over and the dash-lights and indicators came on. Vince pushed a few buttons and smiled. "You are set up in English now. Here is the address of the shopping center. I just set this location up as home. You should be good to go." He got out of his side of the car and walked back around the car to me.

"You're really letting me go by myself?" Fear of being alone surged through me. I reminded myself was safe on the island and I was a big girl, I could take care of myself.

"Why not? You are not a prisoner; I do not want you to feel like you are. The island is safe, and it is the middle of the day. What trouble can you find?" Vince leaned over in between my open door and the car.

"It seems to find me," I muttered. "Okay, I'll be back in a while." I forced a smile and found my courage. I did it on my own in Athens, right?

"You have your phone. If you need anything call me." He stood up and stepped back. "And if you see anything else you need, get it. Do not allow yourself to feel guilty about it."

"Thank you." I closed the door and rolled down the window. "I'll try and not to take too long."

"Have a good time. This will be your last free day for a few weeks so take advantage of it." Vince went back to the door leading to the tunnels.

I hit the button on the garage door opener, turned the key to start the car and nothing happened. All the indicators were on so it was not the battery. I turned the key again and nothing happened. What was wrong with this car? I hit the steering wheel with the palm of my hand.

*You have to push the clutch in, then turn the key to start the car*, Vince thought and I blushed. Duh, I was driving a standard transmission.

I pushed in the clutch, made sure it was in neutral, and turned the key. The engine growled to life. "Thanks," I said, figuring he could hear me. I put the car into first gear, slowly let off the clutch while gently applying pressure to the gas pedal. The car lurched forward a few feet and stalled.

*Are you sure you know how to drive a standard?* I felt his amusement at my difficulty.

"Yes, it's just been awhile." I would not let Vince or this car beat me. I started over, got my timing right and rocketed out of the garage barely remembering to hit the button to close the door before following the driveway to the front gate.

*Please be careful with Theron's car,* was the last thought I heard from Vince before I was out of range. The gate came up before me and opened automatically. I looked at the GPS display and followed the directions to the shopping center. It was just far enough away for me to figure out the clutch and start enjoying the ride.

Shopping in Crete was much more fun than it was in Athens. When I shopped in Athens, I only got the necessities, focusing on traveling light. Since Vince had given me his blessing on getting what I needed I did. I even found a t-shirt for Vince I thought he would like.

I found a café to have lunch at and started reading one of the new books I picked up. I was so engrossed in the story that I did not notice a shadow stop in front of me. When I did, I had no idea how long he had been standing there. I cursed myself for not paying better attention. I looked up to see a young man standing a few feet away from me. He was my height, but gangly like he was just hitting puberty and had not had a chance to grow into his body yet. He had a thin face; his cheekbones protruded, his long narrow nose held up a pair of aviator-mirrored sunglasses. He had shaggy dirty blond hair; it looked like he had not cut it in months. He was not ugly but he was not handsome either.

"Yasou," he said awkwardly as if Greek was not his first

113

language.

"Hi," I said, looking away trying to show disinterest.

"You speak English?" He sat down at my table uninvited, and made himself at home. "There aren't many people on this side of the island who speak it."

"I'm new here." I closed my book, put it in my purse, and pulled out my wallet to pay the bill.

"How long are you going to be here?" he asked, watching every move I made, and ignoring that I was trying to leave.

"I'm not sure. It depends on a lot of things." I put money on the table and stood up.

"Why are you running off?" He pushed his chair back.

"Because I was enjoying a nice lunch when a rude American decided to sit down and bug me without asking." I was being rude in return, but this guy rubbed me the wrong way.

"Look, I'm sorry." He got up and put his hands in the pockets of his cargo shorts. "I thought you were from home, and I wanted to talk with someone from back in the States."

"I'm sorry you're homesick, but I really have to be going." I headed for the car not giving him a second glance.

That was creepy, I thought to myself as I drove back to the compound. When did I start attracting all the weirdos?

I forced myself to stopped thinking about it, and concentrated on the road and the hum of the engine as I tore around curves, enjoying the landscape flying by. There was something to be said about German engineering after all.

I had no idea how long the police had been following me, I was too busy enjoying the ride but when the siren went off behind me I jumped, and froze looking down at the speedometer. I was going a hundred and twenty kilometers per hour in an area zoned for eighty. That was not good. I pulled the car over and tried to keep calm. It was not the first time I had been pulled over.

I rolled my window down when the officer stepped up beside me. "Hi, do you speak English?"

"Yes, do you know how fast you were going?" I could barely understand him with his thick accent.

"Yes sir, I'm sorry this is my friend's car and it got away from me. I'm not use to driving something so nice." I was trying to be polite and innocent.

"Can I see your driver's license and the registration for the car please?"

I took my wallet out of the front seat remembering I was no longer Katie Hunter, but Mary Sims. I gave it to him then leaned over to open the glove box. I found a bunch of papers all in Greek. "I'm not sure what you need." I handed all of them to the man.

Another officer approached my car and started speaking in rapid Greek. The officer stopped looking at the paperwork and put his free hand on his gun. "Please step out of the car, Ms. Sims."

Adrenaline raced through me. What was the problem? Had Theron reported the car stolen? I unclicked my seat belt and opened the door. I got out and stood up waiting for the next order.

"Walk to the front of the car and place both hands on the hood."

"What's going on?" I asked shakily, walking to the front of the car, and putting my hands on the hot hood. "This is really hot; can we do this on the trunk?"

"Stay where you are." He came up behind me and started frisking me. "Do you know who this car belongs to?"

"It's Theron's." Realizing I did not know what last name, he

115

went by. "He gave me permission to use his car while I'm visiting him."

Done frisking me he pulled one arm behind my back and attached a cuff to my wrist, then pulled the other one behind me and cuffed it. "We are verifying that now. He does not take kindly to car thieves." He helped me stand up straight then walked me back to his car. "Where is your passport?"

"In my wallet sitting on the front seat of the car." I prayed Vince had given Theron my alias, if not this could get out of control quickly.

He opened the back door of his car and indicated for me to get in. Not wanting to get into more trouble than I already was, I ducked my head in and sat down uncomfortably with my hands behind my back. If I ended up in jail it would be hard for Lolita to get to me, I thought. That was me, always looking on the bright side of things.

The officer's partner was on the phone talking quickly. He said something to his partner. He must have been on hold. After a few minutes with me praying I would not end up in a Greek prison, and wondering if it would be as bad as a Turkish prison, the man started to speak again. He stopped speaking suddenly as if the person on the other end of the line cut him off. He listened as the voice on the other line became so loud that if I spoke Greek I would have understood it word for word. It was Theron and he sounded mad.

The officer who cuffed me jumped out of the car, opened my door, helped me out and took the handcuffs off. "What's going on?"

"I am so sorry. Please forgive me for cuffing you and putting you in the car." I turned around to see fear in the man's eyes. Theron had more power on this island then I thought. This man looked like he was going to pee himself.

"It's okay, I was the one speeding. You were just doing your job. If I had really stolen the car, Theron would be very happy with you right now. I will take care of him."

"Really?" the man asked as his partner got out of the car and spoke quickly in Greek. He looked worried as well.

"Yes, it wasn't your fault. Am I free to go?" I asked, trying not to scream with relief. I was not going to jail.

"Yes, here is your driver's license and your passport." He handed them to me. "I would appreciate any help with Theron you can give us."

"I'll see what I can do. Thank you for not giving me a ticket."

"Don't worry about it." They went back to their car and got in.

I went back to my car and heard my cell phone vibrating. "Hello?"

"Are you alright? Did they try anything with you?" Vince sounded worried.

"No, they were doing their job. I was driving pretty fast," I said embarrassed.

"Are you done shopping?"

"Yes, I'm almost back to the compound." I started the car but waited to pull back out on the road until I was done talking to Vince.

"I will see you at home. You can leave the car at our house. Someone will move it later." He hung up without saying goodbye, and I had a feeling my relief at not getting in trouble came too soon.

I drove the rest of the way back not going a degree above the speed limit. There was no reason to get pulled over again. I pulled the car up to the house, went back to the trunk, pulled my bags out of it and went inside. I trudged my way to my room with my arms ready to fall off from the weight. Maybe I bought too much?

"How fast were you going when you got pulled over?" Vince asked from the doorway of my room.

"A hundred and twenty in an eighty zone. That car likes to go; I didn't realize how fast I was going." I turned around to face him and put my hands on my hips. "I'm sorry, is Theron mad?"

"He will only be mad if you damaged the car. He is mad at the police for trying to arrest you. I am sure he will be here soon to make sure you were unhurt by his police force."

"The one who handcuffed me looked like he was going to pee himself when he heard Theron screaming on the other end of the line. I'm glad you remembered to tell him my alias. Did you tell anyone else?" I did not want it getting around. If too many people learned it, I would have to change it again.

"Just him, and for this reason. Did you have a good time shopping?"

"Yes, I even got you something." I dug into the bag with the t-shirt in it. I pulled it out and gave it to him. "I know you're not much of a t-shirt guy, but I saw this and thought of you. Since you are going to be my teacher and all."

He smiled after reading it. "You think I am your Yoda?"

"So far, yes. You're my teacher, right? You quoted him at the airport. I thought you would like the shirt." I laughed and began unpacking my new stuff. "Would you mind if I downloaded some songs to put on my MP3 player?"

"No not at all. Are you going to use it when you are running and swimming?"

"That's the plan."

"Good and you did not have a problem finding everything you will need?"

"None. That's a nice shopping center." I stopped emptying the bags and turned to look at Vince. "Thanks for letting me go out on my own. I hope I didn't ruin your trust in me by almost getting arrested."

He smiled. "No, the only reason why they gave you such a hard time was because they thought you stole the head of the Cretan mafia's car. Theron is mad because they pulled you over in the first place. He wants to earn your trust and having you pulled over by his police is not the way to gain it. I find it all very amusing."

"I was only worried for a minute, but I figured Lolita would have a hard time getting to me if I was in jail." I went back to removing the tags from my new clothes and folding them.

"When you are done here, remove your shoes and meet me in the dojo." Vince turned to leave.

"Sure thing I won't be long."

# CHAPTER 17

I climbed the stairs to the dojo feeling both nervous and excited about what was about to happen. I thought back to the shower at Miguel's. I would never let anything like that happen to me again. I wanted to be able defend myself, so an attacker might be able to crawl away, if I let them. I hoped I would not suck at the martial arts stuff.

The door to the dojo was open, and I looked inside to see Vince kneeling on the hardwood floor. His eyes were closed and his hands rested loosely on his lap. I was not sure what to do so I softly knocked on the doorframe.

"Before you enter, bow to the dojo to express your respect for the space," Vince said, without opening his eyes. I bowed and entered the dojo. "Please kneel in front of me." He gestured to the space in front of him.

I walked over and knelt down trying to mimic his stance. I let the back of my thighs rest on the soles of my feet, and placed my hands on my knees.

"Katie, we need to have a serious conversation before we go any further."

"Sure, Vince. What would you like to talk about?" The seriousness of his voice was making me nervous.

"You know my background; I was a gladiator and trained them. I also spent many years in the Far East with my maker. While I was there I studied all different types of martial arts." He waited for me to nod my head in agreement before continuing. "I want to train you to be better equipped to defend yourself. This will be beneficial now and later when you have been changed."

"About that Vince." Remembering I had not had an opportunity to tell him what the prophecy really said. "I need to tell you what the prophecy said about the one who changes me."

"For the time being, we are going to forget about the prophecy. From now on, all we will discuss is your training. My goal is to teach not only to defend yourself but you will also have better concentration, balance, control and humility."

"Okay . . ." I trailed off. It was weird how Vince wanted to forget about the prophecy. He had been the one who would not stop talking about it since we met.

"You will call me Sensei when we are in this room. You will do what I say without question or you will be corrected. It will take time, and you will have to work harder than you ever have before. You are athletic and in above average shape, but by the time I am done, you will have the endurance to fight for hours without tiring.

"You will be in pain, and I will try to minimize it, but there is no way around it. I want you to remember I am doing this to make you stronger." He stopped speaking, sitting silently waiting for my reply.

"Sensei." The title felt weird on my tongue. "I wish to learn all you think I am worthy of learning." I had no idea where the words came from.

"Beginning tomorrow you will start your day with a run around the grounds. It is about an eight-mile track. Then you will take a three-hour break as long as you have not done anything requiring correction. Then you will go for a one-hour swim in the sea. You will then be given a break before we start your martial arts training. During your breaks you will eat, rest, and practice your Greek with Theron and Helen."

I did not think I would make it through one day of training without keeling over dead. It was going to be the most intense physical conditioning I had ever attempted. I had to ask myself if this what I really wanted. Yes, I wanted it; I wanted to be able to take care of myself for a change. "It is a challenge worth undertaking if it means I will be able to protect myself better."

"Good." He closed his eyes and bowed his head. "Theron and Helen will be here shortly. You may leave to prepare for their arrival. Have you eaten since breakfast?"

"Yes, I stopped and had some food at a café before I was pulled over. I should be alright for a while."

"Good, I will make you something for dinner later then."

"Vince, I hate to make you cook for me when you're not going to eat. I can make myself dinner."

Vince's eyes popped open and he stood up looking furious. I wanted to run away. "Stay where you are." He walked behind me to the wall covered in weapons. Crap, what did I say? Was he going to beat me?

"You owe me one hundred pushups. Do you know why?" He came back to stand in front of me holding a sword. It was not metal, it looked like bound together wood. I gulped and seriously thought about quitting before I started.

I thought about what I said in my head before he got mad. I

thought I was being nice. "No, please tell me and I won't do it again."

"Remember when I said, you will call me Sensei when we are in the dojo?"

"I do now, Sensei, I'm sorry." I lowered my head and stared at my feet.

"Do you also remember when I said, you will do as I say without question?"

I remembered, but I did not think I had questioned him, had I? "Yes, Sensei. I didn't realize I questioned you."

"I said, I would make you dinner. You offering to cook for yourself was second guessing me. Do you understand?"

I cringed. I did not understand how it was second guessing him but he was the boss. "Yes, Sensei. I'm sorry I broke the rules."

"Do you know what this is?" he asked, bringing the sword up then down onto his hand. It made a loud smacking noise.

"No." Fear caused tears to roll down my cheeks.

"This is a bamboo sword; it is used in karate as a correction tool. It stings but not too badly. Stand up," he ordered, ignoring my tears while he brought the sword back down in his hand making the smacking sound again.

Flinching from the sound I stood up as quickly as I could, which must not have been fast enough because he swatted the outside my thigh. "Whenever I tell you to do something you must do it as quickly and as soundlessly as you can. Do you understand?"

"Yes, Sensei." I stood up straight. The sound of it connecting with my leg was worse than the bite, it barely stung when he 'corrected' me, and I sighed in relief.

"Good now get into plank position. You have fifty pushups for each offence. They must be perfect."

I got into plank position with my hands outstretched directly below my shoulders. Sensei tapped on my hand. "In karate, one does not do pushups with an open palm. One does them on one's knuckles to toughen them for fighting."

"One hundred." Sensei put the bamboo sword back in its place on the wall.

I collapsed to the floor taking deep breaths. My whole body was shaking from the effort and my knuckles burned with pain. I ended up doing a hundred incorrect pushups for every fifty perfect pushups. To be fair Sensei did not hit me with the sword again, he used it to push my midsection up and tap my ass down.

"You probably have enough time to take a shower before Theron and Helen get here." He moved toward me until his feet came into my line of vision. "Do you need help standing up?"

"No." I was mad at him for the abuse I just endured. There was no way I was going to let him help me up. I pushed myself to my knees before finding my feet and standing up.

"Good. Sometimes being angry will help you fight through the pain. Never let it influence your fighting though. You will always fight better with a clear head. You are free to go and get ready." He took a few steps away from me.

I almost turned and left the dojo before remembering to bow to Sensei, then I stopped at the doorway to the dojo, turned and bowed. I flexed my hands as I walked down the stairs thinking I never wanted to do another pushup.

After I showered and changed into a summer dress, I went

out to the kitchen in my bare feet following the smell of food cooking. Vince had his back to me while he worked over the stove and Theron was leaning against the wall holding a glass of wine at his side in a loose grip.

"Katie, I'm so sorry about the situation with the police." Theron pushed off the wall and came toward me. "I'm going to have them both fired."

"Why? They were doing their job." I took a step back when Theron moved in to give me a hug. Already knowing he wanted me made me want to avoid the hug. "Don't fire them on account of me. I was the one speeding."

"You're sure?" He stopped and looked deflated when he saw me move away from him. Vince snorted and I looked over to see him watching the scene from the corner of his eye. Catching me looking at him, he turned back to the stove.

"Yes, if I had stolen the car you would've gotten it back thanks to those men. Why fire them? Thank you for letting me use your car, by the way. It's amazing to drive." I walked over to look over Vince's shoulder. "What's for dinner?" I saw a pot with noodles boiling and a skillet with a red sauce simmering next to it.

"Spaghetti with sausage and red sauce. There is a salad waiting for you in the dining room." He moved away from me. "We will be in shortly."

"It smells great. Thank you." I went into the dining room where a large Greek salad was sitting at my spot on the table. I sat down and thought about how Vince moved away from me while he was standing at the stove. He had never done that before. In the past, it seemed like he was always stopping himself from touching me. Normally I could feel his affection for me but since I got back from the store it was

126

gone. All I could feel was a low simmering anger or anguish.

I snapped my head around. Why did I care if Vince did not want to be near me? I had sworn off everyone from the male persuasion after Miguel. Vince was my Sensei, and maybe someday he would be my friend, but it was pointless to beat myself up because he could not stand to be close to me.

I picked up my fork and worked on the salad. There was no wine on the table, just a large bottle of water. I wondered if my training meant I could not drink. It did not really matter though. I did not want to drink anything if I had to run eight miles and swim for an hour the next day. Staying hydrated was more important than a buzz.

Vince came in with a plate full of food and set it down next to me. "How is your salad?"

"Very good, thank you." Finished, I pushed the empty salad dish away and pulled the pasta over to me. "Where's Helen? I thought she was coming over too?"

Theron took the chair across from me while Vince sat down at the head of the table. "Something came up. She will come over tomorrow." Theron laced his fingers together and rested them on the table. *I can't believe Miguel already figured out where she is.*

"Miguel knows where I am?" I dropped my fork and pushed back from the table ready to run.

"How did you know?" Theron asked, moving to chase me if I ran.

"I told you she has gifts." Vince looked over at Theron with a small smile playing on his lips.

Ignoring the non-relevant conversation, I looked at Vince. "What are we going to do? Where are we going to go?"

"We are safe here. There is no reason for us to leave. He cannot get to us here, and if he tries, he will die. Right Theron?"

Theron was staring at me in awe. "What? Oh yes, if they step foot on my island they will not leave it. I have forty vampires under my command. It does not matter how old he is, there is no way they will be able to beat us. Don't worry Katie. You're safe."

"Helen is meeting with Miguel right now to make sure he knows what will happen if he steps foot on Crete," Vince chimed in.

"Will she be safe? Did someone go with her?" My mind went back to the shower again.

"Helen has a black belt in jujitsu and has completed my training program. She can take care of Miguel if she needs too. He called today waving a truce flag. If he tries anything he will be the one to pay, not Helen." Theron looked at me as if I was a broken little girl. Maybe I was. "What did he do to you?"

I looked down at my food and knotted my fingers in my napkin. I did not want to tell either of them about the rape. I did not want their pity. It was my fault it happened. I was the idiot who did not leave when I had the chance. "He was mean."

"I promise he will not set foot on this island or come within miles of you." Theron reached his hand across the table. "I promise as long as you are on my island he will not be a threat to you."

"Don't make promises to me." I got up and ran out of the room. I needed to be by myself. I went into my room and shut the door. I fell onto the bed face first and tried to calm my racing heart.

Miguel knew where I was. How did he figure it out? Where was Lolita? Was she coming right behind him? I did not think she would listen to Theron's warnings about coming onto the island, and I did not want Theron to sacrifice any of his vampires for me.

I could leave. There was an airport on the island. They would have no idea where I went. Well, Vince would since he could track my credit card, but he would never tell them where I went. Where would I go? Some place without any vampires. Where would that be? A desert island in the middle of nowhere. I did not know if I could handle it or not but I had to start somewhere.

I got up from the bed and pulled my bag out. I packed the bare necessities I would need. I had just pulled out my laptop to look at flights when there was a knock at the door. I looked up from the computer. "Who's there?"

*Vince, can I come in?*

I closed the laptop, got up and went to open the door. He was holding my plate of food in one hand and a TV tray in the other. "You need to eat no matter what you do."

I drew my eyebrows together. "What do you mean 'no matter what I do'?"

His eyes flicked down to my packed bag. "I have excellent hearing. I knew you were packing. You need something in your system besides vegetables."

"I'm not hungry." I went back to the chair by the window. I took the laptop off the seat and sat down with it in my lap. I opened it and continued to look at flights.

"Can you at least have a bite? I worked hard making this for you." Vince opened the tray and set the plate down on top of it.

I looked at the food and my stomach growled. I had to at least try it. "Fine." I gestured for him to bring the tray over to me.

He sat the tray down, pulled a fork, knife, and napkin out of his pocket and placed them next to the plate. "Can I sit on the bed while you eat or do you want to be alone?"

Vince looked defeated. Like he had failed me, when it was me who was failing him. "Please, make yourself at home." I picked up the fork and loaded it with noodles and sausage before bringing it to my mouth. It was amazing; I had never had better spaghetti in my life. "Wow, this is great." I dug in, my appetite coming back. "Thank you."

Vince nodded his head but did not say anything. He just watched me eat. He looked more like the Vince I knew with every bite I took, but he did not say anything. When I was done, I scraped the empty plate with my fork and licked it clean. "That was so good."

"You can lick the plate; I will not tell anyone." He got up from the bed, took the plate, and left the room leaving the door open.

I wanted to laugh Vince made a joke. It was progress, but it did not matter. I needed to think about where I wanted to go. Home was the first place to come to mind, but once they found out I was not here they would look there, I could not go home. Anywhere on the main continents were out; it would be too easy for them to find me. A small island with a small population would be best. One where there were too few people to keep a vampire fed. I picked up my laptop and starting looking into safe places.

"Where are you going to go?" Vince leaned against the doorframe.

"You're not going to try and stop me?" I looked up, locking eyes with him.

"Why? If you think you can protect yourself better than Theron's forty vampire warriors and me, then why would I try?" He crossed his arms over his chest and one leg over the other.

Tears pricked the back of my eyes. "I believe you can protect me. It's just . . ." I trailed off. "I just don't want him to know where I am. He scares me almost as much as Lolita."

"Again, where will you to go? You might as well tell me. I will be able to track you, but I will not follow you."

"I don't know. An island with a population small enough there wouldn't be enough food for a vampire to live there." I looked down at the island I brought up on a map program.

"Good idea. Are you prepared to live the rest of your life on that island? Never see your family again? Ignore their cries for help when Lolita gets tired of looking for you and tries to draw you out by hurting them?" Vince stood up straight and pulled at the bottom of his shirt to make sure it was hanging correctly. "I did not realize your will to live and be safe came before everything else in your life." He turned to leave.

"Wait, maybe I haven't thought this through. Do you really think Lolita will go after my family?"

"I would not put it past her. As for Miguel, we will know more when Helen gets back. I know he tried to make you his slave, but what are you not telling me?" He put his hands on his hips.

I looked out the window; I was so ashamed I did not leave with Vince when he offered the first time. I did not want to admit to him that I let myself get into a situation where Miguel could rape me. "Nothing important." I tried to put a brave face but a tear betrayed me and ran down my cheek.

Vince was in front of me in a second, kneeling in between my legs, and using his thumb to whip the tear away. "You do not have to be brave right now. You can tell me anything. I will not judge you. I will do anything for you."

His words made me lose the little control I had, and the tears fell in earnest. I took a gasping breath and tried to find my voice. "He wanted sex, but I didn't want to. I tried to ignore him. He . . ." My sobbing drowned out the words. Vince pulled me into his arms, rubbed my back, and for some reason I let him. Even though the thought of any man touching me repulsed me, I was safe with Vince.

*It is alright, you do not have to say any more.* Pure rage was pouring off him, yet he held me with a gentleness I did not know he possessed.

"I tried to fight him off, but he punched me and I fell then he just . . . just did what he wanted. I never want to be that weak again."

*I am sorry. Stay, and I will make sure you will never feel weak again.* He rested his head on top of mine.

"You won't let him near me, right?" I looked up at him. His mouth was so close to mine, our eyes locked, and it all went away. Everything about Miguel was instantly forgotten. All I wanted was for Vince to kiss me and tell me everything was going to be alright.

*Never, I will kill him for what he did to you.* He did not look away but he did not move closer either. *Please stay.*

"I will as long as you can keep me safe," I whispered, licking my now dry lips.

*Anything for you, Katie. Anything.* Vince blinked, let go of me and pushed back.

I let go of him and watched him retreat to the doorway. "You are going to have a long day tomorrow. You might want to get some sleep."

"Good idea." I wiped the tears from my face and stood up from the chair.

*If you need me, just call and I will be here.* Vince

closed the door behind him.

I went into the bathroom and looked at my tearstained face. No wonder he did not kiss me, I thought. I looked like a drowned rat. Why did I want him to kiss me? Men had been nothing but trouble for me. I should not want anyone to kiss me. I blew out a frustrated breath, washed my face, took my clothes off and crawled into bed dreading my first day of training.

# CHAPTER 18

Vince wanted to take off after Miguel and challenge him to an old fashion duel. He raped her. How could he rape 'The One'? Hell, who cared that she was 'The One', how could he rape Katie? She was an angel. She was pure and everything around her was tainted. Basking in her presence alone would polish some of the tarnish off a soul. The bastard.

Vince flew down the hall and back into the dining room where Theron waited. Theron took one look at Vince and knew his sire was in one of his moods. "What happened? Is she leaving?"

"No, she is staying." He could not sit down; he was too angry. He paced up and down the room running his hands through his hair.

"Vince, why are you so mad? What happened?"

"He raped her," the whispered words left his lips before he could stop himself. Vince stopped and turned to Theron. "Do not tell anyone what you just heard."

"As you wish, Master." Theron looked bewildered. "How could he? That's not Miguel. He has never had to force a woman to have sex with him, yet he forced 'The One.' When did he turn into an idiot? He waited over a hundred years for her to show up, and then he rapes her? He's gone off the deep end."

"You are right; I want to get my hands on him right now.

Where is he again?" Vince looked at his watch, calculating if he could get to Miguel and back before the sun came up. He needed to be here for Katie's first day of training.

"It's too late for you to get to the island before the sun rises. Helen is barely going to make it back. You need to clear your head. Do you want to go spar for a while?"

"No, that is not a good idea. I might hurt you while I am in this mood."

"What do you want to do then?"

Vince stopped pacing and looked toward Katie's bedroom. "I want to make all of her hurt go away. How could he?"

"I don't know her very well but she has a magnetism. When I'm with her I want to do whatever she asks. She's an amazing woman. I'm sorry I started this whole mess, but wait, I didn't tell her Miguel was close by I only thought about it. Are you going to tell me what is going on?"

"Do you remember what the prophecy says?" Vince asked, forcing himself to take a deep breath and stop pacing. There was nothing he could do about Miguel tonight.

"If this is about the prophecy then let's get another glass of wine." Theron stood and walked into the kitchen.

Vince followed Theron and took the glass he offered. "She is 'The One,' how could it not be about the prophecy?"

"I know you're right." He took a sip of his wine and thought for a moment. "I remember the gist of it, but I don't have it memorized."

"She will hear what is in our hearts . . ." Vince trailed off.

"You mean she can read our minds?" Theron put his wine glass on the counter and crossed his arms over his chest defensively.

"Not everything, but when you project your thoughts she picks them up."

"Is that how she knew I wanted to fuck her last night?"

"And that Miguel is nearby," Vince downed the rest of his wine and went to fill it up again. If he could not kill Miguel, he might as well get drunk.

"Thanks for giving me the heads up about it before now." Theron said mockingly.

"Forgive me if I have been a little preoccupied. Just watch what you think from now on."

"Can you hear her?"

"No, she said while she was under the slave bond with Miguel she could hear him though."

"What a prick."

"I am stunned she did not tell me what he did to her." Bringing up Miguel's name made him sick to his stomach and he put the wine down on the counter, no longer wanting to get drunk. "I thought we trusted each other."

"Vince, you have known her for a week. It takes time to form the bond you want. She thinks it's her fault. She's not one to tell the world about her mistakes. She doesn't see herself as the victim, but as a dumb girl who should've seen the signs and left before it happened," Theron said gently, seeing the pain in Vince's eyes.

"When did you learn so much about women?" Vince silently agreed with everything Theron said. He could use her anger at herself to make her stronger and fiercer. He would make sure she would never be in a situation where she could not defend herself ever again.

"When I made Helen. Women don't think like us. They analyze everything that happens. They look at a situation and wonder how it could have turned out differently." He paused to take a sip of the wine. "In cases like this, they blame themselves. It's not her fault, you know it and I know it, but it is going to take time for her to know it. In any case it is better you know. Now you can make sure you don't push any of the buttons that will put her in shutdown and drown in self-misery. How did you get her to stay?"

Vince took a sip of wine, ran his fingers through his hair and sighed. "Guilt trip."

"I'm surprised it worked with how scared she is. She must trust you."

"I am getting there. Too many men have fucked with her. Earning her trust is going to be a long process, but it will be worth it." Vince looked down at Theron's pocket where his cell phone was vibrating.

Theron fished it out and looked at the display. "It's Helen." He swiped the screen and brought it up to his face. "What's the word?"

"Miguel wants to see Katie. He and Lolita have parted ways. He says he wants to apologize to her. He feels terrible about what happened. He wants to earn her forgiveness, but he knows better than to step foot on Crete without your permission. He says he will stay where he is until she forgives him for what he did." Vince heard Helen say, even though the phone was against Theron's ear.

"He's not planning on telling Lolita where Katie is?" Theron asked, raising his eyebrows at Vince.

"No, he blames Lolita for most of what happened in San Sebastian. He admitted to starting the fire at Vince's because he figured out Vince helped Katie escape."

"Katie's dream came true; he did burn the town down." Vince would have to talk to her about her dreams.

They were prophetic; they were going to have to pay closer attention to them.

"Where are you?" Theron asked, looking at his watch.

"I just got off the boat. I'm heading home."

"Good, find me when you get here I want a full report." He hung up the phone after she gave him an affirmative.

"What are you going to tell Katie?" Theron looked down the hallway toward her bedroom.

"The truth." There was no way he could tell her anything different if he wanted to earn her trust.

"How do you think she will take it?"

"I cannot be sure, but I cannot risk a half truth or a lie with her. She has been lied to too many times. Even a white lie will have her leaving us behind to spend her life hiding on an island trying to avoid all of us."

"You know her better than I thought." Theron put down his empty wine glass and moved toward the door. "Let's go to my house and wait for Helen to return."

"I can talk to Helen about it tomorrow," Vince said, following him to the door. "I want to stay close by in case she needs me."

"She is not even in your bed yet and you are whipped." Theron laughed, opening the door. "What are you going to be like after she is yours?"

"I am sure it will be entertaining if it ever happens. Good night, Theron." Vince closed the door in his face then went into the den to continue his search for Lolita.

# CHAPTER 19

Lolita threw the newspaper across the room, she had struck out again. Angel's death notice was not what she wanted to find when she read the *El País*. The girl had failed her. Looking back at her plan she knew it was overly optimistic. Vince had enjoyed the poppy seed many times, even if it was long ago. Of course he would be able to keep his head and kill the spy she had so painstakingly molded into the blood whore she needed to infiltrate Maria's home.

Time for the next plan. There had been no sign of Vince or Katie and it worried her. The longer no one heard from them the less of a chance she would have to bring the girl down before she was turned.

She had another plan in the works though. She got out of the hotel bed she had been lying in, and went into the bathroom to get herself ready for the little party she was throwing. After showering and dressing in a long black silk nightgown, she picked up the phone and dialed the front desk.

"Sí, Señora?" asked the voice on the other end of the line.

"There was a bellboy who helped me the other day and I was completely out of money to tip him. I think his name was Antonio. Could you please send him up to my room? I want to pay him for his work.

"Antonio? I am sorry Señora, he is not here today. If you would like, you can give the money to me and I will make sure he gets it."

"Thank you but no. I would like to thank him personally. When will he be back to work?"

"He is scheduled to work tomorrow. I can send him up to your room as soon as he arrives."

"Very well," Lolita said and hung up the phone.

Antonio would tell her what she wanted to know or he would die trying not to. She laughed. Who was she kidding? He was going to die no matter what.

# CHAPTER 20

I woke up remembering the night before. Great, now Vince and Theron knew what happened with Miguel. I wanted to take the incident to the grave, but my fear of Miguel made it too big to hide. Just the thought of Miguel knowing where I was had my heart pumping double time.

Vince said he would keep me safe. I believed he would, and by extension Theron. I remembered hearing his voice yelling at the police for pulling me over. They would do everything they could to keep me safe, but I needed to learn how to defend myself, and there was only one way to start. I had to get up and face Vince.

Thirty minutes later, I emerged from my room ready to face the day. I was dressed in my running shorts, tank top, sports bra, and my new running shoes. I went to the kitchen and looked longingly at the empty coffee pot. The last thing I needed was a cup of coffee, but I longed for it anyway. I found an orange in the fruit basket on the counter and peeled it instead. Then I joined Vince in the dining room, where he was waiting for me.

"Good morning Vince," I said in a small voice, hoping he would not bring up the night before. He was sitting in the same spot he always did, only now he had a laptop sitting in front of him. I sat down in front of a covered plate and took the cover off it. There was a healthy breakfast of yogurt, fruit, and dry multi-grain toast. "Thanks for making me breakfast."

"Good morning and you are welcome." Vince looked up from his computer. "How did you sleep?"

"Better than I thought I would." I picked up my spoon and began eating the yogurt. "Sorry I freaked out last night."

"You have every right to be upset. I wish I would have known what he did to you. Maybe I could have broken the news to you in a different way."

"I don't think there is a way to keep me calm when you mention his name." I kept eating trying not to think about him.

"Did you charge up the watch you bought yesterday?" Vince asked, changing the subject.

"Yeah." I extended my wrist to show him the fitness watch that would log my miles and pinpoint where I was located on the property. Being tracked might put some people off, but it made me feel safe. Vince would know where I was for my entire run. If something happened, he could get help to me.

"Good, I will keep track of your progress with it." He looked back down at his laptop while I continued to eat.

When I was done, I took the MP3 player out of my pocket and plugged my ear buds in. I downloaded some of my favorite workout music and loaded it on to the device before Theron came over the night before. "I guess I'll head out. Wish me luck." I got up to make my way to the backdoor leading to the terrace.

"Your goal should be to run for the entire eight miles. Which means you should not drop to less than three miles

144

per hour. For every thirty seconds you do, you will owe me ten pushups. Do you understand?" Vince turned his computer around to show me a map of the grounds.

I gulped. This was going to be harder than I thought. "Yes, Sensei. I'll do my best not to disappoint you." I bowed, I am not sure why, it just felt like the appropriate time and place to do so.

"If you fail, you will not only be disappointing me but yourself. I know you can do it. You need to prove to yourself you can. Good luck," Vince said, before going back to his computer.

With the conversation over, I went outside, took the stairs down to the beach, and started my run. Theron had quite the compound, I counted five other homes on the property besides the mansion and the house Vince and I were staying in. I wondered who lived in the other houses as I ran by. They were all set up for vampires with heavily tinted windows to keep the burning rays of the sun out.

I hit the end of the cove, followed a dirt path up a hill, and passed by a few outbuildings. The landscape was green; the air was hot and humid. If I was going to be doing this run every day, I needed to get up earlier, and run when it was cooler. When I got to the top of the hill leading away from the beach, I took my tank top off and shoved the straps in the back of my shorts. I had sweat completely through it. I looked down at my watch thinking I would be near the five-mile mark, but no luck, I had barely run two miles.

I ran in place for a few moments trying to catch my breath when I felt a tap on my shoulder. I whipped around with my fists up to see the annoying guy from the café, holding his hands up surrender. I pulled one of my earbuds out. "Can I help you? Aren't you the guy who hit on me yesterday? What are you doing here?"

"I was going to ask you the same thing," he said with an awkward smile. "You have to be crazy to be running in this heat."

"I'm in training." I looked down at my watch. "I have to get moving." I continued down the path leaving him behind.

"What are you training for?" he asked, catching up to me.

"To become a better fighter, to defend myself better." I really wished he would leave me alone.

"Is someone after you too?" He ran past me, got in front of me, then turned and ran backward forcing me to look at him.

"It's always important to be able to protect yourself," I said between breaths. "You should turn around or you'll trip."

He looked over his shoulder and saw the stairs coming up. "Thanks, I'm Alex by the way." He flipped around to run next to me.

"I'm Katie."

"How long have you been here? I haven't seen you around before." We got to the stairs and started climbing them.

"A few days." I concentrated on the steps trying not to trip.

"Great." Finally, at the top of the stairs, I thought he would stop allowing me to get on with my run, but he kept pace with me. "How long are you going to be here?"

"I'm not sure probably till the end of the summer unless things change."

"Me too, it'll be nice to have someone to hang out with who will go outside during the day."

"Who said I wanted to hang out with you?" I was trying to be funny.

"Oh, well I see how it is. I'll let you be then." He sounded defeated.

"I was kidding. I'm going to be pretty busy while I'm here, but we can see how it goes. What are you doing here?" I wondered if he knew a vampire was hosting him.

"Same as you." He paused for a moment as if he was trying to find a way to explain it to me without telling me too much. "I'm lying low until a few people stop looking for me."

Enough said, I thought. "You don't have to keep running with me." I looked down at my watch. "I have four more miles to go."

He winced. "That's okay I'm bored and I need the exercise."

"Suit yourself." I plugged my earbud back in and we ran in silence for the next hour.

Vince was right; one circuit of the compound was almost eight miles. I barely finished without passing out from heat exhaustion, but I did it and it gave me something to be proud of. After making it to the terrace of the house, I bent over and grabbed my knees. I was seriously thinking about throwing up, but I did not want to in front of Alex.

"Are you alright?" He bent over, breathing hard, trying to catch his breath.

"I'm not sure." I slowly stood up straight. "Are you?"

"Umm, no." He staggered to the railing and started puking. The breeze was coming right at me; I caught a whiff of his vomit, raced to the terrace next to him and threw up.

At least I did not start it; I thought to myself then staggered over to a chair and sat down. "That was brutal." I hung my head between my knees trying to take deep breaths.

"You're telling me? I still have to go back to my place."

"I'll go get some water," I said, heading for the door. "I'll be right back."

In the kitchen I grabbed two cold bottles of water and was about to go back outside when Vince walked in. "Who is that?" he asked, looking through the tinted glass at Alex who was sitting in a chair with his forearms resting on his thighs.

"Alex." I opened one of the water bottles and chugged the contents. "He's staying at the last house on the beach." I came up for air and pointed in the direction of the house.

"Give him the water and send him on his way, then meet me in the dojo." Vince took a few steps away from me and put his hands on his hips. He did not look happy about the appearance of Alex.

I went back outside and gave the bottle to Alex. "Hey, don't take this the wrong way but you have to go." I drank the rest of my water.

"Alright, but why?" he asked, opening the bottle, and chugging it down as I had.

"My Sensei's orders are not for me to question," I said solemnly.

"Really?" Alex looked skeptical.

"Those are the conditions I must abide by if I want him to train me. He looked pissed off when he saw you though. You better go." I moved toward the door. "It was fun, well as fun as running eight miles in the middle of the day can be. I'm going to get up earlier tomorrow if I have to do it again. Feel free to join me."

"Yeah, alright." He gave me a quizzical look. "See you around." He headed for the stairs leading down to the beach.

I went inside, grabbed a towel from my bathroom, and went upstairs to the dojo. The door was open and I could see Vince kneeling in the same spot as yesterday. He looked so relaxed, confident, and at one with himself. I did not think I had ever felt that way.

"Sensei?" I asked, then remembered I was supposed to bow whenever I entered the dojo.

"Katie, remove your shoes and socks and join me." He didn't bother opening his eyes.

"Yes, Sensei." I quickly took off my shoes and socks, and entered the dojo, enjoying the feel of the cool wood beneath my aching feet. I walked over to Vince and knelt in front of him with about two feet between us.

"Close your eyes and empty your mind, Katie," he said in a quiet but irritated voice.

I closed my eyes and tried to empty out all the thoughts from my mind, but it was no good. My legs were cramping, my feet were asleep and I was in a mild panic over how many pushups I owed him for slowing down when Alex joined me.

"Think about your breathing. Inhale and hold it for ten seconds." I could hear him inhaling with me. "Good, now let it out slowly." He exhaled with me. "Again." We inhaled together and exhaled together.

I had no idea how intimate it could be to just breath with someone. It was not sexual but it felt like we were coming together as one, bonding in a way.

"Do you know why you are going to be punished?" he asked after we were both calm.

"I slowed down when Alex joined me because he snuck up behind me. It took some time to get him to run with me instead of bug me." How long could it have been? It could not have been more than a few minutes.

"Very good, you did not stop but you went below the minimum speed. You owe me twenty pushups."

"Yes, Sensei." I took a breath and got in plank position on my knuckles. I groaned in pain. They still hurt from the day before. I

149

thought twenty pushups would not be too bad, but since my hands were already bruised, it was worse.

"Stop." Vince got up and went to the weapons wall while I held my plank position. He casually came back and corrected my form for each pushup. When he finally told me I was done, I crashed on the floor. It was becoming a habit.

"You have two hours to eat and relax," Vince said as I stood up. "You will meet me back here with your swimming suit on in that time."

"Yes, Sensei." I bowed wondering if I would be able to find the energy not to drown in the sea.

"Keep in mind, if you had not slowed down you would have had three hours of rest before your next session begins," he said, before leaving the dojo.

I did not want to move. I could have slept for hours on the hard floor but my bed sounded better. Grabbing my shoes from outside the dojo, I went down to my room, but the smell coming from the kitchen made my mouth water.

I ducked my head into the kitchen to find a gyro with couscous sitting on a plate next to a sports drink and a bowl of ice for my knuckles. I dropped my shoes where I stood, took the plate of food, the drink, and the ice to the dining room table. I alternated one hand in the ice while the other hand fed me. I was starved but my knuckles hurt too.

After I ate, I decided I could not get into bed until I took a shower. I rinsed off in the coldest water I could stand, put on a t-shirt then looked at the clock. I had forty-five minutes until I had to be back in the dojo. Being late was not an option; I did not want to do any more pushups.

I set the alarm clock to go off thirty minutes later and hit the bed. I swear I had just closed my eyes when the alarm started to go off. I turned the alarm off and winced, the pain in my knuckles woke me up more than the alarm. I crawled out of bed and put on my one-piece swimming suit before thinking about what I was doing. I put on some flip-flops, grabbed my goggles, and went back to the dojo.

It was empty when I got there. I looked at my watch, I still had five minutes to spare. I went over to the windows and watched the waves crash on the beach below me. The clearing of a throat had me spinning around and bowing before I had time to think about it.

"Next time when you arrive early I want you to kneel and find your center." He walked into the room and knelt in what I now called his spot on the floor.

"Yes, Sensei." I remained standing since he did not tell me to join him on the floor.

"I want you to swim in the sea for sixty minutes. Did you put sunscreen on?"

"No, Sensei, I forgot," I answered, hoping I would not get in trouble for forgetting.

"Put some on and hit the water. Don't forget to start your watch." He rose, walked over to the window, and looked out at the sea.

"Thank you." I bowed at the doorway and hurried to my room to get the sunscreen. After applying it everywhere I could reach, I went in search of Sensei with my goggles in one hand and the bottle of sunscreen in the other. I found him in the kitchen staring out at the sea.

"Sensei, would you please put some sunscreen on my back? I can't reach."

"Bring it here." I gave it to him and turned around. He rubbed it into my skin impersonally. "Once you get past the break I want you to swim back and forth between this house and the end of the cove." He pointed to the outcrop of land. "You can use any stroke you like."

"Thank you." I went out the terrace door and down to the beach. I left my flip-flops near the edge of the water and tested the temperature with my feet. It was a lot warmer than the Atlantic had been. There was a three-foot break I was going to go through to get to calmer waters. With my goggles around my neck, I made my way toward the break. When the water was up to my waist I dunked myself under the water and came up to put my goggles on. I could still touch the ground when I got to the break. Instead of going under the wave, I braced myself and let it break around me. If it had been any bigger I would have lost my footing and been swept into it. I would have to remember that for next time. I moved away from the break some distance then set my watch for sixty minutes.

I had swum in the ocean before but never seriously. It was harder than swimming in a pool. It must have been because the Mediterranean is so much saltier then a pool. I floated more than I normally did. I went from the forward crawl, to backstroke, to breaststroke and back again. If I stopped for a break, I would have to add the time onto the end of my swim. Not wanting to add any more time to my torture, I kept going even though I was slow. My watch buzzed me at the end of sixty minutes and I almost cried in relief. I swam back to shore and tried to body surf the break. It did not go well and I ended up being sucked into the wave and rolled around between the sand and the water for a good twenty seconds. When I was finally free, I gulped in air and tried to shake the sand out of my swimming suit, it felt like there was at least a pound in there.

"Are you alright?" A voice asked me from the beach. I looked up to see Alex sitting on the beach with shorts and an unbuttoned white and blue striped shirt on.

"Yeah, just using nature's exfoliator," I said, walking up the beach stumbling but not falling. Great land sickness, I thought.

"Whoa." He jumped up and grabbed my arm to steady me. "You must have been out there for a while."

"A little over an hour." I braced myself against him to put my flip-flops on. "Thanks for the help."

"No problem." He let go when he saw I could stand on my own again.

"I better get back up to the house and rid of all this sand." I moved my legs back and forth feeling the grains rake my skin.

"I'll see you around," Alex said.

I turned midstride. "I'm sure you will since you're stalking me," I said with a singsong voice, kidding with him.

"See how you are?" He turned and walked back to his house. I noticed he was limping a bit. He was not used to running eight miles either.

I stopped at the shower at the base of the terrace steps and rinsed off. I wanted to take my bathing suit off and get all the sand out, but I would have to put it back on to get in the house. There was almost nothing more miserable then putting on a wet bathing suit, and I was not walking up the steps and into the house naked. Vince would probably give me more pushups to do. I got the sand out as best I could then walked slowly up the stairs. When I reached the terrace I found a towel waiting on the table, and I wondered how Sensei got it there without being fried by the sun.

I dried off, went into the kitchen, and found a protein bar and an energy drink waiting for me. I took them both, went into the dining room, and sat down to eat them. Sensei came in soon after I finished the protein bar and was half way through the sports drink.

He took the seat across from me with a stern look on his face. "Tell me about the boy."

"There's not much to tell. He hit on me at the café where I had lunch yesterday. I blew him off because I want nothing to do with men right now. He saw me running today and joined me. He said he was staying here, lying low for a while. He was waiting for me when I finished my swim. I think he's lonely." I finished the drink, and got up to grab a bottle of water out of the fridge in the kitchen.

"What name did you give him?" He sounded paranoid.

"Katie."

"I need to talk to Theron about him, but he has been busy all day punishing Ben. I will talk to him later about it. How was the swim?"

"Harder than I thought it would be." I took a swig of water. "I was more buoyant in the sea than I am in a pool. It felt like I had to work harder to pull myself through the water."

Sensei smiled. "That is why you are swimming in the sea and not in the pool." He got up. "Hit the shower. Theron and Helen will be here within the hour to start your Greek lessons."

At least I would get a break from exercise for a while, I thought making my way to my room.

When I came out of my bedroom, clean, in shorts and a t-shirt, a little while later, I found a strange vampire sitting on the couch in the den. When she saw me, she stood up and nodded her head in greeting. She was short, with brown hair pulled back into a bun. She looked close my age with an oval face and piercing brown eyes. She was stocky, not fat just curvy and muscular. "You must be Helen." I went to her, offering her my hand in greeting.

"Yes, and you're Katie. It's nice to meet you." She took my hand in a vise grip and shook it.

"You too. I heard you went to see Miguel last night. How did it go?"

"As well as I expected. He is completely enamored with you. He wants you back but he wants your forgiveness more." Helen resumed her position on the couch.

"He's not going to tell Lolita where I am?" I sat down on the seat across from her. Why were men all of a sudden going crazy over me? They never had before I came to Europe. I was over it.

"No, they had a falling out. We will not have to worry about him running to her, and he knows better than to set foot on this island without Theron's permission. You are safe from him."

"It's the best news I have heard in a while." I let out a cleansing breath and felt the tension I had been carrying around since I found out he was so close, relax inside me.

"There you are, Katie." Theron glided into the room taking the seat next to Helen. "Helen gave you the news about Miguel? You don't need to worry about him while you are here."

"Yes, thank you both for all your help." I sat back in my seat and waited to hear how they were going to teach me Greek.

"I guess we should get started," Helen said, getting up and turning the television on, then she went to a laptop hooked up to it and powered it up. "We're going to go over some basics to start. Then we'll stop speaking English all together and speak only in Greek. Vince told me you have a latent talent for it. If you do, then it won't take us too long to bring it forward."

155

Two hours later, I walked blindly into the kitchen and found Vince cooking again. "What are you making? It smells fabulous."

He turned to look at me questioningly. "I do not understand English," he said slowly in Greek.

I hit my hand to my forehead leaving it there. My brain was too full of confusing Greek phrases. It felt like no meant yes and yes meant no and the words were hard to form in my mouth. I had spoken to my mother in Greek, and I had been able to read and speak Greek once in a while, but learning it was killing me. Bringing my hand down I found Vince staring at me, waiting for me to start over in Greek.

I tried and he laughed but replied. "I'm making a seafood stew with rice for dinner." At least I think that is what he said.

"When will dinner be ready?" I asked slowly, trying to make sure I got every word right.

"In ten minutes." Vince turned back to the stove. "Do you want to practice your Greek while you wait?"

"No, I'm going to go watch the waves crash on the shore." I wanted some time to myself, mostly because I did not want to speak Greek anymore. I brought a chair to the edge of the terrace, sat down, leaned my arms on the railing and looked out at the sea. Watching the swells come in and crash on the beach below was Zen for me. I closed my eyes and just listened. Before I realized it, the sound carried me into dreamland.

I found myself in a dimly lit room. I looked up at the arched ceiling at least thirty feet above me covered in

Frescos, but it was too dark to see the details. The room was filled with pews facing me. I was in a church with the altar at my back. The only light was coming from flickering candles. I had never been much of a churchgoer, but I found their insides alluring. The stained glass depicted everything from Christ's birth to his death. The artwork and the ornate altars and candelabras always left me in awe.

The church was empty, and I wondered why I was there. I did not think my mother would show up here. From what I understood, she hated Christianity since it stole many of her followers. I heard voices coming from outside the closed doors at the back of the church, and I moved to hide behind one of the pews.

"What do you mean this woman is going to pull us away from the church?" a male voice asked as the door opened.

"She believes in the old ways and is convincing other vampires that we must go back to the pagan ways and worship our so-called creator, Asteria." A voice I prayed I would never hear again said.

I peeked over the edge of the pew and looked at the two vampires who were making their way down the aisle toward the altar. I froze in place, unable to breathe at the sight of Lolita. She was dressed more somberly then she typically did, in a long black dress with a black hat and veil covering everything except the blood red lipstick she wore. Her hair was pulled back low on her neck.

I forced myself to duck back down behind the pew before she saw me. She had tried to kill me in a dream before; I did not want to fight her in my dream again.

"But you say she is not a vampire. What do we need to worry about?" asked the man, going up to the altar and lighting more candles.

"You are aware of the old prophecy my brother swore by? Well he seems to think she is 'The One'. The followers believe if she is turned she will rule us all." Lolita followed the vampire around explaining.

"The only one who rules us is Christ." The man stopped to look at Lolita. "What do you need?"

Lolita pressed her lips together in a tight smile. "I may need your help getting to her once she is found."

"Very well. The brotherhood will be of assistance if it is warranted."

A hand on my shoulder woke me from the dream. I turned to see Vince smiling down at me. He said something and I looked at him lost. What language was he speaking? Then I remembered he was only speaking to me in Greek. "Your dinner is ready; do you want to come in and eat?"

I looked around, the sun had set, the temperature had dropped a few degrees and there was an offshore breeze blowing toward me. I shivered and looked up at Vince. "Dinner sounds good." I got up and went inside. "I had a dream."

Vince sat down across from my spot. "What did you dream?" He sounded concerned.

"Lolita is recruiting help from the Catholic Church." I pulled the lid off my plate and forced myself to eat. I did not have much of an appetite, but I was not done for the day and I needed fuel.

"Tell me everything you remember in detail." Vince looked shocked at my statement.

I told him everything I could remember about the dream, leaving nothing out. We knew my dreams could come true; we needed to take them seriously.

"She is trying to find allies. She is expecting a war,"

Vince said more to himself than to me. "Do you have any idea where they were?"

"No, I'm not even sure they were speaking English. I wish I could be more help."

"Don't worry. Just having the dream is enough. Theron and I will look into where she might be later."

Finished eating, I was at a loss. "What do we do next?"

"We are going to put all thoughts of Lolita on the back burner for the rest of the night. If you dream of anything like that again tell me immediately."

"I will. It scared the crap out of me."

"Fear is good thing sometimes, but do not let it rule you. Let's move on from this. We will begin karate tonight. It is the most basic martial art you will learn. It has facets in the other styles as well," Vince explained in Greek. It was becoming shockingly easier to understand him. "I will give you an hour to digest, then get dressed and meet me in the dojo."

I took my plate into the kitchen and began doing the dishes. I felt bad leaving them for Vince. He cooked for me; there was no reason for him to clean for me too. By the time I finished it was time to get dressed for my first karate lesson.

When I went into my room, I found a white outfit laid out on my bed. There was a pair of pants with a tie at the waist, and what looked like a very short robe for a top. It opened in the front, and it had little ties like robes do to keep from coming open. There was a white belt with no way to secure it. I thought it was called a gi, and I thought I put on correctly, but I could not figure out the belt so I took it with me.

I walked up the stairs to the dojo barefoot and slid the door open. Vince was kneeling in his spot with his eyes closed. I stepped into the room and bowed. I did not know if he could see me or not, but at least I knew I had followed the rules. I went to the same spot as I had last time, knelt in front of him, placed my white belt on the floor between us, and closed my eyes.

I tried to empty my mind, but the tops of my feet were bruised from kneeling earlier and my legs thought they had enough for the day. I was thinking how bad everything hurt and how much it was going to hurt tomorrow, when I heard Sensei let out a breath.

I snapped to attention, automatically inhaling with him, and exhaling with him. I found my center and emptied my head of everything except for my next breath. A few breaths later, I felt him lean forward and pick up my belt.

"Stand Katie."

I opened my eyes and quickly stood up. "Why are you not wearing your belt?" he asked in Greek.

"Sensei, I'm sorry I could not figure out how to put it on," I said slowly, trying use the correct words, and not breaking eye contact with him.

"Very well, turn toward the mirror. I am only going to show you how to do this once." He moved behind me, unrolled the belt, and held one end with his left hand while he wrapped the rest around me until the end was short, then he took the short end he started with and tied a simple square knot.

"Thank you, Sensei." I tried to memorize how he tied the belt.

"As I said earlier, tonight you are going to begin to learn karate. It is a Japanese fighting style focusing on hand-to-hand combat. For now we will make this non-contact." He moved to stand a few feet in front of me. "Show me your fist."

I clinched my hand together resting my thumb on

160

the outside of my hand, on top of my knuckles. "Good, at least you know the proper way to make a fist. Now watch and copy me." He moved his feet shoulder width apart. He held out his right hand in a fist while his left was turned and pulled back by his hip. His shoulders were square and he slowly made his arms trade places moving his left fist out, and bringing his right fist back to rest next to his hip, in a slow punching motion.

After watching him a moment I copied him. We were not going for thrust or power, but form. "Watch my hips." Sensei continued in slow motion, every time he switched arms, his hips rolled just a little bit. I tried to copy his movement but it felt awkward. "Keep going." He stopped his demonstration, walked behind me and put his hands on my hips. "I will guide you until you get it," he said in my ear.

If we had been in any other situation his statement would have made me a little hot, but not there. I swear it did not make me the tiniest bit hot. I kept punching in slow motion thinking about what my arms were doing and not how the rest of my body felt with him standing so close with his hands on my hips. With every punch, he gently moved my hips the way he wanted them to go.

After a few minutes he moved his hands away and stepped in front of me. "Now you have it." He watched from each side. "Watch yourself in the mirror, pretend you are fighting yourself. Look for weaknesses. Speed up and put some force behind the punch."

I did as he instructed and watched myself in the mirror. He walked over to the wall of weapons, picked up the bamboo sword and came back to me. I tensed thinking he was going to hit me with it, but he pushed my shoulder back with it instead. "Keep your shoulders square; use your hips to send the power of the punch through your arm."

I tried but it looked sloppy. I was using my hips too much and

161

not at the right time. He went behind me again and placed his hands on my hips. "Like this." He jerked my hips at the precise moment when my punch would hit its intended target. After a few punches he let go and walked back around me. "Very good."

My arms were starting to burn, but I could not stop until he told me to. I did not want to do any more pushups, or some other muscle building torture.

"Use more power now, think of your hips. Use your body to power the punch not just your puny arm." He tapped my arm lightly when it was no longer parallel with the floor. I was struggling and breathing hard. "Think about your breathing, match it to mine again."

I took a deep breath and watched him, I breathed with him, continuing to punch my reflection in the mirror. He corrected me a few more times but the punching went on and on.

"Shake it out," Sensei finally said, walking over to a switch on the wall. He flipped it on as I let my arms drop and shook them out. The windows began to retract letting in a breeze. "Grab some water, then we will continue." He threw me a water bottle. I caught it, barely. I chugged the water and put it on a shelf by the door.

"Follow me." Sensei moved to the middle of the room facing the windows. "Face me and do as I do."

Once I was in position I watched him slowly lift his leg, bring his knee up and extend his calf and foot. Then he slowly brought it back down where he started. I tried to do as he did. I brought my knee up, slowly extended my calf then brought it back up and set it down.

"Flex your foot; you want to kick someone with the

162

ball of your foot, not your toes. Otherwise you will break them." He continued kicking his leg out and back. "The motion should come from your hip joint, the rest of your body should not move, otherwise you will lose your balance, giving your opponent the opportunity to sweep your foot out from under you and kill you."

I put my foot down, bent my knees slightly, and started again making sure only my leg and hip were doing the kicking. "Better, now speed it up." He quickly brought his leg out and snapped it back to show me how. It seemed like most of the motion was coming from the knee. I needed to pull my knee up, kick out quickly from the knee and bring it back just as quickly.

"Good." He walked around me to check my form. "Stop." He moved to face me. "I want you to kick me as hard as you can."

I almost questioned him before remembering I would be punished if I did. I kicked him, not with everything I had, but with some power behind it. As soon as I made contact with his chest, pain radiated from my toes half way up my calf. I hopped around trying not to put any weight on my foot and shake the pain out of it. "You want to connect with the ball of your foot, not your toes." He shook his head looking at the floor.

"I'm sorry Sensei." I limped around still shaking my foot out. I was fighting back tears of exhaustion. I had to tough this out. I stood in front of him again and continued with my right leg making sure to flex my foot. It still hurt like hell, but I did not think anything was broken, thank god, I did not try to kick him as hard as I could.

"Switch to the other leg now."

I did as he instructed, starting out slow to learn the form and create muscle memory. I gradually increased the speed and made sure I flexed my foot. "Good," he said at last. "Grab some water."

After I chugged some water he showed me fighting stance, and how to punch and kick while in that position. Next, he showed me a roundhouse kick. Even with the offshore breeze coming in through the open windows it was still hot, and I was starting to wobble on my feet.

"That is enough for tonight," he finally said and I realized for the first time since I met him, I could not gauge his feelings. It was as if he locked them up in a box so even he could not feel them. "Kneel." He stood about three feet from me.

I did as he asked, but my muscles were so sore it was not very graceful. He knelt where he stood. "Today was a hard for you, but you never gave up, well done. Now close your eyes and center yourself." He closed his eyes.

I closed mine and breathed, feeling overjoyed, I received a compliment from him. When had his approval become so important to me? I quickly cleared my head and matched my breathing to his. I was almost asleep when he started talking again.

"Go through that door and take a shower, then lie face down on the massage table, there is a sheet to cover yourself."

"Yes Sensei." I stood, and walked to the door with my aching body protesting every step. He cleared his throat reminding me to bow. I turned and bowed. "Thank you, Sensei." The thank you was more for the reminder to bow before leaving the dojo than for the workout.

I went through the door into a small room open to the sea. There was a door to the right; I opened it to find a basic bathroom, with a sink, toilet, and shower stall. I peeled off the gi and my underthings before stepping into the shower. I let the water run cold on my skin and just stood there for a minute before I washed the sweat off my body. I dried off with a towel and laid down on the table in the adjoining room.

I was asleep when Sensei came in; his hand on my shoulder woke me up. "Relax, it is just me," he said in English, running his hand down my back and legs. "When we are here you may speak freely and in English." He ran his hand back up my other leg and the other side of my back. "I am going to give you a message; it should keep you from being sore tomorrow. You can talk about how today went, or go back to sleep if you wish."

"Why did you turn into such a slave driver?" I asked, relaxing into the face rest as he pulled the sheet back from my right leg and tucked it under my left leg. I heard him squeeze something into his hands, rub them together then start to knead my upper thigh and buttock. I let out a moan, it felt so good.

"If you want to beat Lolita and become the queen of the vampires you are going to need to be strong. If I am nice to you, you will not learn to be fierce." He worked down my thigh to my calf.

"How do you do it?" I groaned as he dug into my calf.

"Do what?"

"Turn your feelings off." I snapped my mouth closed realizing I just admitted I could sense his mood. "Right now you are enjoying what you are doing, but I could not get anything from you today."

"When were you going to tell me you could sense our emotions?" He tensed for a second then continued to move down to my foot. I kicked out in defense of the tickle he caused.

"Sorry, I'm a little ticklish." I tried to use mind over matter to overcome the feeling. "I can hear what's in your heart remember?"

"When I was human, I made the mistake of caring about one of the other gladiators and it showed a little too much." He covered my leg back up with the sheet and moved to the other side. "I was the number one gladiator in our school at the time, and the number two

165

gladiator wanted my position. He found out I cared for the boy and beat him to death to try to throw me off my game."

"I'm sorry." Vince started working on my other leg, and I was a blob unable to move. "What happened to the gladiator who killed him?"

"I killed him. I was punished for killing him, but I could not let him get away with killing the boy," Vince said as if he was talking about a mosquito he smacked. "From then on I made myself lock up my emotions. I find there is a better outcome."

"I don't like you when you are like that." I forced myself to be honest.

"When I am your Sensei, I do not care if you like me or not. I only care if you follow directions." He finished my leg, covered it up and pulled the sheet down to the small of my back.

I had nothing to say so changed the subject. "What am I going to be doing tomorrow?"

"The same as today, eight-mile run, an hour swim and martial arts training. It would not hurt to practice karate on your own too."

"I can't wait." I closed my eyes remembering a question. "Can I work out with Alex? Having another person around will help keep me motivated."

"I am going to find out tonight why he is here and then we will see."

"Okay." Without anything else to say I matched my breathing to his again and fell asleep.

"Time to get up Katie." Vince shook my shoulder.

"Huh?" I asked, trying to remember where I was.

"There is a robe at the end of the table. Go take a

shower and get some sleep." I heard the soft click of the door closing behind him as he left the room.

I got up slowly and put the robe on. My gi and under clothes were gone. I wondered where they went. I slipped out of the small room, crossed the dojo to the stairs and went straight to my room. A shower and bed were the only things on my mind.

# CHAPTER 21

Vince watched Katie as she slept on the massage table, and held himself back. He wanted nothing more than to take her in his arms and make her his. He shook his head. He had to follow his rules. If they started something now, her training would suffer and defeat the purpose of everything they were trying to achieve. He needed to wake her up and get her to bed, he wanted to join Theron and see if they had any hits tracking Lolita down. Instead, he stood and watched her sleep.

Katie was nowhere near ready to take on Lolita, but she would get there. She was picking everything up quickly, and her speed was already as fast as most human black belts, but if she was going to beat Lolita, she was going to have to be faster than human, faster than a vampire. He was not sure if she would be able to be as fast as she needed to be as a human, but it was looking promising. He did not think she noticed how fast she already was, but her only comparison was himself. He decided not to tell her yet. She needed to figure it out for herself. She needed confidence, but he did not need her to get a big head.

After waking Katie and sending her to bed, he took the golf cart to Theron's house. He parked it at the front door and entered the mansion without knocking. It was lit up as usual, inside Theron's vampires were busy with their nightly duties making sure the island was protected and running smoothly.

He made his way to the second floor and Theron's office; passing a few of Theron's vampires on the way. He paid them no mind; except for a female, he did not recognize. She stared at him as if she knew him, but he could not place her. He nodded his head to her and continued to Theron's office.

He stopped outside the door and took a step back thinking about what Theron had accomplished as a vampire. It made him proud; he had chosen a smart and innovative man to turn. Sometimes he wished he had carved out a spot in the world to rule as Theron and Miguel had, but he was not meant to rule alone. He was a fighter and bodyguard, he did not think he knew how to rule, only take orders. He took care of himself, and built a fortune that would allow him to create his own territory if he wanted to. Yet his place in this world was not as a dictator, but a protector.

What would he do if he and Katie became lovers? She was going to rule the vampires, he had no doubt, but would he be able to rule at her side? If he did, he would have to find good bodyguards for the both of them. Once he found his way to her side, she would prove to be an endless distraction.

He shook himself. She may hate him by the time she completed his training. Maybe he would always be her bodyguard. Keeping her safe from those who would want to take her place or take her. But what if she took a lover? Could he stand by protecting her while she shared a bed with another? He knocked on Theron's door forcing himself to stop thinking about the future, and entered when Theron gave him permission. "Good evening," Vince said, closing the door behind him and nodding at Theron and Helen. Theron sat behind his desk looking at a computer monitor while Helen sat in one of the visitor chairs.

"How did the karate lesson go?" Theron asked, looking up from his computer as Vince took the other visitor chair.

"As well as expected. She is picking it up quickly. She is already as fast as the fastest human, and she is picking up Greek quickly."

"Yes," Helen turned so she could look at Vince. "I believe it's all in there, she just has to stop fighting it."

"Agreed." Theron folded his fingers together and rested his hands on the table. "Do you think she will be ready to fight Ben?"

"I will make sure she is." Vince leaned back in his chair, he wanted to sleep, but first he needed some answers. "What is going on with Miguel? I know what you told Katie. Is there anything else we need to consider when dealing with him?"

"He has been beaten," Helen looked at Vince. "He knows he ruined his chances with her. He blames himself and his sister; he banished her from San Sebastian. He guessed you would bring her here. It was sheer luck he was right. All he wants to do is make it right with her and beg her for forgiveness."

"Should we get rid of him?" Theron asked and Vince turned back to him thinking.

"As much as I would like to shred him for what he did to Katie, he may still be useful. Leave him for now; he is in a self-imposed exile. He can stay there pretending to watch out for Katie." Vince got up and paced around the room.

"If we are done with this subject I need to go. I have some things to take care of before I am off for the night." Helen got up to leave.

"Have a good evening Helen." Theron nodded his head and

watched her leave the room.

"Any word on Lolita's location?"

"She's moving around in her typical fashion. She moves from town to town every few nights. The problem is, we are only finding out where she has been, not where she is going next. It doesn't look like she is actively trying to find Katie, but she is up to something."

"I may be of help there. Katie had a dream about Lolita this afternoon. She was in a church; she was trying to make allegiances with a vampire priest. I think she is trying to build an army. She was using religion to convince the priest from what Katie remembered."

"How do you know her dreams are reality?" Theron sounded skeptical.

"Katie dreamed Miguel would burn San Sebastian to the ground, and a week later it happened. It is enough for me to believe it."

"Very well." Theron stretched his arms over his head. "Is there anything else?"

"Yes," Vince stopped in front of the desk. "Who is Alex and why is he here?"

"How do you even know about him? He should be keeping his head down. The people who are after him have spies everywhere."

"He found Katie yesterday when she was having lunch, then he joined her on her run this morning and watched her swim this afternoon." Jealousy raged through him. What he would not give to have been out there running next to Katie.

"He has been here for a few months. I'm sure he is just lonely for human companionship. He's a mercenary. He was spotted on his last mission and he needed a place to lie low for a while. He's done some work for me in the past and it went well. I offered him sanctuary, thinking I'll get a discount next time I require his services." Theron leaned back in his chair.

"Katie asked me if she could workout with him." Vince ran his hand through his hair and blew out a loud breath. "Do you think I can trust him?"

"In what way?"

"Will he hurt her? Will he watch out for her? Protect her?" Vince asked automatically, even though he was thinking of a completely different scenario.

"I think he will. He sees women as the weaker sex. He will automatically want to protect her, but his motives may not be pure. He has not been laid since he's been here. His blood tastes off, and no one will play with him. After what Katie went through with Miguel I doubt you have anything to worry about."

"Thank you for putting the idea in my head Theron." Vince went back to his chair and sat down hard.

"You were already thinking about it. Maybe you should reconsider your rule about not being romantically involved with your student."

"You know I cannot. She will not be as strong as she will be if I took our relationship there. I can deal with the jealousy. I will be fine."

"Are you going to let Alex workout with her?" Leaning back in his chair Theron laced his hands behind his head. He enjoyed watching his maker be uncomfortable, it did not happen very often.

"If I do not allow it, she could hold it against me. I need to trust her as much as she trusts me. I will allow it for now. If this human becomes a distraction though, I will be forced to end it."

"A reasonable plan." Theron got up and came around the

desk. "What are you plans for the rest of the night?"

"Sleep, I have not had a good night's sleep in over a week." Vince got up as well and moved to the door.

"That sounds boring." Theron moved behind Vince. "Why don't you join me for a snack?"

Vince thought about it while opening the door. He felt a small tinge of hunger but sleep called to him. "Tomorrow night perhaps, I need sleep."

"Very well, have a good night Vince."

"You too, Theron."

Vince drove back to the house and parked the golf cart at the front door. He went inside and stopped outside Katie's door. He listened to the steady rhythm of her heart and breathing. She was no doubt asleep after the day she had, but he needed to make sure.

He went down the hall to his room, wanting to sleep as well. At least Katie was safe for the time being.

# CHAPTER 22

The next day I woke up to my alarm, which was odd, I did not remember setting it the night before. It was nine in the morning. I rolled out of bed and stretched, every muscle hurt, I was not sure how I pulled the muscles in my jaw but even they hurt. I shuffled into the bathroom, took care of the necessities then got dressed in my running gear.

When I went out to the kitchen, I found Vince and Alex sitting at the table. Alex had a cup of coffee in his hand while Vince had his hands folded on the table.

"Good morning," I said, passing by them on my way to the kitchen where I opened fridge for some juice. I wanted coffee, but if I was going to run eight more miles today, coffee did not sound good to my stomach.

"Good morning," they said at the same time.

I poured my juice, took the plate filled with eggs and bacon over to the table, and sat down. They looked at me then my plate. "What?"

"You're going to eat all of that before your run?" Alex already looked green around the gills.

"It's your fault I puked yesterday." I dug in to the eggs. "The smell of your vomit made me vomit."

"I'll buy that." Vince smiled. "Alex is going to be your daytime workout partner as you requested."

"Are you sure you are up for it, Alex?" I gave him a sideways look.

"Yes, I'll be able to keep up just fine." His voice was cool as if I had no right to question him.

"Alright don't get your panties in a twist." I shoveled another fork full of food into my mouth.

"When you are done eating please come to see me in the dojo." Vince stood to leave.

"How are your legs feeling today?" I asked.

"They're okay, a little stiff, but I'll get by just fine." He leaned back in his chair balancing it on the back legs.

"Good." I scraped the last of the food from my plate onto my fork and shoveled it into my mouth. "I might need you to carry me later." I got up and took my plate to the sink. "I'll be back after I talk to Vince then we can get started."

"I'll be waiting." Alex brought his chair back down to the floor and smiled at me.

Before I entered the dojo, I bowed to Sensei then walked in. "You wanted to speak to me Sensei?"

"Yes, about Alex." He gestured for me to kneel across from him. I knelt and he continued. "He is a mercenary who works for Theron once in a while. He is here lying low after someone spotted him on his last job. He is a very dangerous man. Theron and I both think you will be safe with him, but keep in mind, he is a gun for hire, and you should not trust him completely."

"Thank you, Sensei, for telling me about Alex and what I need to look out for." Alex, the puny skinny kid downstairs was a mercenary? It was almost laughable, but he

176

had kept up with me the day before. He would be the perfect assassin; everyone would think he was a computer geek at first glance. If he was a mercenary, then I would be safer with him than by myself. What could the harm be?

"Good luck on your run; I may not be here when you get back. Theron or Helen will be here to help you with your Greek after your swim." He stood up and gestured for me to stand as well. "Make sure you take at least a three-hour break between your run and your swim and eat at least an hour before you go swimming."

"Thank you, Sensei." I stood up, bowed to him then went back to the kitchen to get Alex.

"Are you ready to go?" I asked as I came back into kitchen.

"Let's do it." He got up and went to the door leading outside.

We did not talk much on our run, we just ran. He ran at my pace, if had to keep up with him I would have died. It was harder than yesterday, my legs and my arms were tired, but there was no vomit this time. When we got back to the house, I got us both a sports drink to enjoy while we stretched out.

"What are you doing during your break?" Alex asked grabbing his foot behind his back to stretch out his quad.

"Yesterday I ate and slept." I copied the stretch he was doing. "Today I think I'll eat and catch up on current events. I haven't watched the news in forever. What about you?"

"Eat, sleep, sounds pretty good to me." He looked toward his house.

"I have food if you want to eat lunch here." I motioned toward the kitchen.

He thought about it for a moment. "Sounds good."

"Okay, come on in, I'll put something together." I went through the door and held it for him.

"Thanks."

177

I made ham sandwiches, and found some chips to eat with them. I put the plates on the table and sat down. "I feel better today than I did yesterday at this time." I picked up the sandwich and took a bite. As I chewed, I noticed Alex had not touched his and he was staring at me. "What?"

"Nothing, it's just—" He stopped himself.

"It's just what?"

"It's just; I've never seen a woman who isn't afraid to eat when she is hungry." He picked up his sandwich taking a bite.

"Then you are hanging out with the wrong kind of women." I took another bite, chasing it with water.

"Maybe you're right." If I had not known any better, I thought he might have been hitting on me. "Are you sleeping with Vince?"

"Me and Vince?" I asked, scrambling for how to make him back off but not piss the mercenary off. "No, I just got out of a completely fucked up relationship." At least I was being honest. "I'm taking a break from men for a while."

"Duly noted." Alex finished off his sandwich and got up with his plate.

"That doesn't mean I'm not enjoying your company though." I watched as he made his way to the sink with his plate. "I could really use a friend to hang out with."

He put his plate in the sink, turned around and leaned against it looking at me. "Normally, I don't make friends with women." He watched for my reaction, which was blank. "But you're tough and funny so yes I'll be your friend."

"Great," I said sardonically. "I'm going to go grab the laptop and do some web surfing. Do you want to join me?" I asked to be polite; I really did not want him to join me.

He must have read it on my face because he said. "No thanks, I am going to catch a nap before our swim." He made his way to the door. "What time do you want to meet?"

"Two?" I asked, looking at the clock.

"I'll see you then," he said before leaving.

I went into my room and took my laptop out of its bag. I went into the den and got comfortable on the couch. I stared at the blank search screen. I wanted to type my name into it, but I was not sure if someone could track me if I did. I could not log into my Facebook account, and I was scared to search for my parents. I finally decided San Sebastian's newspaper was the safest way to see what else had happened there. Since it was a tourist town, it was in both English and Spanish.

I thought I would have to scroll through days and days of information but on the second page, there was an article about me.

Have You Seen This Woman?

Katie Hunter, is 23 years old, 1.7m, 68 kg with short black hair, American. She was last seen on June 2nd at the bar, Sed De Sangre, around midnight.

Hunter, was backpacking through Europe with her boyfriend. When their relationship ended. Her last known residence was *El Campamento de Mount Urgull*. According to the authorities her identification, passport, and wallet were stolen from her and were found on a prostitute who was hit by a car the same night as her disappearance.

Her parents told our reporter that they are afraid she has been hurt, and she speaks very little Spanish. If anyone has seen her, please contact the police. They have also set up a website for people to leave tips or any information on

179

finding their daughter.

I hesitated a moment before I clicked on the link to open the webpage. There was a photo of me in the middle with the words, *Help Us Find Our Katie.* I scrolled down to read what my dad had written there.

*We are heading to Spain at the end of the week to talk to the police and canvas the town in hopes that someone will have word on what happened to our Katie. Please pray we will find her and bring her home.*

I did not want them to worry. I wished the police had said it was me who was dead and not the prostitute. They could have burned the body before my parents could claim it. If they went to San Sebastian now Lolita could kidnap them to try to get to me. *Fuck,* I thought then picked up my cell phone and called Vince.

"Katie, what is wrong?" he asked after the phone rang once.

"I need to talk to you about my parents." I tried to keep my breathing even. "When are you coming home?"

"I can be there in ten minutes; I am already on the way." He ended the call.

I looked at the clock it was one-thirty, where had the time gone? I needed to get ready for my swim with Alex, but I needed Vince to do something to keep my parents safe and away from the 'evil ones'.

I hurried to my room, put on my swimming suit and a pair of shorts then went back out to the den to wait for Vince.

"What is wrong?" he asked as soon as he entered the room.

"My parents are going to San Sebastian to look for me." I held my hand over my face trying not to cry.

"I am sorry, but what is the big emergency? They will look, but they will not find you." He sat in the seat next to me.

"You have no feelings for anyone beyond yourself, do you?" I got up and started pacing back and forth across the room. "What if Lolita uses them to get to me?"

"Why do you care? They are not even your real parents." He was angry with me for some reason.

"They were the only parents I ever knew, Vince. I love them. I hate that they are out there looking for me, and there's nothing I can do to let them know I'm safe." I wanted to beat some sense into him.

"I understand where you are coming from but you need to let them go. They will mourn you eventually then they will be able to move on with their lives." It sounded like he was speaking from experience.

"Vince, if Lolita gets her hands on them and threatens to kill them, please believe me when I say I will go to her to save them." I stormed out of the house and headed for the beach.

Alex not arrived at the beach when I got there, and I did not wait for him. I was too mad to wait. I left my shorts and my flip-flops on the beach and ran to the water. The break was smaller today and I had no trouble getting through the waves. Once I was a good distance out, I started swimming.

Vince had no idea what I was feeling. My parents, were the people who adopted me, fed me, sent me to school, and loved me. They were going into danger because of me. It was my mess. It was because of me they were going to end up in the middle of this. He had been a vampire too long, I decided after I made my turn and headed back to my starting point.

He needed a wakeup call with reality. I was dead serious

when I told him I would go after my parents if Lolita took them. They were innocent in all this. I was not sure how I was going to get away from Vince, but he said if I wanted to leave and go out on my own he would let me. I hated to be that woman, save my parents or I am leaving, but I did not see a way around it.

Alex was treading water when I got back to my starting point and he looked pissed. "You were supposed to wait for me," he almost yelled.

"I'm sorry I had to blow off some steam." I did not care if I sounded upset.

"What happened?"

"I got into a fight with Vince." I looked back at the house. "Look, I can't talk about it, let's just swim okay?"

"Okay, let's get it done." He said turning to me. "But Katie, I have been through a lot of shit if you need to talk to someone I promise I can handle it without judgment."

"Thanks Alex." I put my head down and continued swimming.

After our swim, Alex and I lay on the beach catching our breath. "That sucked worse than yesterday." I sat up and stretched my arms above my head.

"I'll have to agree with you." Alex was sitting up next to me. "But only because I didn't swim for an hour yesterday. I got to watch."

"Must be nice." I pushed his shoulder back trying to get him to fall over in the sand. He did not move. Man, I was a weakling.

"Why are you doing this?" Alex asked turning our conversation serious.

"Doing what?" I pretended I did not know what he

182

was talking about.

"Training like an Olympic athlete. What is so bad that Vince wouldn't be able to protect you?"

"Vince will always protect me I think, no matter what," I said in a faraway voice. "But I need to be able to take care of myself too."

"I understand, but this seems a little extreme doesn't it. Wouldn't some self-defense training work just as well? With a lot less pain?"

I thought about what he said. I was not sure how to answer, *I am the prophesied queen of the vampires*, was not going to work. He might know about vampires since he was staying at the compound, but he did not need to know too much about the prophecy or me. "It might be strange to you, but I want to be the best at what I do. This is Vince's training program, and I'm going to stick to it."

"Then I'll stick with you on the workouts." He looked back at the house. "Do you need to get back up there?"

"No, I have time before the next session, but I need something to drink. I swear the salt just pulls the moisture right out of you." I got up dusting the sand off my ass. I walked over to my shorts and slid them on.

"I have some sport drinks back at my place if you want to come over for a while." He sounded shy.

I looked at him then back to the house. I needed to get everything figured out with Vince, otherwise I needed to pack, and figure out how I was going to keep my parents out of Lolita's grasp. "Can I take a rain check?" I slipped on my flip-flops. "I need to work this out with Vince before I'm going to be much company."

"Sure thing, I'll see you tomorrow at nine to go running, right?" He got up dusting the sand off his shorts.

"Sounds like a plan." I started walking toward the house. "See you."

"Yeah, see you," he said, walking back toward his house.

Vince was in the kitchen cooking when I walked in. I was wet from the shower at the base of the stairs, and I did not want to stand around dripping on the floor. I said hi, and then took off for my room to put some dry clothes on.

When I came out there was a lamb dish waiting where I normally sat and Vince was sitting opposite of me. He had a sports drink sitting next to the plate along with a bottle of water.

I sat down at the table and did not say anything until I had a long chug of the sports drink and water. "Thank you for making dinner." I looked at the spread. "Why are you always cooking for me?"

"I want to make sure you eat balanced meals while you are in training." He looked worried.

"They have all been great, thanks." I picked up my fork and knife to cut into the food. It tasted better then it smelled and I could not hold back a smile.

"Are you going to leave to find your parents?" he asked, sounding and feeling nervous, he must be worried if I could feel him.

"It depends." I took another bite of the lamb with some broccoli. "Is there anything we can do from here to stop them from coming to Europe and getting close to Lolita?"

"I have been thinking about it." He did not sound confident about his idea. "And I have spoken with Theron at length about it, the only thing we can think of is telling them you witnessed a horrible crime, and the Spanish authorities put you in witness protection. We can tell them, if they come to Europe they are not only going to put you at risk but risk themselves as well."

I thought about it while I chewed my dinner. "That's not a bad plan, as long as we make it look real. Maybe who ever talks to them could give them a letter from me?" I ate a piece of bread.

"Good idea." Vince stared at a spot behind me. "Can you write it before we go up to the dojo? Then I can give it to the vampire who will meet with your parents after we are done for the night."

"Yes, of course." I finished the sports drink. "Thank you for arranging this Vince."

"I am sorry if I seemed to be uncaring." He forced himself to meet my eyes before looking past me again. "I have not had anyone close to me, like you are with your parents, in a very long time. I forgot how much humans cared about each other. It is something I miss."

"I hope someone will care about you like I do my parents someday."

"There is always a chance." He walked down the hall to the door leading to the tunnels. "Be in the dojo by nine."

"Yes, Sensei," I murmured, taking my dishes to the kitchen and washing them.

I went to my room to I find my gi, and the clothes I wore the day before sitting on the bed clean and folded. I would have to ask Vince if he was doing my laundry as well as the cooking for me.

Pushing the thought away for the time being I found a pen and notebook and went back into the dining room to write my parents a letter to convince them I was safe, and assure them I would see them again someday even if I had a hard time believing it.

*Dear Mom & Dad,*

*I'm so sorry I can't call you and tell you I'm alright. The people who are after me may be bugging your phone. I can't get into what is going on. This is a life or death situation, but please don't*

185

*worry. I have some amazing people keeping me safe.*

*I don't know who will be delivering this letter, but you can trust them. Please don't come to Europe looking for me. It would only cause more harm than good. I want you both to be safe and happy. The people I am with will die to protect me.*

*I'm sure you are wondering if I really wrote this letter and not someone else. I'm racking my brain for a way to prove it's me. Do you remember when I was in kindergarten and I was playing on the monkey bars? I fell off and chipped my tooth. I didn't tell anyone because I thought I would get kicked out of school. When you finally came to pick me up I smiled and you saw it. No one could believe I kept quiet when I was in so much pain.*

*I hope this proves to you that your daughter is writing this letter. Please don't look for me. I'll come to you when I am safe.*

*I love you both, thanks for picking me that day,*
*Katie*

I finished the letter, folded it, put it in an envelope and sealed it with a kiss. I wiped the tears off my face and placed it on the table. I stared at it for a minute praying what I wrote would convince my parents I was safe and not to come looking for me. They may not be my blood, but they made me the person I was, they taught me right from wrong and to be a good person. No matter who your real parents are, the ones who raised you, and loved you like their own are the ones you owe respect to.

I looked at my watch, it was only eight, but I went into my room and put my gi on anyway. I went up to the dojo, opened the sliding windows, knelt, and thought about nothing but my breathing. After a while I heard Sensei enter the dojo and I moved to get up. "Stay where you are. There is no need to bow when you greet me like this."

"Thank you, Sensei." I relaxed back into the pose.

He knelt in front of me and closed his eyes. My breathing was already calm and my thoughts were of nothing but my next breath. I listened as he matched his breathing to mine. It was odd but still intimate. I was proud to be the calm one; he had to match my breathing for a change.

"Stand and start with your punches." He got up and went to get the bamboo sword.

I did as he said, moving through the workout as he directed. He was more forceful with the corrections that night. I was going to have a few bruises, but I needed the corrections. After punches and kicks, we moved on to blocks. Lower blocks and upper blocks. I was beginning to tire when he gave me a water break.

When I was done with the water, he ordered me to a wide line in the middle of the room. He handed me a pair of sparring gloves and showed me how to put them on as he put on his.

"We are going to spar, slowly to start. When you spar in class there is a light contact rule, if you hit harder than a tap you will be punished. No punches or kicks below the belt are allowed. Before we begin, we bow to each other to show respect for the fight. We will move around the room, if you see a punch coming block it, same with a kick. If you see a window or a weakness take advantage of it and use the skills you learned to attack me. Do you understand?"

"Yes, Sensei." I was nervous and excited.

"Hajime," he said and we both fell back into our fighting stances.

Vince bounced around on the balls of his feet and I mimicked him keeping my arms up, with my elbows slightly bent and my hands fisted. He took a quick step forward and I took a step back not letting him get into striking range.

"You cannot just dance around all night." He moved in and out again. "Are you going to hit me?"

"I'm still looking for an opening, Sensei." I was afraid if I moved in he would block me or hit me and it would hurt.

"Remember this is light contact. I am not going to hurt you."

I moved in and out looking for an opening. I faked with my left hand and came in fast with my right. He blocked it easily, letting the wind out of my sails. I failed.

"The fight is not over because I blocked one punch Katie. It was a good fake, but I saw your punch coming from a mile away. Think about the quickest way to punch me without allowing me to grab you and throw you to the ground."

"Yes, Sensei." Before I could even think about trying something else, he came in with a punch to my face. My arm whipped out and blocked the punch automatically. My arm hurt where we had made contact but it was better than my face hurting.

"Good." He danced around me, forcing me to keep up.

I lashed out with a roundhouse kick aimed at his ribs but I was not quick enough. He caught my foot and pulled. Before I knew what was happening I was on the ground with him above me with a fist cocked, ready to pummel my face. I brought my arms up to protect my face and I flashed back to Miguel on top of me in the shower. Fear spiked through me, and I kicked my leg up connecting with his groin. I would never let that happen again, I thought to myself. His face turned green, he grabbed his groin and rolled away from me, curling into the fetal position. I jumped up quickly and resumed my fighting stance.

He rolled to his feet and said, "yamete," in a wheezing voice. "Katie, did you not hear me say, no below the belt hits?"

"Sensei, I'm sorry." I looked down at my feet, I did not want to tell him it was because of Miguel, but he needed to understand. "I had a flashback."

He stopped rocking and moved his hands from between his legs. His mouth opened and closed but nothing came out. He ran his hands through his hair and let out a breath. "I am sorry if I caused you to have a flashback. I am sure you could not help your impulse to protect yourself. That being said, please try to remember this is a safe environment, no one here is going to hurt you." He put his finger under my chin and pulled my chin up until I met his eyes.

"Yes, Sensei." I was trying not to cry, I disappointed him.

"You have your first fight in less than two weeks. We are really going to have to work on sparring if you want to win." He let go of my chin and walked away. I wondered how he could turn is compassion on and off like that. I did not think I would ever understand him.

I wanted to ask him why he made the bet, but I did not want to do more pushups then I was already going to have to do for kicking him in the balls. It would have to wait until we were in the massage room.

"Let's go again." He walked behind his line in the floor.

As we continued, I found myself relaxing and getting into the rhythm of the dance. We would come together punching, kicking, or blocking then move apart. I was sure Vince was taking it easy on me. He got in a lot of hits, but he let me get in a few too. I was feeling more confident, but I was not ready for a cage fight.

189

After our last session, we bowed to each other. "There is only one more thing you need to do tonight." He went to get his trusty bamboo sword. "You owe me one hundred pushups."

I wanted to protest, but I broke the rules by kicking him in the balls. I groaned, he was right. Fighting him on it would only earn me more.

"You were protecting yourself when you kicked me, but breaking the rules always has consequences."

"Yes, Sensei." I got into the plank position. My body was tired. It had been a long two days, but I did everything I could to do my pushups perfect every time. I only had to do twenty extra for a change.

When I was done Sensei sent me into the back room for a shower, then he came in to give me my massage. It was somewhat odd, let me kick your ass and make you so tired you cannot move then I will massage you and make you feel better.

"How are you feeling tonight?" he asked as he worked on my legs.

"Tired and sore." I flexed my hands. "My knuckles are killing me."

He left me, and I heard him open a door, pick up something then close it. He picked up my hand and I felt an icepack being wrapped around it, then he went to the other side and did the same thing on the other hand.

"That feels awesome." I closed my eyes as the cold soothed the burning. "Thank you."

"I have done my fair share of knuckle pushups. They hurt, but are worth it. They will save you a lot of pain when you really punch someone." Vince went back to his work on

190

my legs.

"Why are you having me fight Ben? He's a vampire, a new one, but he'll still be a lot better than I'll be in two weeks."

"You need to believe in yourself more. You are picking everything up very quickly. You will beat him." *Plus, he does not know you will be able to read his mind.*

"I can't read your mind." But I wished I could sometimes. "I can only hear you when you want me to."

"I think if you try you will be able to. We are going to start working on it tomorrow."

"I hope you have a plan because I have no idea how to do it." I closed my eyes.

"I do have a plan." He moved to the other side of my body. "What do you think of Alex?"

"Oh, he's a nice guy, and it's nice to have someone to workout with." I cringed, thinking about how he flirted with me. "He's a good listener and doesn't push for information."

"You have not told him anything?"

"No, and I don't intend to. I don't want to drag any humans into this." I stiffened wondering if Vince would leave Alex out of it.

"Relax, it is a good call." He pushed his hand down on my leg until he felt me relax. "He may be a good guy to have on our side if the need presents itself, but for the time being I am glad he is nice."

"Yeah, it's nice to have someone to talk to who doesn't know how fucked up my life is." I closed my eyes again.

"I would not say it is fucked up. It is just full of challenges that will make you stronger."

"That's one way to look at it." I was not sure I saw it the same way. "What's the plan for tomorrow?"

"Same as today, plus in between your run and your swim we are going to meet in here for a few hours to work on mind reading.

Then after your swim, Theron or Helen will come to help you with your Greek."

"I left the letter for my parents on the dining room table. Will you make sure it gets to them?"

"Yes, Theron's man is leaving just after midnight. I should have plenty of time to get it to him."

"Thank you, Sensei. You have no idea how much this means to me." I yawned; the massage was making me drowsy.

*Anything for you, Katie*, he thought; I had a feeling he did not mean for me to hear that.

# CHAPTER 23

I was standing outside the temple when I opened my eyes. Everything looked the same as it had in my last dream; it was beautiful and well kept. The doors to my mother's temple were open waiting for me.

"Mom?" I called out. "Are you here?"

"Yes, dear I am here," she said from beside me. "You look tired."

"Vince has been working me really hard." I looked down at my purple knuckles. "He's trying to prepare me for the coming battles. He said I should be as strong as possible before I change."

"Did you tell him what the prophecy said about the one who changes you?" She held my hand and walked us into the temple.

"I haven't, I keep forgetting to tell him, things have been strange."

"What do you mean? From what I have heard he is being a good protector and teacher."

"He is, but he becomes a different person when he's training me. I have a hard time talking to him when we are in training mode. The only time I feel like I can talk to him is at the end of my day, and I'm so sore and tired I forget to tell him about it. I will the next time he talks about changing me."

"Do not forget to tell him." She squeezed my bruised hand and I tried to pull it out of her grip but she would not let go.

"Mom," I yelled. "What are you doing? It hurts."

"Healing your hands dear." She finally let go and took a step back. "Did you not realize that you are healing much faster than before?"

"I did and I meant to ask you about it." I looked at my hand and made a fist without pain for the first time in a few days. "Are you the reason why the bite from Lolita healed so quickly without scarring?"

"Yes, I did not want you to be reminded of her for the rest of your life."

"Thank you." I did not want the reminder either.

"You are doing well with your training. You will be a warrior for our cause. I can already see it. Stay true to your training, listen to your instincts and all will be well child." She gave me a hug as I closed my eyes and breathed in the scent that was solely the Goddess.


The next day after my run with Alex and a shower, I went up to the dojo, as Sensei indicated the night before. I could not find my gi so I wore lose fitting shorts and a tank top.

He was waiting for me when I entered. I bowed and joined him on the floor kneeling. I closed my eyes automatically and matched my breathing to his.

*Is your mind quiet?* He asked.

"Yes, Sensei," I answered in a calm voice.

*I want you to break into my mind and see what I am thinking.*

"I'm not sure how." I left my eyes closed and pulled my eyebrows together.

*Remember how Lolita and Miguel tried to control you with their minds? Try to do that to me.*

"I'll try." I thought about how his mind was able to speak to me. "Can you please speak to my mind again?" I needed somewhere to start.

*You can do this Katie; I believe in you.*

As the words formed in my mind I tracked how they got there. It was almost like there was a cell phone tower in my head that received thoughts, and he had one too. I sent my mind out and found his tower. I could tell it was Vince from the way he sounded in my mind. His feelings were mellow and optimistic. I pushed through the feeling and found a wall or a dead space. Something was happening just beyond it but I could not get through.

*Breathe Katie, you are turning blue,* Sensei thought and the force field became thin for a second. I saw an opportunity, pushed through the thin barrier and I was in his mind. It was calm except for some growing trepidation. What did he tell me to do? Breathe, I took a breath and he calmed. *Can you hear me?* I asked him with my mind.

Sensei jumped and I fell face first to the hard floor. He was standing over me before I could open my eyes. "Are you hurt?" He bent down and helped me to sit.

"I was there in your mind and you kicked me out." I ran a hand over my face. The floor was hard and my face hurt where I hit it. "I'm fine, could you hear me?"

"Yes, it was like someone screaming in my ear." Sensei stuck his figure in his ear and shook it like there was water in it.

"I guess I'll have to whisper my thoughts to you when I'm in your head." I almost laughed.

He smiled. "You did it though." He was emanating pride.

195

"You were able to get through, this is great."

"Did you think I wouldn't be able to?" He seemed confident about it last night when he mentioned it.

"I did, but I was not a hundred percent sure. I was a little concerned when you stopped breathing though. Do you know what happened?"

"I was in your mind, but I was on the outer edges, there was a force field I could not get through. I forgot about everything but breaking through the force field." I thought I could get back into his head anytime I wanted now. I created a door. "Could you feel me in there before I spoke?"

"There was a small almost tickling sensation. If I did not know you were trying to get in I do not think I would have noticed it." He got up and walked to the mirror. "That is how you are going to beat Ben."

"Really? The only way I found a way in was when you thought something to me." I rolled my eyes. "How am I going to get Ben to think to me?"

"Are you questioning your sensei?"

Danger Will Robinson. Backtrack, I thought to myself. "No, I'm just pointing out the hurdles we need to overcome in order for the plan to work." I was trying to sound diplomatic.

"That is why we started working on it now. Tonight when we spar I want you to try and intercept what I am going to do before I do it."

"I look forward to the challenge, Sensei." I lied, I was dreading it. It would help in the fight against Lolita, but somehow, I did not think I would master it without a few bruises.

"Why don't you go and get something to eat? You

196

need to let it settle before your swim."

"Thank you, Sensei." I got up bowing to him. "Would you like to join me and hang out for a while?" I really wanted to ask him about the meeting with my parents, and I needed to tell him about the prophecy, but I did not want to risk any more pushups.

"I am sorry but Theron needs me up at the mansion, we can talk tonight."

So much for talking to him about a few things I thought he would find very important. I went downstairs, got something to eat then I went to practice my punches and kicks.

That night, after a good swim with Alex, practicing my Greek with Helen and a yummy dinner of fish and rice, the real work began.

Sensei and I danced in circles while I tried to enter his mind and figure out what his next move was going to be. It did not go very well.

"Let's take a break." He pulled me up from the floor where I landed after walking into one of his kicks instead of blocking it. "You have to be able to listen and to move at the same time."

I almost said: "Tell me something I didn't know," but I caught my tongue before it was too late. "Yes, Sensei," I said instead and picked up my water bottle from the floor.

"What do you hear when you are in my head? Are you getting what I am going to do before I do it?"

"I do, but your thoughts are very fast, you think it a split second before you do it." I was trying to put something into words that there were no words for. "Then, when you do something like, kick or punch it feels like I'm the one doing it. I think that's why I stepped into that last kick."

"What do you see when you are in my head?" He leaned against the wall thinking.

"It's confusing. I see you from my eyes. Wait, I can't really

197

see through your eyes, but I get an impression of what you are looking at, which is me and it throws me." I looked over at him wanting him to understand what I was saying.

"Why don't we try this?" He moved to the center of the room. "Stand next to me."

I put down the water bottle and did as he asked. "Now enter my mind and mimic everything I do. Learn how I move when my brain tells me what to do." He stood at rest with his hands in fists hanging in front of his black belt.

I copied him and entered his mind. I kept my eyes open which was a struggle. I wanted to close them and follow by letting his mind lead me, but that was not what we were trying to accomplish.

We took a step to the left with a low block, then we took a step in the same direction and did a standard punch. We turned one hundred and eighty degrees and did two low blocks followed by a punch.

I was beginning to see how he thought. We turned ninety degrees back to the way we started and blocked a high punch three times stepping forward with each block. Instead of copying him, I began to read what his mind was telling me to do. I let his brain impulses guide me in my movements. We turned blocking and punching then turned again blocking and punching. We finished at the same time; it was like a choreographed dance we had practiced hundreds of times.

"That was a kata." He moved around in front of me. "I felt when you let my brain take over and guide you through the moves, it was beautiful to watch." He looked bashful admitting it to me.

"Yes, when I let go, I let your impulses guide my

movement." I was still reeling from it. It was an intense sensation, a very personal one.

"What is wrong?" He noted the cringe on my face.

"I feel like I invaded your privacy. I saw how important the moves were to you and how much you wanted to get every movement perfect."

"Good." He moved closer to me. "That is what I wanted you to feel. I do not mind since I asked you to do it, but please stay out of my mind when we are not training."

"Of course, Sensei." I did not want to be in his mind in the first place.

"Let's try and spar again. Your biggest challenge is going to be reading my move and forcing yourself to do the counter move, not mimicking the move I am going to do." He moved into fighting stance.

We sparred for hours, slowly I was able to wrap my mind around anticipating and countering the moves he threw at me. We were not up to full speed but we were making progress.

Later, while lying on the massage table after we were done, and I was able to speak freely I asked if my parents received my letter.

"Yes, Theron's man met with them last night and explained what was going on." He found a knot in my back that had me gasping in pain. "They did not believe anything he said until he gave them the letter. I am glad you wrote it. It helped deter them from coming to Europe."

I held back my tears. "I'm so glad they're staying home. I hope Lolita doesn't go after them."

"I do not think she will. Her humanity was so long ago that she does not remember family and what humans are willing do for the ones they love. I do not think she had much of a family when she was human anyway."

"I had a dream last night." I needed to tell him what the prophecy said before he did something stupid like change me.

"Did the goddess come to you?" He paused for a moment, then continued working my muscles.

"Yes, or I went to her." I thought back. "She reminded me to tell you about what I read when I looked at the original prophecy."

"You mentioned you needed to talk to me about it." He moved to the other side of my body, like the prophecy was no big deal. "Why didn't you mention it before?"

"Well you haven't been one for conversations lately unless I'm so exhausted I can barely think," I snapped. He was the one who was cold and distant most of the time. "You haven't been very approachable."

"Are you mad at me?"

"You changed when we started training." I racked my brain trying to find the right words. "We used to talk about lots of things, but now the only thing you talk to me about is training. You said being cold would give me a better outcome, but I miss my friend who saved me from the monsters." I did not know why I chose that moment to unload on him but there it was.

"That is what this time is for, Katie." He dug his hands in a little harder than was necessary into my back. "Besides you and Alex are becoming pretty chummy." I felt jealousy bleed out of him.

"Alex is a kid; he is company to workout with, a friend. He's not someone I can talk to about the prophecy and my dreams." I was frustrated at his was jealousy, but there was no point calling him out on it, it would serve no purpose.

"Alex is much more than a kid. Never doubt it, and I believe he wants more than friendship with you."

"I told him when we started working out that I'm taking a break from men. If he can't take a hint, then I'll talk to him again."

"I think he will respect your boundaries but keep it in mind. I wish I could be out there running and swimming with you," he said in a soft voice.

My heart melted just a little bit at his tone. "I would like that too."

"No, you would not because I would push you harder every day to make you faster and stronger. We are going to change things up tomorrow." His voice was hard again, he had closed down. "What were you going to tell me about the prophecy?"

"A part of it was translated wrong." I wanted nothing more than to get up and go to bed, but he needed to know what was going on. "What I read and my mother confirmed is: The one who changes her will suffer putrefaction in Tartarus for all days."

"What?" Vince stopped his hands, leaving them on my back as if he was frozen in stone. "How could that be?"

"I'm just calling it like I read it. Mom confirmed it with me last night. She was upset I hadn't told you about it yet."

"This changes everything. I am going to have to come up with a new plan now." His fingers returned to their work but they were digging even deeper and harder than before. "I wish you would have told me sooner. I would have changed your entire training schedule."

"I tried to tell you the first night we were in the dojo. You said you didn't want to talk about the prophecy anymore." I grunted in pain. "Can you lighten up please? You're hurting me."

He ignored me, wrapped up in his own thoughts. I tried to move off the table but he held me fast. With no other option, I found my way into his head. *Vince, snap out it! You are hurting me.*

201

"Didn't I ask you to stay out of my head unless we were training?" he asked, removing his hands from my back.

"I had no choice. You were hurting me and talking to you wasn't working." I sat up with the sheet wrapped around me.

He shook his head. "I am sorry I was hurting you. I planned to change you myself when your training was done. Then we could take care of Lolita sooner rather than later."

"Were you going to ask me if being changed was something I wanted or were you just going to make the decision for me?" He was starting to remind me of Miguel and not in a good way.

"I had not decided yet . . . But now . . ." He was digging a hole he was going to have a hard time getting out of. "I will put my life on the line for you Katie, but I will not spend my afterlife in Tartarus."

"Well," I stood up from the table, "I'm glad I know where you stand in all of this." I pulled the sheet tighter to my body and left.

*Katie, wait,* Vince thought to me. I moved across the dojo but stopped at the tone in his voice. I whirled around, put my hands on my hips.

"Why Vince? I thought you respected me. Thought you would include me in your grand plan. I guess I was wrong. You're just like Miguel, trying to get me where you want me, and make me into a tool for your own reasons. I will not be treated like that. I have put up with your training because it's what I want, not because you wanted me to. I would've quit the first day if I thought it wasn't something I knew I needed. I just want to take care of Lolita. Then maybe I can do what I want for a change and not what I have to. I will not be your tool, and I will not put up with your bullshit."

"Will you let me explain?" Vince moved in front of me during my tirade.

"Do you want to try?" I mocked. "Do you think I am going to believe anything you have to say?" I spun toward the door; I did not want to listen to him anymore.

*Please, you are the most important thing I have in my life.*

*Vince, leave me alone*, I thought breaking into his thoughts. I did not care if he did not want me too. What I just found out hurt more than finding out what Miguel had planned for me.

I went into my bathroom and started a bath. I was too wired to go to sleep. I sat in the bathtub with bath salts and closed my eyes. I had blocked Vince's thought from my mind. I could feel him trying to think to me, but I blocked him out. It was the first time I was able to block him.

Vince planned to change me without finding out if I was ready or if I wanted to be changed. I wanted to know if he was going to do it to take Lolita out of the equation as soon as possible, or because he wanted to rule at my side, but either way I did not want to talk to him. I needed to cool down or I would talk myself into leaving and trying to make it on my own.

Leaving was not a bad idea. I would not have to train every day. I would not have to worry about the damn pushups or bowing. The other side of it was, how would I live? Where could I go where no one would find out where I was and still survive? I would need to get a job, stop living off Vince and I would never get to see my parents again. I could never risk something happening to them because of me.

I would not leave, I thought, dunking my head under the water. I wanted Vince to teach me everything he knew. I was mad at him but he did not lie to me. It was a first for the men in my life, one who told me the truth. I was still mad at him, but I was going to have to work with him, I did not see any other way of making myself safe.

I was supposed to be queen, but I just wanted to be safe. I wanted my enemies neutralized and to live like a normal twenty-three-year-old for a change. I had to stay where I was and learn everything I could from Vince before I would get a chance to be normal. Mind made up, but not feeling any better about Vince, I got out of the tub and crawled into bed. The training helped with sleep, normally I would have tossed and turned all night overthinking everything that happened, but I was so tired I slept dreamlessly.

# CHAPTER 24

The following few days dragged, I got up, ate, ran with Alex, ate, worked on my mental abilities with Sensei, swam with Alex, practiced my Greek, sparred with Sensei, got a massage, went to sleep. I stopped trying to talk to Vince. I did not see the point, he wanted me to be a warrior so I did as he said and only spoke when spoken to. He would drop his cold act letting me know he was there if I wanted to talk during my nightly massage, but I had nothing to say to him.

He started to time me on my runs and swims. If I did not get my eight miles done in less than an hour I would have to spend five minutes for every minute I was late punching a two-by-four post covered with a piece of carpet. He gave me a piece of cloth to wrap my knuckles with while I punched it, but it only helped to not pull the skin off my knuckles, they were still purple and red from bursting blood vessels. I kept expecting my speedy healing to make them heal quicker, but since I was doing the same thing day in and day out, they never got the chance to heal completely. On the third day, they cracked and bled.

Alex shook his head when he saw them and bandaged them for me, but it did not help when we swam that afternoon. I was in so much pain; I finished my swim in tears trying not to choke on the snot clogging my throat.

When we got back to shore my eyes were red and I cradled my poor hands in each other. Alex looked like he was ready to storm up to the house and start a fight with Vince. "Alex," I called to him as he began stomping toward the house. "Stop, please let me explain." I stopped at the shower and turned it on to rinse the salt water out of the cracks in my hands.

"Why? Doesn't he care that you're suffering?" He turned to face me and put his fisted hands on his hips.

"It's only pain. It will be worth it in the end."

"How can you say that? What can be worth this kind of pain?"

"Being able to live my life without worrying that someone is trying to kill me and my parents." He deserved an answer. It was not the whole truth, but it was as much as I could tell him.

"Come with me. I'll protect you; you won't have to worry about all this training. I will treat you like a queen." He took my hands in his and turned them around in the water.

He was serious, by the look in his eyes. "I wish it was that easy. I won't be safe until I kill the one who's after me. I don't want you involved Alex. It would kill me if anything happened to you because of my problems."

"Tell me who it is and I'll do it for you."

"I can't let you do that. No one else can take care of her but me, but thanks for offering. You're a good friend Alex. I better go change." I kissed him on the cheek and ran up the stairs before he could say anything else.

Alex did not have much to say to me after that, but he was there every day to help me run and swim faster. He brought some plastic bags and rubber bands to wrap around my wrists so the seawater would not get into my cuts.

I was determined to follow the training regime Sensei laid out for me. I might be mad at him, but I needed to be stronger and faster. At night we would spar, it was getting easier. He got out a large fifty-pound punching bag and hung it in the middle of the dojo. With my sparring gloves on, I would spend at least an hour practicing my combinations on it. I was not sure what was worse, punching the two-by-four or the punching bag. They both hurt, they both made me bleed.

After my karate workout, Vince would massage me and bandage my hands. He was careful, and I felt his compassion as he took care of me. *This will make you tougher*, he thought to me before I blocked him out.

Every morning when I met with Alex he would look at my hands and wince. He never brought up the conversation we had on the beach again. I was glad, he was a nice guy, but I did not want him to get involved. He still did not understand why I needed to be able to take care of myself when I had all these people protecting me. I did not think Alex would ever get it.

I told him repeatedly, I just wanted to be able to take care of myself. I believed it, if I did not think I needed this training then I would have quit.

Two nights before the fight, I went up to the dojo for our normal karate class. It had been a good day. I had beaten my time in running and swimming. Thankfully, my hands were beginning to heal. I entered the dojo and bowed to Sensei who was kneeling in the center of the room. I knelt and found my center.

"Tonight, you are going to spar with Alex." He got up and went to the door of the massage room. He opened the door and Alex came out dressed in a gi. "You have ten minutes to warm up before we begin," Sensei said, leaving the room.

"This will be fun," I mumbled to myself as I began to warm up.

"It will be," Alex said, doing his own version of warming up.

Sensei came back into the dojo a few minutes later carrying two sparring helmets, and new gloves. I was happy to see the gloves since I split mine the night before on the punching bag.

"Put these on." He put both pairs on the floor between Alex and me. "Then we will begin."

I took the helmet and the gloves, put them on and began to roll my shoulders around. Alex did the same.

"Are you both ready?" Sensei asked.

"Yes," we both said stepping up to the lines in the floor.

"We are going full strength on this one, Katie; your goal is to have him tap out. There will be no hitting below the belt, if you do you will get an hour with the board tomorrow," Sensei said to both of us.

"Yes, Sensei." I bowed to him.

"I agree," Alex said.

"Hajime." Sensei moved back to watch the fight.

I jumped into my fighting stance and brought my arms up. I knew why Sensei had Alex spar with me. I would not be able to read his moves from his mind, I would have to look for his tells and anticipate him.

We bounced around the room feigning in and out, getting an idea of what our range would be. I had a feeling Alex would not want to make the first move on a woman. With a thought, I faked a low kick, he blocked it easily and taking advantage of his arm being low, I punched him hard in the face. He moved back quickly, wiping blood from his nose.

Part of me wanted to apologize, he was my friend, but this was sparring, and it was going to make me better. He came after me then, with punches and kicks. I could not block them all and took a few hard hits to the body while I protected my face.

I moved backward to gain some space between us, but he would not let up. Finally, I planted my foot, and while he hit me hard in the chest, I brought my other leg around in a roundhouse kick hitting him in the kidneys. The blow knocked him onto his butt and Sensei called time.

I offered Alex a hand up and he took it smiling. "You're getting pretty good," he said as I pulled him up. "I didn't hurt you did I?"

"I'll have a few bruises, but nothing's broken." I walked back over to my line. "How is your nose? Sorry I made you bleed."

"Not broken, I hit it pretty hard a month ago. It barely takes anything to make it bleed." He touched it gingerly.

"That was good," Sensei said. "You used the element of surprise to catch him off guard; you need to be faster coming up with a plan when you are on the defensive though. Every blow you take is going to slow you down. You need the fight to be quick and decisive."

"Yes, Sensei." I understood I did not mess up, he was coaching me.

"Let's go again, only with minimal contact this time." Sensei looked at Alex's swelling nose. "You need to be ready to fight in two nights; I do not want you injured."

I found sparring with Alex very different than sparring with Sensei. Since he was human, I felt like I might have a chance against him if it was a real fight. I was out of Sensei's league when it came to fighting; I would never be as good as him.

Sensei would not shut up during my massage. "You did very well tonight. Alex has been through a lot of combat training and you surprised him. Toward the end, he was having a hard time keeping up.

"Tomorrow you will only run and swim half of what you normally do. I want you to do some relaxing and meditation. You need to visualize fighting Ben; think about how you are going to defeat him. I want you to see yourself winning.

"We will have a light workout here tomorrow night, the next day you will do even less." I tuned him out but he kept talking until I was asleep.

"Katie." A hand was shaking my shoulder. "Katie, wake up I need to check your side before you go to bed."

I opened my eyes remembering I was still in the massage room. "Why?" I sat up and pulled the sheet with me to cover myself.

"Alex kicked you pretty hard in the ribs. I want to make sure they are not broken or cracked.

"Okay." I got up and felt a slight stitch in my side.

"You are going to have to move the sheet," he said gently.

I dropped the sheet. I was naked, but I was so tired I did not care anymore. It was not like he had not seen me naked before.

I heard him draw in a breath. "Hold your arm over your head." He bent down to look at my side. He might have gotten an up close and personal look at my boob as well, but I was beyond caring. I held my arm up so he could smooth and press his fingers into my side. "Does it hurt when I do this?"

210

"It's a little tender but no sharp pains." He moved back and straightened.

"I think you are just bruised." He was trying to look at me in the face, but his eyes kept moving down to my breasts.

"Great, thanks." I moved around him to grab the robe hanging on the wall and shrugged it on. I was too tired to have a bath even if it sounded amazing. "Good night." I moved around him again walked to the door.

"Katie." He remained facing the opposite wall.

"Yes, Sensei?" I paused with my hand on the doorknob.

"I am sorry I did not tell you my plan."

"You are now." I crossed my arms over my chest and shivered even though it was warm in the room.

"My plan was to push you hard, get you into the best shape possible and ask you if I could change you. Then we could take care of Lolita before she gained any more allies."

"Why didn't you tell me this from the beginning? I wanted to tell you how I understood the prophecy. If we would've talked, we wouldn't be where we are at now." I moved to look at his back.

"Where are we now?" He turned to look at me.

"I feel like the man who saved me is a liar who's afraid of telling the truth. While you did not lie straight out you lied by omission. If I never had the chance to tell you about the prophecy and you changed me all would be lost. Do you think I want you to suffer in Tartarus?"

"Maybe it is what I deserve." He looked and felt deflated, I had blocked him out for so long I had no idea how he had been feeling.

"No, you don't. You're a good man and you thought you were doing what the Goddess asked of you. I'm still here because you care."

"Does that mean you have forgiven me?"

"I'm not sure yet, but I hate how we have been acting around each other. I don't know why you don't want to include me on your plans. I want to know what you're thinking."

"I don't have a plan right now except to complete your training. Maybe we can come up with something together."

"We can talk about it, but not now. I need sleep."

"Very well. Are we okay?"

"I don't know, but I think we'll get there." I went to the door and down to my room.

# CHAPTER 25

Vince was lying in bed thinking about Katie. He hoped their conversation had helped bridge the gap between them. If she had not been in training, he would have made it up to her already, but he felt like he had to hold himself back to ensure her training would not suffer. She had no idea how good at combat she was. She only had him and now Alex to spar with and they were both experts. She had no idea she matched her speed to her partners. When he sparred with her, she moved at his pace. He was a little worried about how Alex would fair when she could move so quickly. He was surprised when she slowed herself down and moved at Alex's pace. She still lacked the confidence she needed, but giving Alex a bloody nose helped. She did not think she was good enough, but she was practicing at a level that people took decades to achieve. If only he could find a way to get it through her head. Maybe after she fought Ben she would understand. He smiled; he could not wait for her to beat him to pulp.

He jerked when she entered his mind. What the hell? He thought to himself. He asked her not to enter his mind without permission and here she was doing it. What did she hope to gain by listening in? He heard her mumbling and realized she was sleeping. It was a bad dream; someone was chasing her. He got up and went to her bedroom door, put his hand on the knob, but stopped himself from going in. He wanted to go to her and wake her from the nightmare, but remembering what Miguel did while she was sleeping; he took his hand off the doorknob. It would be better to wake her up from outside her room. She was hyperventilating, she needed to calm down, and he did not think he would be able to wake her until she was calm.

*Breath with me,* he thought to her.

# CHAPTER 26

I did not sleep well that night, it was the first night since we arrived on Crete that I tossed and turned. My dreams were scattered. At first, Vince and I were doing a kata in sync only instead of doing the same motions I was doing the kata and he was the attacker who choreographed the moves. When it was done, he grabbed me and kissed me long and hard. I kissed him back, we grabbed and fumbled with each other's gis trying to get them off. I went into his mind and his fangs were coming out, he wanted to bite me. I pulled away and ran through the door.

Then I was in the ocean treading water. Alex was a hundred yards in front of me calling for me to help him. I swam toward him, but never got any closer. I stopped, realizing it was a dream and tried to make myself wake up but the dream shifted again.

This time I watched Lolita drinking a man dry, he looked familiar. I snuck closer not wanting her to see me. I wanted to get a better look at him. His face was slack except for a grimace on his lips. He looked familiar, but I could not figure out who he was.

His eyes sprung open startling me. "She's coming for you." It was Antonio, the nice man who helped me in San Sebastian, the one I told to leave and never go back. His eyes closed and his head lolled back.

Lolita pulled her head up from her meal and locked eyes with me. "You will never be my queen," she hissed, showing me her bloodstained teeth.

I turned and ran, she chased after me. I wanted to turn and fight, but I was not ready to face her. I had too much to learn before we met again. Then I understood, I had to be the one to bring her down. Vince would not be able to take her.

Then I was back in the dojo. Sensei was kneeling on the floor. *Come and breathe with me.*

I walked over and knelt so close our knees all but touched. I was breathing hard; I could not seem to catch my breath. *Close your eyes, listen to my breathing.*

I closed my eyes but my breathing was too loud, I could not hear his. "I can't hear you." Panic filled me thinking, I would never be able to catch my breath.

He took my hand and placed it on his chest. *Feel it then.* He pulled in a lung full of air held it, then released it slowly. I forced my chest to expand, then contract as his did. It took a long time, but finally my breathing went back to normal. *Thank you, Sensei.* I reached into his mind.

Then I felt it, the most incredibly pure emotion I had ever felt. There was pride, adoration, excitement, anticipation, protectiveness, and contentment. I had never felt anything so warm and strong and bright before. It was love in its purest form. Tears trickle down my face jealous of the feeling. *What is wrong?*

*Your love is so pure; I've never felt anything like it before. Somehow, I don't think I ever will. It makes me sad.* I did not know how else to describe the envious feeling I had and feared I never would.

*You will, it was written in the stars. You too will feel this one day.*

I opened my eyes to find myself alone in the dojo. Someone was pounding on the door and I turned to face it. Fearing it was Lolita I jumped up and ran to the wall of weapons. I took a katana off the wall, I did not know how to use it properly, but I had to try to kill her.

"Katie, let me in," the voice said, it was muffled but male. It was not Lolita. Was it Miguel? I was not sure. "Katie, wake up!"

I jolted awake to someone was pounding on my door of my bedroom. Had I locked it? I got up, put on a robe, and I checked the knob, it was not locked, but the pounding continued.

"Who's there?" I asked, rubbing my eyes, they were still wet with tears.

"Vince, please open up."

I turned the knob and pulled the door open. "It wasn't locked."

"Are you ok?" He came into my room, forcing me back.

"I had a bad dream." I moved back to the bed and sat down. "Why didn't you come in and wake me up?"

"This is your room; I did not want to come in without your permission." He looked around like a bad guy was hiding somewhere nearby. "You have had bad experiences with people who let themselves into your room."

A flashback of waking up next to Miguel popped into my mind. "Thank you for your caution." I pulled my knees up to my chin.

"You entered my mind while you were dreaming." He paced back and forth in the small room.

"Oh, I'm sorry. Was I talking to you?" Who did he love so purely? Did he see anything from my side? This was embarrassing.

"Yes, but most of it was garbled. I thought you were doing it on purpose at first, but then I figured out you were dreaming. Do you

217

want to talk about it? You look upset."

I thought it about for a moment. "I guess I should since they have a habit of coming true."

"When you are ready." Vince went to my chair and turned it around to face the bed.

"It jumped around a lot, so I'll tell you the important parts." He did not need to know about the make out scene. "I was swimming, and Alex was drowning pleading for help but I could not get to him.

"Then it jumped and Lolita was drinking from Antonio. I told him to leave San Sebastian and to stay away from vampires at the airport. I hope it was just a dream. He said she was coming for me." A chill took me and I wrapped my arms around myself. "Anyway Lolita said I would never be her queen and chased me. I wanted to fight her, but I did not think I was ready yet.

"Then I was in the dojo and you were helping me catch my breath. When I finally caught it, I opened my eyes and I was alone. Someone started pounding on the door and I thought it was Lolita or Miguel, but it was you."

"Was it like the dream you had about San Sabastian burning or was it like an ordinary nightmare?" Vince leaned forward and rested his elbows on his knees.

"I'm not sure. I think it was just a nightmare. It didn't feel as real as San Sabastian burning."

"Well, we will have to wait and see." Vince stood up.

I rubbed my temples, I really wanted to go back to sleep, but I was not sure if I wanted to face the nightmares again. "What time is it?"

"Almost five." He looked at his watch and walked toward the door. "You should go back to sleep for a while."

218

"Yeah, I think I'll try." I got up to take my robe off. "Vince?"

"Yes?" he asked turning back from the door to face me.

I wanted to ask him to stay and make sure I did not dream anymore, but I could not. "If it happens again will you come in and wake me up?"

"With your permission I will." He almost smiled, then turned back to the door.

"Thanks."

"Good night," he said quietly, shutting the door behind him.

"Night," I murmured, taking my robe off and getting back under the covers. I stared at the ceiling for what felt like hours before I fell asleep. I kept wondering which part of the dream I was getting from Vince. The part about Lolita was not coming from him but the rest of it? Who was he in love with?

I might have fantasized that he loved me like that and I loved him too. It might have been why I was able to fall back to sleep.

# CHAPTER 27

It was nice in some ways to have a short day, but the short run and short swim left me feeling restless. I was normally so tired at the end of the day I could not think. Now with some down time I was not sure what to do with myself. Vince was up at Theron's again and Alex said he had things to do.

I took a long shower after my swim; I had not really practiced any kind of a beauty regiment for weeks. I shaved my legs, my bikini line, and my pits. I deep conditioned my hair. It was starting to get long and gangly. Maybe after the fight I could ask Vince if I could go into town and get it cut. I was not planning to leave it short but it needed to be trimmed and shaped.

After I was done with my do-it-yourself spa day, I decided to top it off with some tanning. I put on the tiny bikini I bought in Athens and put a pair of shorts on over it.

I picked up the book I had started a few weeks ago but had been too tired to read. I went out to the pool and sat in a lounge chair. I started on my back and undid the straps of my bikini top. I tried to get back into the book, but I kept thinking about everything that had happened to me in the past month.

I had changed, I been a girl traveling through Europe when this started. I wanted to do one big thing with my life before settling down with a typical life: house in the suburbs, kids, husband, career, even a minivan. I was not a naive little girl anymore. The girl who believed nothing bad could happen to her.

Now, I was a woman training for the fight of her life, and if I won, I would be the queen of an entire race. I was harder, I was much less trusting, and I was not going to let anyone be in charge of me.

I thought about Vince, was he in charge of me? He told me what to do and when to do it, but he was not forcing me. I wanted to do what he asked. I could walk away if I wanted and Vince would let me. I let him tell me what to do because he was molding me into the person I wanted and needed to become if I was going to rule the vampires. The real question was; did I want to become a vampire? Part of me looked at their speed, beauty, and grace, and thought, why would not I want to become one of them. The other part of me thought about everything I would miss if I became one.

I flipped over taking the top of my bikini off but leaving it close by. I would miss the sun, lying out and letting the rays turn my skin bronze. I was not sure if I would miss not having children, and being an only child I would not even get to experience being an aunt. I did not know why I was worrying about it. No one would want to change me after hearing what the prophecy said about the one who did. It still worried me though, how was I going to rule them if I was not one of them.

I rolled over again thinking about what I learned from Vince. I could enter his mind and see what he was going to do next. Some of the things I picked up on in my dream were his real feelings I had no doubt. I wondered how far away he had to be for me not to pick up his thoughts. I was worried about worming my way into Ben's head. I would not be able to beat him without the mind trick.

I closed my eyes and reached out with my mind. I tried to find those little blips I picked up from Vince. I found a few in the area. They were far away but I could sense them. Vince would probably be pissed, but I had to try, and as long as I did not think anything to them, they would never know. Vince said it was like a tickle, and he would not have paid it any mind if he did not know what I was doing.

I picked the closest blip. I found my way to the force field and poked it with my thoughts. *What,* I heard and it was all I needed to get into Theron's head. He was thinking about the fight; he wanted me to win, just to put Ben in his place, but he did not think I had a chance. A human woman against a male vampire, it was a long shot. He was worried about Vince. He had been coming up to the house everyday just to be alone. There was something bothering him and he would not talk about it. Theron even offered to cancel the fight thinking he was worried I would lose and get hurt, but Vince was adamant that the fight happen.

I jumped out of his head wondering what was going on with Vince. Was his need for solitude was because of the fight we had over the prophecy? He said he planned my training based on the idea that he would change me soon and we could kill Lolita. It could have something to do with what I picked from him in my dream, maybe he missed his lover and wanted me taken care of, then he could back to her. I did not see a way to find out; I could not just ask him.

I shook my head and realized what I just did. I jumped into Theron's mind and it was easy. All I had to do was poke Ben's force field and I would be in.

Too excited to sit still I went back into my room and changed into some comfortable shorts and a sports bra. I went out to the lawn on the east side of the house. It was flat and in the shade. I practiced the katas Sensei taught me, my combinations, and made up a few new ones. I kept myself loosen just going through the motions. It felt good.

When Sensei entered the dojo that night, I could feel the pride beaming off him. He knelt across from me as he normally did and matched his breathing to mine. After a few moments, he thought *open your eyes I would like to talk.*

I did as I was told, and locked my eyes with his. "Yes, Sensei."

"Theron told me something odd happened to him today. He was thinking about the fight when he got a small headache. You understand the only way vampires get a headache is if they are hit in the head, most likely multiple times with something like a hammer." There was a glint in his eye. "Did you have something to do with it?"

"Yes, Sensei." I broke eye contact and stared at a knot in the wood floor. "I just wanted to see how far away I could do it. He was the closest."

"I am proud of you." He gave me a genuine smile when I looked up at his words. "I was not sure if you were practicing anything outside of your normal schedule. What did you find out?"

"He's looking forward to the fight and he wants me to win, but he doesn't think I have a chance." I agreed with him.

The smile on Sensei's face vanished. "Well, we are going to prove them all wrong." He got up and stepped back a few feet. "Let's warm up then we will do some light sparring."

Later as I lay on the massage table Sensei brought up the dream again. "You told me about your dream, and I thought about it. Antonio heard where we were going in the car." Vince stopped working on my back. "This is bad."

"I forgot to tell you. I'm sorry. After you dropped me off, he tried to take me to Miguel. He wasn't your slave after all. Miguel took him back."

"How did you escape?" Vince moved to my head and pulled a chair up so we could talk face to face.

"I think he had been given enough vampire blood to allow me to compel him. I made him take me back to the airport, made him forget our traveling names, that we were together, and where we were going. Then I compelled him to leave town and stay away from vampires."

"Do you think your compulsion worked?"

"He took me back to the airport instead of the villa."

"Is he the only human you have been able to compel?"

"He's the only one I have tried it on. It was an emergency. I wasn't going back to the villa."

"Could you tell from your dream if he had told her anything?"

"I don't think he did. He was still trying to help me. I think she was changing him."

"I wonder why she would change him. He is not her type."

"I think she's building an army. She believes there is going to be a war."

Vince got up and moved to my side to resume his work on my back. "I hope she is wrong. I have seen enough war in my life."

# CHAPTER 28

I did not dream that night. When I woke up, I felt relaxed and calm. My body did not hurt for the first time in weeks. After the fight, I would be right back at it, but I would take whatever breaks I could get. Remembering the fight had me tense in seconds. I was going to fight my first vampire, he was a jerk, but still he was a vampire.

Sensei drilled into my head that I had to believe I could win, visualize I was going to win. I tried, but somehow, I could not see how I would win.

Vince was in the kitchen when I came out of my bedroom, he had just finished making me a huge breakfast. I sat down to eat saying, "Thank you Sensei."

"Do not feel like you have to eat all of it," he said, washing the dishes. "You need to have lots of energy for tonight, but I do not want you too stuffed to move."

"Yes, Sensei." We kept a companionable silence while I ate and he cleaned. When he was done, he sat down at the table and waited for me to finish eating.

"How did you sleep?"

"Good, no dreams last night." I got up, taking my dish to the sink.

"Good, I want you well rested. If you feel like you can, take a nap this afternoon."

"Yes, Sensei." I placed the dish in the drying rack.

"The fight is going to be on the beach at eleven tonight." He looked out the window. "It is a little later than when we normally practice."

"Okay," I went back to the table and sat back down. There was something on his mind; he was trying to work himself up to saying it. "Just spit it out."

"This is going to be a hard fight." He rubbed his thumb and pointer finger in between his eyebrows. "You will win, but I feel like you are having a hard time believing you will. What can I do to convince you that you will win?"

"I don't know," I said, rubbing my temples. "I have only been training for two weeks. I feel like I have so much more to learn, and I'll never learn enough to beat Lolita on my own, but I have to."

He sat in silence looking at me as if I had lost my mind. "Why would you say that? You are not fighting Lolita; you are fighting Ben. An upstart little shit who thinks he can treat everyone on this island any way he wants. He is a guppy compared to Lolita."

"Because this is the first step to get to her, and I'm not ready to face her, which means I feel like I'm not ready to face anyone." I put my head in my hands.

He blew out a long breath. "You are right, it is the first step in getting to her, and as your Sensei believe me when I say, you are ready to fight Ben. If you were not ready I would not let you fight." He paused looking stressed. "You cannot let her get to you. You are not fighting her tonight. You fought well against Alex, and bested him in some areas without your mental gift. What else can I do to prove it to you?"

"I don't know." I grabbed my too long choppy hair and pulled it. "I won't know what I can do it until it's done."

"Then you will do it and afterward we will celebrate." He looked like he had something else on his mind though. "What did you get from me in you dream the other night?"

"Do you really want to know?" I looked around, trying to think of a way to put it without naming the emotion.

"Yes, more than anything." He folded his hands, giving me all of his attention.

"It was the purest, most honest, and unselfish feeling I have ever experienced. You were helping me breathe because I had been running from Lolita, and I was having trouble calming down." I paused, looking down at my hands. "I don't think you were feeling it for me since I was sleeping, and you were who knows where, but it was a feeling that I'm envious of."

He smiled the biggest smile I had ever seen from him, it almost looked like it hurt. "Good, I think you will get to enjoy the feeling someday too." He stood to leave. "I am going to Theron's to make sure everything is ready for tonight. I think Alex will be coming over soon. You should take him to the pool and relax with him for a change.

"You want me to hang out with him outside of training?" I asked as he moved down the hall toward the tunnel.

"Yes, have fun, but please take a nap," he said before he disappeared around the corner.

I wanted to cry. From what he said, he was not in love with me. Why should I care? He was my protector and sensei nothing more, right?

Alex knocked on the door, and I forced myself to put a happy face on. "Hey there, cowboy." I tried to sound up beat. "Vince told me you were coming over to hang out. What do you want to do?"

"Pool, I'm tired of smelling like the ocean. I'd rather smell like chlorine." He sat down in the chair Vince had vacated. "Hurry up and go change. Don't forget, we're in Europe, tops aren't allowed."

"Please, you would pass out if you saw me without my top." I got up and walked to my bedroom. "I'll be back in a few."

"Are you ready?" I asked when I came back into the kitchen ten minutes later with a towel over my shoulder and my pool bag in my hand.

"I've been waiting for hours it feels like." Alex stood up from the chair he was lounging in. "Let's go."

I followed him to the pool where I set up my chair. He took the one next to me throwing his towel on it then diving into the pool and splashing me in the process.

I shrieked when the cold water hit me, and pulled my bag containing my phone, and my MP3 player into me to try to block the water from hitting it. "Ass. You better not have gotten my stuff wet." I opened the bag and set it on the lounger. Then I bent over, pulled my phone and music player out making sure they were dry.

"Did they get wet?" Alex asked from the edge of the pool.

"No, you would've had hell to pay if they were." I stood up turning to give him an evil eye.

"It still would've been worth it." He pushed back from the wall and glided through the water to the other side.

"Why do you say that?" I moved my bag to the front of the chair so nothing would get wet if he splashed me again.

"The view while you were going through your bag would've been worth just about anything."

I had no idea what he was talking about so I ignored him. I took my cover-up off and began rubbing sunscreen onto my arms, legs, and mid-section. "Can you please come and put some sunscreen on my back?"

"I would love to." He swam back over to my side of the pool and pulled himself out in one motion. All the running and swimming was helping him out. He was looking more toned and solid. He still was not handsome; his face had not grown into his body yet.

"Thanks," I said, handing him the lotion and turning my back on him.

"Believe me it's my pleasure." He squirted the cold liquid on my back and I shivered before he started rubbing it in.

He was enjoying this too much, I thought, and his comment about the view clicked in my mind. He was watching my ass when I bent over. "You need to get laid, Alex."

"Are you offering? A lot of athletes like to get it on before the big game. They claim it helps them relax."

"No, I'm not offering, dick." I took a step away from him and turned around I did not care if he was done or not. "Thanks." I took the bottle out of his hand and put it back in my bag being careful not to bend over where he would get an eyeful.

"Do you always put sunscreen on before you go swimming?"

"Yes, a sunburnt back sucks."

"Who puts it on for you?"

"Vince, why?"

"Just wondered why you never asked me before."

"We always meet at the beach; I hate bringing stuff down there so I have him do it before I come down."

Alex made a non-committal noise then jumped back into the

pool. I jumped in after him and we enjoyed swimming around for a while then ended up lying in the floating chairs.

When I was completely pruney, I got out of the pool and settled onto the lounge chair with my book. Alex stayed in the pool humming to himself. After reading for a while, I nodded off to sleep.

A shake to my shoulder had me jumping awake. "What time is it?"

"Time to eat." Alex waved a hand toward the patio table now covered with food. "Vince made it. He wants to make sure you have plenty of energy for tonight."

After we ate Alex went home to get ready for the evening, and I went inside to meditate. The dojo was always different in the middle of the day, but it did not matter, the room was becoming a place of peace for me. I knelt and thought about everything I learned in such a small amount of time. It felt like I had been training for two months instead of two weeks. I could protect myself against humans if not vampires now. I wondered if I would ever be as fast as a vampire while I was still human. My abilities seemed to be coming quicker and quicker, I wished speed would show up before tonight. It was my biggest fear; that I would be too slow to fight a vampire.

I spent the rest of the day a nervous wreck. I forced myself to eat a light dinner and drank lots of water. Vince came in right at sundown and told me to get dressed and meet him in the dojo.

I went into my room and found my gi, but not my belt. I put on what I had and began searching my room. I looked under the furniture thinking maybe it fell off the bed and was shoved under the bed or dresser, but it was not there. I checked the closet, the floor, the hangers, and the shelf on top, I could not see up there but could feel. I was starting to panic. This was not how I wanted to start my night. I checked the bathroom, I had no idea why my belt would be in there, but I was at my wits end. What would Sensei do if I lost my belt?

With nowhere else to look, I dragged my feet up the stairs to the dojo. When I got to the door, I bowed then entered to find Sensei kneeling with a belt on the floor in front of him. I wordlessly knelt in front of him and matched my breathing to his.

"What took you so long?

"Sensei, I couldn't find my belt. I looked everywhere. I'm sorry, I think I lost it."

He looked down at the belt between us. "You did not lose it. I did not give it back."

I let out a sigh of relief I had not lost it. I wanted to yell at him for adding to my stress; he could have clued me in before I tore my room apart looking for it. Remembering I was in the dojo, I kept my mouth shut.

"You have only been training for a few weeks," he said, looking from me to the belt between us. "In that time you have proven to be a dedicated and a natural fighter.

"Normally it takes years for someone to earn a black belt. You have shown you are worthy of the belt, but you have much more training to do before you have earned it. However, you will wear it tonight as a sign of what you will become." He picked up the belt with both hands and held it out to me.

"Thank you, Sensei." I bowed taking the belt with both hands. "I hope one day I will earn the right to wear this."

"I know you will, but we need to talk about tonight," he said, getting up and walking around the room. "Each round will last three minutes; it will be full contact. There will be no hits below the belt, to the back of the head or neck, and no biting."

"Yes, Sensei." Adrenaline spiked through me, this fight was really going to happen.

"Ben, is arrogant and selfish." He picked up a bag and brought it over to me. "He thinks this will be an easy fight. He has done nothing to prepare for it. He will try to finish you in the first round. You must be prepared to get into his head as quickly as possible." He knelt down close enough that our knees almost touched. "Give me your hand." He took a roll of gauze out of the bag. I gave him my hand and he started to wrap the gauze around it.

"Do you have any questions?" he asked as he wrapped athletic tape around the gauze covering my hand.

"No." Butterflies erupted in my belly as I watched him wrap my hand.

"Breathe with me." He moved to wrap my other hand.

I closed my eyes and matched my breathing to his. *You can do this; I know you are nervous. Find your center when you enter the ring. Relax, think of nothing but breathing in and out.*

It took me a while to let go of the anxiety I was carrying around about the fight. I breathed with him, forgetting he was wrapping my hands to protect them and let my fears go.

*It is time to start warming up.* He got up and opened the sliding windows.

I opened my eyes, got up rolling my shoulders, and shook out my legs. They were used to kneeling on the wood floor, but they still liked a good shake when I stood up. I bent over and picked up my belt. I was still in awe that he had given me a black belt. I did not feel like I deserved it. I think he gave it to me to help build up my confidence. I wrapped it around myself and tied it in a knot. The only thing different with this belt compared to my old white one was the color, but when I looked in the mirror I noticed how nicely the two-inch thick belt broke up the stark whiteness of the gi. I looked good, like a badass. It kind of made me feel like one too, maybe his plan worked.

I began to jog around the room to wake up my muscles. To my surprise, Sensei joined me. We jogged for ten minutes then started stretching, and with Sensei's help, I kept my breathing in line with his and stayed calm. The butterflies were there but they were not overpowering, they might have been from excitement.

"It is time to go."

I stood and bowed deeply to him. "Thank you for training me Sensei. I will bring you pride."

"I have no doubt you will." He moved to the stairs and led the way to the beach.

# CHAPTER 29

There were roughly thirty people standing around the makeshift ring. Most of them were vampires with a few humans scattered among them. Alex was standing by my corner with a stool and a cooler.

I tensed as we moved closer to the crowd and the ring. The butterflies in my stomach took over, and I felt like I was going to throw up from the nerves.

*Breathe with me*, Sensei thought matching my stride. *I want to see the bad-ass woman who walked into the bar in San Sebastian. The one no one wanted to fuck with.*

I found his breath and matched it. The badass wannabe from San Sebastian was so long ago. She was a fake, but I was not a fake any more. I was unproven, but I was a badass. Start acting like it, I thought to myself, pulling my shoulders back, holding my head high and lengthening my stride.

The crowed parted as we moved through them. Some were cheering, more were murmuring quietly. Most of them had never seen me before. They had only heard of me, and I had no idea what was being said about me.

Ben was already in the makeshift ring, which was composed of a rough rope tied around stakes to form a square. He smiled an 'I am going to fuck you up' smile at me. I returned it and went for his beacon. I got his feelings first; they were bored, arrogant, holier-than-thou, and punchy.

"Go and kick this guy's ass." Alex put my gloves on over my wrapped hands. "I know you can do it."

I smiled at him, "Thanks." I turned to Sensei who was staring daggers at Ben. I bowed to get his attention.

"You will be successful in this endeavor," he said, returning the bow.

I stepped under the rope and the butterflies ceased. I found my breath and zeroed in on my target. Helen stepped into the center of the ring and held her hands up.

"Ladies and gentlemen welcome to our very first fight night," she said and the small crowd yelled and applauded. There must not be much to do at night here, I thought before she continued.

"Tonight we have Ben versus Katie. This will be a full contact match with standard rules. Each round will last three minutes with a minute rest in-between." Ben and I moved to either side of her as she spoke. "Do you agree with the rules?"

"Yes," we said together.

"Very well. Bow and go to your corners." She moved to the perimeter of the ring.

I bowed, Ben did not. *You stupid bitch, I won't bow to you,* he thought and I had my way in. I smirked and backed up to my corner. I caught Sensei with my eye and gave him a nod to let him know I was in Ben's mind. He nodded back. *Well done. I have been meaning to tell you something, you are just as fast as he is.*

My mouth dropped open and I thought my eyes might bug out of my head. How could I be as fast as Ben? I did not have time to ponder the answer as the bell rang and I took my fighting stance moving to the middle of the ring.

Ben ran toward me, he wanted to end this quickly, but he had too much time to think as he came across the sand. His thoughts told me what he was going to with enough time to block the punch to my face with my left hand and punch him hard in the gut. He stumbled a step, bent over, and grabbed his middle, looking surprised I had hit him. He quickly stood up and came after me with a battery of punches, leaving me no choice, but to block for what felt like an endless amount of time.

*He will not stop what he is doing unless you stop him,* Sensei thought to me.

Thinking fast I came up with a plan, it would hurt but I had to do it. I dropped my arm, allowing him to hit me in the solar plexus. I attacked with a roundhouse kick to his face. It threw him off balance and he landed on his ass with blood flying out of his mouth. I heard the crowd distantly yelling something but I could not make out what it was.

My side was killing me from his punch but now was my time to end of it. Before he could get up, I moved quickly, straddled him and punched his face over and over again. He blocked his face with his arms but I was still doing damage. Blood splattered the ground around me hitting the white sand and staining it crimson. I felt no sympathy as I continued to hammer him with punches.

I heard a bell in the back of my mind thinking I was hearing things; there was no way three minutes were already up. I felt someone pull me off Ben and I turned to see Helen.

"Go to your corner, didn't you hear the bell ring?"

"Sorry, I thought I was hearing things." I went back to my corner where Alex set the stool. I sat down and he shoved a water bottle in my face. I took it, rinsed out my mouth then drank some it.

239

"You are doing great out there," Alex said before Sensei gestured for him to be silent.

"You are doing well," he said in a low voice. "A few more kicks to the face and you will have him beat. Hitting his body will do more damage to you than him. If you can get him back on the ground, straddle him and hammer his face. To win you need to disable him so he will not be able to continue."

"Yes, Sensei." I got up looking over at Ben's corner. He was leaning against the ropes with his head hanging down as if he was trying to catch his breath. There was a skinny girl in a bikini hovering over him who looked like she had no idea how to help him.

The bell rang and he shoved her out of the way and moved fast to get to me. *You are going to die bitch*, was all he had running through his mind. When he was almost on me, I turned to the side and tripped him.

He went down. I jumped on him and started punching him in the face. He squirmed, rolled, and before I knew what was going on, I was underneath him.

With no grappling skills, all I could do was protect my face while he started hammering away at it. I was still able to see where he was going with his attack the problem was I could not think of a way to get out of it. The pain in my arms was becoming a distraction. I wanted to put them down just to give them a break. I did the only thing I could think of; I head butted him. Pain exploded across my forehead. He reared back; I arched my back and bucked him off. I jumped to my feet swaying a bit as the world rocked back and forth as if I was on a boat. I shook my head and the world righted itself. Head butting hurt more than I thought it would.

Ben was shaking his head back and forth trying to clear his vision. *Knock him out or break his leg*, Sensei thought to me. How was I supposed to do either of those? I aimed a kick at his head, and he blocked it with his arm. Somehow, I caught the perfect angle though. There was a loud snapping sound as my leg connected with his arm, like a thick stick being broken in half. Ben screamed and fell to his knees. Halfway between his elbow and his wrist both bones in his arm were broken. The lower half of his arm and hand flopped around as he tried to catch himself, but unable to, he went down face first into the sand while screaming in agony.

The bell rang and the crowd exploded in excitement. I moved to where Ben was lying in the sand and offered him a hand. "It was a good fight."

"Get the fuck away from me you bitch." He pushed my hand away and spit in my face. "This isn't over."

Helen held my wrist it in the air before I could worry about the last comment from Ben, or the bloody spit running down my cheek. "The winner is Katie," she yelled, letting go of my arm.

I smiled to the crowd and wiped the spit off my face. I turned back to Ben and bowed not taking my eyes off him in the process. I turned and walked back to my corner where Sensei and Alex waited.

I heard Ben think, *I am going to kill you.* I turned in time to see him streak toward me with his fangs out. He wanted to win, one way other or another. Instinct took over, I knelt on one knee as he approached and lashed out with an uppercut catching him on the point of his chin. Pain radiated up my arm, but I was unable to take my eyes off Ben. He stood up straight for a second with a dazed look in his eyes before falling backward on to the sand. He was out cold.

Alex and Sensei ran over to me while I shook my hand to try to dissipate the pain, but it only made it hurt more. "Are you all right?"

I looked at them and smiled. "I'm fucking fantastic."
I quickly bowed to Sensei then hugged Alex.

"You fought well," Sensei said but he did not look pleased.

"Thank you, Sensei." I could not help smiling. I beat a vampire; I could not believe it. "Why didn't you tell me I was that fast?" I asked, but before Sensei could answer, Theron joined us.

"Great fight, Katie." Theron stopped in front of me. "I'm sorry Ben's a sore loser."

"But are you?" Vince asked, placing a hand on his shoulder smiling.

"No, in fact I have a party planned for everyone. If you will let your pupil out to play for a while." Theron gave Vince a look like he was no fun most of the time.

"It was a good fight." *Do you want to go to a party?* Vince thought to me.

I nodded my head, a party sounded fun.

"Yes, we will join you in a little while." Vince moved to my side. "I am sure Katie is going to want to shower and tend to her injuries before she comes up to the mansion."

"Yes, I really need a shower." The sweat made my gi stick to me with a layer of sand in between it and my skin. Every time I moved it felt like sandpaper was taking off a layer of skin.

"Then we'll see you both later." Theron looked to Alex. "Are you coming, Alex?"

"Yes, I'll head up with you." He looked at me. "I'll see you in a while. You did great."

"Thanks see you in a while."

Vince and I walked toward the house. "Are you going

to be my sensei tonight or Vince?" I asked as we walked beside each other.

He laughed. "Tonight I will be anyone you want. You did very well. You did not panic, you were cool and calculating." He rested his hand lightly on my lower back as if to guide me. "But my favorite part was after the fight, when that little fuck came after you and you floored him. No one should fuck with you for a while."

"That scared me more than the entire fight." I was enjoying his hand on my back. "He was going to kill me because; I humiliated him in front of his friends and family."

"I would not have let it happen." Vince stiffened for a moment. "I will protect you with my life."

"Isn't that why you are training me?" I laughed. "When I'm done you won't have to put your life on the line as often?"

He turned in front of me and stopped. "I am training you because if I do lose my life protecting you, I want you to be able to run away or win without me." He was dead serious.

"Vince, I don't know how to thank you for all of the help and training you've given me." I reached out to take his hand. "I pray you will never have to sacrifice your life for me. I would never want you to. I don't know what I would do without you.

"I know I've been pissy with you lately, but don't think for a moment I could do this without you. I need you more than you know." I did not know why I just spilled my guts to him but I needed him to know how much he meant to me.

"Katie," he said quietly, he wanted to say more but he dropped my hand. "Let's get you cleaned up so we can get to the party before it gets out of hand."

"Wait, why didn't you tell me how fast I am?" I was kind of mad he did not tell me until right before the fight. He knew how stressed I was over it.

"Because I wanted to give you a confidence boost right before the fight."

I thought about it for a minute. If I had known how fast I was yesterday, would I have still won the fight? Would I have gone into the fight over confident? I would never know. "I'll give you a pass on withholding information this once."

"Thank you," he said as he opened the kitchen door for me.

He pulled a stool out from under the bar and indicated for me to sit down. I boosted myself up and gave my hands to Vince. He carefully pulled the gloves off my hands then pulled out a pair of scissors to cut the tape off. "Your adrenaline will start to fade soon." He inspected one hand; the knuckles where my fingers met my hand were already turning purple. "The pain is going to kick in pretty fast. You cannot show any pain at the party. Take some pain killers before we leave, then hold a cold beer in your hand." He took my other hand to inspect it. "It looks like you might have cracked a knuckle." He lightly ran his finger over it and I hissed in pain.

"Do I need to go to a doctor?" The pain from such a light caress was debilitating.

"No, with how you quickly you heal, there is nothing to do but let it heal. Try not to punch anything for a while." Vince chuckled. "You are going to have to deal with the pain. Take off your top; I want to check your ribs and your side. You took some pretty hard hits to the midsection."

Doing as instructed I took off the black belt, and undid the strings holding the top closed. I took it off and hissed as the sleeve of the shirt touched my knuckle. "Damn, getting dressed is going to be fun with this." I pulled it the rest of the way off.

"Arms up please." Vince turned on the overhead light in the kitchen.

I put my arms over my head and felt the pull in my muscles. Wow, I was going to be sore. Vince looked, poked and prodded. When I did not scream in agony, he moved on to my forearms that had blocked so many punches. They were tender and would bruise, but there was no permanent damage. He took a pen light from his pocket and shined it in my eyes checking for a concussion since I head butted Ben. He finally said I was good to go and told me to hit the showers.

After a long hot shower, I took the painkillers and anti-inflammatories he suggested then put on some makeup. I did not have the right stuff to cover the bruises, but they were a badge of honor right? I went to my closet thinking I would wear one of the sundresses I bought. I had not worn real clothes in weeks. It was an odd feeling. I picked out a bright yellow strapless maxi dress and put on matching sandals.

When I came out of my bedroom, Vince had changed from his gi and was waiting for me. He had lightweight khaki pants on and a white linen shirt. His hair was slicked back in a low ponytail. He looked good.

"Shall we?" He offered me his arm.

"Sure I just want to grab an icepack for my hands while we are on our way up there." I moved toward the kitchen.

"I already have them in the golf cart."

"You're the best." I took his arm and let him lead me out the front door to the waiting golf cart. He helped me get the ice in the right spots before we took off toward the party.

"What should I tell people?" I did not want to invite trouble or another fight.

"As little as possible. They will likely be able to tell if you are lying, just like you can tell if they are lying, so be honest but vague."

"That won't be hard or anything." I chuckled to myself.

"How are you feeling?" He sounded concerned.

"I'm stiff, my hands hurt more than anything else probably because I move them more."

"We will see how they are in the morning before we move on to the next phase of training." He pulled up to the front of the mansion.

"Great." I groaned inwardly. I would have loved a few days off.

Before I got out of the golf cart, I took off the icepacks wishing I could bring them in with me. Vince held open the front door for me, and I thanked him as I passed through the door. We followed the sound of music and talking toward the main living area and terrace. We passed a few people on the way mostly in pairs talking, or locked in embraces moaning quietly. I did not want to think about why they were moaning.

When we entered party central all talk stopped and the applause began. Vince took a few steps away from me and I bowed to the applause. "Thank you." I looked around the room making eye contact with a few people.

"To the victor," Theron said, moving to me with a glass of champagne in both hands. He handed one to me and held up his in toast. "For a fight well fought."

Everyone held up their glasses saying "salut" and waited for me to take a sip. I brought the glass to my lips but something told me not to drink it. I brought it back down, wondering why I did not want it.

Theron was looking at me suspiciously. "You don't like champagne?"

"It doesn't sound good right now is all."

*What is going on?* Vince squeezed my arm.

*There is something up with this drink. I don't know what and I don't know why I know, but something's not right.* I thought to Vince jumping into his head for a moment. I did not think he would be upset given the situation.

"Theron, can we have a word in private?" Vince indicated a closed door on the wall to our left.

"By all means." Theron lead the way to the door then held it open as we passed through it.

It was a small room and it took me a second to realize we were in an elevator. "Where are we going?" I looked to Vince.

*To my office,* Theron answered. *It's sound proof. I would like to keep this conversation private.*

The door dinged and we exited into a long hallway. Keeping quiet, I followed them to a set of double doors at the end. Theron opened the door waiting for Vince and me to pass through before entering and closing it behind him.

"Please have a seat Katie." Theron went around the desk to his chair and sat down after I sat in one of the visitor's chairs. Vince did not sit down but moved to stand behind and to the side of me with his hands behind his back. "What's this about Vince?"

*Give me your glass,* Vince thought to me. I handed him my glass watching as he pulled it up to his nose and inhaled.

"What is it?" Theron drew his eyebrows together as Vince passed the glass to him.

"Tell me what this smells like."

Theron held the glass under his nose and inhaled.

"Was I right? Is there something wrong with it?" I asked, looking from Vince to Theron while they stared at each other.

"Yes, there is something wrong with the champagne." Vince crossed his arms over his chest. "Can you explain why there is vampire blood in this glass Theron?"

Vince moved in front of me as Theron hurled the glass at the wall and it exploded with liquid and glass flying all over the room. "I don't know, but I can guarantee I'll find out."

"There was vampire blood in the champagne?" I asked, beginning to shake. "Who would want to make me their slave?"

"That is why I wanted a quiet word with Theron. Who else knows who Katie really is?" Vince sat down in the chair looking upset.

"No one and it wasn't me. I know what the prophecy says about making her a slave. If I wanted Katie, I would woo her on my own; I would never do what Miguel did to her."

I listened intently to his feelings as he spoke. He was mad as hell that someone was trying to get to me, but it was not him. "He's telling the truth."

"Are you sure?" Vince turned to meet my eyes.

"Yes, I can feel how pissed and betrayed he feels."

"Where is Ben? Did he have a chance to tamper with it?" Vince uncrossed his arms and crossed one leg over the other.

"He's in the dungeon. After his arm heals he will be punished for going after Katie after the fight was over. It wasn't him." Theron leaned back in his chair and laced his hands behind his head looking at the ceiling. "Looks like you have another enemy we didn't know about."

I rested my elbows on my knees and put my hands over my eyes. Just what I needed, another enemy who wanted to make me their slave. "Vince, did you jilt any of Theron's vampires?"

"How is that relevant?"

"Because if you two are the only ones who know who I really am then there must be another reason why someone would try this."

He was quiet for a moment in thought. "I do not think so, but it has been many years since I have been here. What do you think Theron?"

"Katie makes a valid point. Last time you were here there were quite a few females who wanted you. I don't know if they got anywhere though. You were busy helping me the entire time if I recall."

"Yes, it was nasty business and required my full attention. Did you change any of the donors from back then?"

"I will have to look. Can you think of any other reason someone would go after you through Katie?"

"No, I try not to make enemies."

"If we stay up here much longer, people are going to start to wonder what happened to us. Let's go and enjoy your victory party and worry about this tomorrow." Theron got to his feet.

"In the meantime Katie, do not drink from anything you did not open or watch someone open." Vince got to his feet and waited for me to stand up.

"Maybe I should just go home and let you two enjoy the party." I was scared, hurt, and deflated. How had I managed to gain another enemy?

"Nonsense," Theron moved to the door. "You can't let them know you're scared. If you are to be queen, you must show them you are fearless."

I stood up slowly feeling every sore muscle. He was right, but a party did not sound like as much fun as it did before. I clinched my hands holding in a gasp of pain. "Then get me an ice-cold beer and let's pretend to have some fun."

We went down the hall and got back into the elevator. My bed was calling me, but Theron was right. If I was going to be queen, I was going to have to look tougher than I felt most of the time.

*You look beautiful by the way,* Vince thought as his hooded eyes met mine.

A small smile snuck across my lips and I gave him a nod in thanks. When the elevator dinged, I pulled my shoulders back and pasted a fake smile on my face before the doors opened. I exited first trying to show everyone I did not need a vampire to escort me, but I was relieved when I felt Vince close behind me. His presence was always reassuring. I saw the bar and walked in that direction. "What will you have?" the bartender, who was human, asked.

"Beer in the bottle please." He pulled one from the cooler, opened it and passed it to me. I wrapped my hand around it and stifled a groan, the cold glass felt incredible against my hand. "Thank you." I turned to Vince who was standing behind me.

"There are a lot of people who would like to meet you, if you are up for it." Vince offered me his arm.

"Lead the way." I took his offered arm gingerly. "I wish I could get away with double fisting beers tonight." The light grip I had on his arm made pain shoot up my arm.

"We will trade sides often so you can move your beer from one hand to the other." We approached a small group of people and I recognized Theron and Helen.

"There she is, the woman of the hour." Theron acted as if we had not just had a conversation about who was trying to enslave me. He held his glass up to me. "Katie, let me introduce you to George and John a few of my men."

"Nice to meet you." I let go of Vince, moved my beer to my left hand and extended it to shake everyone's hand carefully trying not to wince in pain.

"You fought well, I can't wait to show you some jujitsu," Helen said.

"Sounds like fun," I said, looking over to Vince expectantly.

"Yes, Helen and Theron are well versed in other martial arts, and I talked them into helping with your training."

"It will be nice to have different partners for a change." I flexed my hand hoping I would be given a few days to heal before the next hell began.

"We were all impressed with your fighting style," Theron commented. I could not help feeling he was going to try something. "You were very good at anticipating your opponent's next move. Did Vince teach you how?"

"Vince helped me hone the skill, but I would call it more of a natural talent." I narrowed my eyes and imagined punching him in the face. He knew I could read minds but apparently, Vince had not told him about my extended mind reading skills.

"It's quite the talent," George said. "I wish I was better at reading my opponent."

"You just have to watch people and learn their tells." I was making it up as I went but I was not in the mood for small talk. I chugged the rest of my beer and looked around for a waiter. One saw me look and hurried over. "Can you please get me another beer in the bottle but don't open it?"

The waiter nodded and left to do my bidding. *Are you going to get drunk?* Vince asked raising his eyebrows to me.

*I don't know, maybe. I think I deserve to blow off some steam tonight.* I replied turning back to George. "Sorry, I needed another beer. What were we talking about?"

"You're a good fighter and almost as fast as us. You say it's a natural talent, but are sure it's not because you belong to Vince?"

I do not know why I had not thought of it before but I must look like Vince's slave to all the vampires who watched the fight. If what Theron said was true, they had no way of knowing who I really was. I was not sure it was good thing. I looked over to Vince and shook my head. "It might." I did not have any other way to explain it without telling this guy who I was. The waiter returned with the beer bottle, and I took it from him. "Please excuse me I need to get some air," I said to George, twisting the beer cap off and finding my way to the terrace, looking for a place to be alone.

There were people all over the place. I headed for the stairs and went halfway down them. Once I was in the dark and out of earshot, I sat down on a step, bent my head to my knees and let the tears come.

They thought I was Vince's slave. How could they think anything else? They had no idea I was "The One" and I was not about to tell them. I had been property before and I did not want anyone to think of me like that ever again. What choice did I have though? If we told everyone who I was it would just invite more trouble, and the news could easily be leaked to Lolita. I was not ready to face her yet. I did not know if I ever would be.

I felt someone sit down on the step next to me. I ignored them and stayed in my little bubble until I felt something touch my arm. I looked up to find a handkerchief dangling from Alex's fingers. I took it and offered him a smile. "Thank you." I took it from him and used it to blot my eyes. Then I ran it under them to make sure I did not look like a drowned rat with mascara down my cheeks.

"No problem. You clean up pretty well for a fighter."

I looked down at my dress and let a small smile touch my lips. "Thanks, it's nice to have a reason to get dressed up."

"I know what you mean." He looked down at his button up shirt.

"You look very handsome." I touched his collar.

"Thanks." He looked away into the darkness. "Do you want to talk about it?"

"Just homesick and tired," I lied, joining him in staring at the dark night.

"I've never been homesick." He folded his hands together. "I hated being home. What's it like?"

"I'm sorry you didn't like your home." I had to pause and think about it. "It's missing your family and friends, but it is also missing the comfort of home. Knowing your dad is going to be yelled at by your mom because he didn't take out the trash. Sleeping in your own bed, and not having to remember where you are when you wake up in the morning."

"I'm sure it's hard." He put a hand on my back and rubbed it in circles. "You'll be okay, what do they say? Home is where you hang your hat."

"It's been a long few weeks and I'm tired." I sat up. "But I'll be fine."

"You were great tonight." He pulled his hand back. "I'm very impressed."

I turned and looked at him. "Thanks. I'm really glad we're

253

friends. I don't think I could've done it without you."

He winked at me. "I think you could've, but I like being your friend so I will take the compliment."

"I better get back up there." I stood up and turned around. "It's my party after all. Right?"

"It is, go have fun. I'll be back; I have to check on something."

"Okay, see you up there." I went back up to join the party.

Vince was waiting for me when I got there. "Are you alright?" he asked, turning to look at me.

"Everyone who saw the fight thinks I'm your slave."

"I did not think of it until it was too late. I am sorry would you rather tell everyone the truth?"

"Don't be a dick, Vince. I'm not mad at you, I just don't like the situation. I've been a slave before, and I hate that they think I'm yours. There's nothing we can do about it now except roll with it."

He hung his head. "I did not mean to sound like a dick. I wish I could fix it, but other than telling them the truth there is no other way to explain your speed."

"You're right. I never want to be someone else's property again and I hate that they think I am yours."

"Believe me, I know how you feel. After Livius changed me, I still felt like a slave. It was not until he retreated to Mount Vesuvius that I felt free for the first time in my life. I did not know what to do with myself. I met Miguel and his maker; they were traveling to Delos to do research on the prophecy. Livius had mentioned it in passing; he made it sound like an old wives' tale, but I was curious and joined them. There I learned everything about

254

the prophecy and helped them develop a strategy. I moved to San Sebastian not long after Phillip met the sun and I became Miguel's second in command.

"At first, I felt like I was a slave again, doing everything Miguel asked. I was so mad at myself for letting it happen. I left the city for a few years just to prove to myself that I belonged to no one. Miguel understood, and took me back with open arms. Our relationship changed then, he became more of a friend than a boss. I found ways to question him and not do everything he asked. It took years."

"And here I am crying over people thinking I'm a slave. You were one for decades or centuries I guess. I was one only for a few days. Thank you for putting it in perspective for me." I turned to look at the people grouped in small clusters around us.

"That was not my point." He put his hand on my shoulder and turned me back to face him. "It does not matter what other people think. As long you know who you are, they cannot hurt you." His stare bored into my eyes, it felt like he was trying to drill his point home. I stared back at him thinking about how hard it must have been for him to learn how to be free after hundreds of years as a slave.

"Okay, I belong to no one. I will make it my mantra." I forced a smile and looked away.

"Good," he said, and when I looked back up at him, he was still staring at me as if he wanted something.

I took the chance and moved into him, wrapping my arms around his thick torso. "Thanks, you really made me feel better."

"You are welcome," he said in a small voice as he pulled back from me.

"George and John seem nice, and I'm excited for Helen to teach me jujitsu." I needed to change the subject or I was going to start crying again.

"She will be a competent instructor for you." He looked around at the people outside. "Can you pick anything up from the people out here?"

"No one is thinking at me so no." I felt like an idiot for not thinking of it sooner. I should have been trying to figure out who spiked my champagne instead of feeling sorry for myself. "I'm too tired to force my way in right now."

"It's alright, just keep it in mind." He must not have seen anyone he thought was capable of hurting me since he steered me back inside.

We mingled, talked to a few other vampires and humans. We tried to determine if any of them were our unknown enemy, but after a while my body started to protest the sandals I was wearing. It did not seem like we were getting anywhere so I found a free sofa and sank into it.

I put my warm, empty beer bottle on the side table and contented myself with people and vampire watching.

Helen saw me sitting on the sofa and came over with a beer in her hand. I smiled as she gave it to me and I let out a sigh of relief when the cold penetrated my hand.

"I bet your hands are killing you. Would you mind if I sat down?"

"Sure," I moved over to make room for her and opened the beer, "they are killing me, so are my feet. I haven't worn heels in weeks."

"I remember the feeling." She looked down at her three-inch heels.

"How long have you been a vampire?" I asked in a low tone she would be able to hear, but the humans around us would not. "If it's not too personal to ask."

"Not at all." She smiled. "Theron changed me right

after the war." It looked like she was thinking back.

"Forgive me, but which one?" Wondering if it was one of the world wars, or the Peloponnesian War.

"World War II." She laughed a little in spite of herself. "It's a good question though; you never know how old one of us is by looking at us."

"No kidding." Not knowing what to say I looked around the room for Vince, he must have been behind me because I could feel but not see him.

"He's behind you. You two are very cute together. I never thought I would see Vince in love."

I almost spit out the sip of beer I was drinking. "We are not together," I said quickly. "He's my protector and mentor, nothing more."

"I'm sorry." She looked taken aback. "The way you two move around each other, I thought you were lovers."

I almost said, "I wish," but thought better of it. "No, he's helping me train to be able to protect myself better. He's a wonderful man, but I don't think he sees me like that." I took a sip of my beer.

*I think that he will surprise you when the time is right,* Helen thought. "Well that's none of my business anyway."

"Why do you think he'll surprise me?"

"I didn't say that out loud." She gave me a wary look.

"No, you didn't." I smiled at her. "You thought it."

"You can read minds?" She looked like she wanted to bolt.

"Only vampires," I said, and quickly added. "Until recently it was only when they were projecting their thoughts but I recently found a way to get into their minds."

"That's how you did it?" She moved closer to me. "How you beat Ben?"

"It wasn't all of it, I still had to hit him, but yes. That's how I

257

was able to anticipate his moves." I lowered my head and voice. "Don't worry I'm not going to get into your head unless we need to for training. We'll tell you the rest tomorrow."

"I'm sure it will be enlightening." I could feel her becoming more and more uncomfortable.

"I didn't mean to make you uncomfortable. I just wanted to give you an idea of what I can do." I was trying to find the words to reassure her. I had no intention of reading her mind all the time. "I told you because Theron said we can trust you."

"You can trust me. I have known Vince for a very long time, and he's a good one." She hesitated, looked at her hands and then back at me. "No one has ever been able to read my mind; you can understand why I'm not very comfortable right now, right?"

"Yes, you should have seen Vince when he figured out I could hear him. Well, I guess I couldn't see him since it was the middle of the day and he was stalking me, but you get the idea."

"Yes, I think he and I are going to have a long talk about this." She got up from the sofa. "I am going to retire for the day. I will see you tomorrow night."

"Goodnight, Helen." I hoped she was not going to freak out on us.

Vince and I left the party after I fell asleep on the couch. I told him about the conversation I had with Helen and he laughed.

"I was completely freaked out when you heard me the first time, but then I saw the tattoo and I added it up quickly." He parked the golf cart at the front door of our house.

We got out and made our way inside. "I didn't overstep anything did I? By telling her I mean," I asked as we walked in the front door.

"No, it was a good idea. Now she will have time to think about it before tomorrow night; let it sink in and get used to the idea." He closed the door behind him.

I walked down the hallway toward my room. "Good, what's the plan for tomorrow?" I asked, wanting to crawl into bed and never get out.

"You have the day off." He followed me and stopped when he reached the door to my room. "We will continue after your hand heals, but you might want to go for an easy run, just to loosen up."

"A day off really?" I was so excited I did not know what to do. I opened the door and turned to him.

"Yes, a day off." He smiled bringing his hand up to brush a piece of hair out of my eyes. "And do not worry we will find whoever tried to enslave you."

Speechless at his gesture and trying to ignore his words, I moved in and kissed him on the cheek. "Thank you for everything Vince. I'll never forget it."

He stiffened and I took a step back. "Goodnight." I backed into my room trying not to let my broken heart show and closed the door in his face.

# CHAPTER 30

The next day I slept until I rolled on my cracked knuckle and woke up with a yell. Vince was pounding on my door within seconds. "Katie, are you alright?"

"Yes, I just rolled onto my hand." I flexed it experimentally. It was swollen enough I could not make a fist and my whole hand was black and blue. The other hand was better but not by much.

"Go back to sleep," Vince said from the other side of the door. "It is early."

"No point now, my hand hurts too much." I threw back the covers and got out of bed. "I'll be out in a few minutes."

"If you are sure." I heard him walking toward the kitchen.

I had to brush my teeth with my left hand, which is harder than it sounds when I had been using my right hand for my entire life. Getting dressed was hard too. I had to wear a sports bra since I could not pinch the ends of a regular bra together to hook it. I was down to a t-shirt and pull on shorts since there was no way I could fasten a button.

When I entered the kitchen twenty minutes later breakfast was waiting for me along with a bowl of ice for each hand and some painkillers. Vince was sitting at the table reading something on his laptop.

"Were you able to narrow down the vampires who might be after you?" I asked, taking my seat, and grabbing the coffee cup with my left hand. It was not too bad, at least I could still feed myself, I thought as I took a sip of the hot liquid.

"No, I am waiting for Theron to give me a list of the vampires who were here the last time I was here." He looked up and winced at the sight of my bruised face and hands. "How are you feeling?"

"Like I got in a fight." I said, deadpan. "I'm going to need more recovery time then I thought." I dug into the eggs and sausage. "Thank you for making me all this food."

"I should have wrapped your hands better." He gently lifted up my right hand and looked at the bruising. "If I would have wrapped it tighter you would not have broken your knuckle."

"Don't blame yourself." I took my hand back and rested it in the ice. It stung like a bitch but it would help me get better quicker.

*But I always will*, he thought to me. *If it was not for me, you never would have been in a fight, and the ordeal with the champagne would never happened.*

"Like you said, I needed the practice," I said around a mouthful. "Now I know what it feels like to be in a real fight, and how much pain I will be in the next day. How were you supposed to know someone here has it out for you? We'll get through this."

"It does not mean I like seeing you hurt." He glanced at my hands and shook his head. "It is going to take a while to heal. I think you are going to have to take a few days off."

"Yeah, I can't even make a fist." I tried to close my

262

hand and winced when I only made it halfway. "I should be able to go running though." Then I thought about every step reverberating up my hand and pain shooting up my arm. "But maybe in a few days."

"We can only work with what we have." He turned his head toward the kitchen door. "Alex is here. I will be in the den if you need me. Helen will be here just after sunset, please be ready to meet with her. Do not drink anything that looks suspicious. I do not think Alex would do anything to hurt you, and he is not anyone's slave, but be careful." He got up and left the room.

Alex knocked on the door, and I yelled for him to come in. He took a seat at the table next to me, looked at my hands and my face. "Well I hope Ben looks and feels worse than you do."

"Thanks, me too." Finished with my food, I took the painkiller sitting next to a glass of orange juice and swallowed it. "This hurts pretty badly."

"You'll survive." He smiled, grabbed my plate and took it to the sink. "Looks like we aren't running today huh?"

"Thanks, I could have done that." I followed him into the kitchen. "No. Every time I move pain radiates up my hand."

"Why don't we have a movie day then? I have a bunch of DVD's. We can camp out in the den, watch movies, and you can move as little as possible."

"That sounds awesome." I put my empty orange juice glass in the sink. Alex followed me with the bowls of mostly melted ice and my coffee mug. "Let me check with Vince, the den is his office."

I went down the hall to find Vince was sitting with his laptop. "Hey, did you hear the plan?" I moved into the room to see him.

"Yes, I think it is a good idea. I will work in my bedroom."

"Why don't you join us?" It felt weird having to ask. "It'll be fun and you can make sure I keep ice on my hands."

"It is fine. I think the saying is, 'three is a crowd'. I do not want to cramp your style."

"Three isn't a crowd if you're all friends." I was surprised he thought I wanted to be alone with Alex. "It would be nice to hang out with my guys together. Do some bonding."

"If you are sure." Vince started picking up the papers scattered around the coffee table.

"One hundred percent. I'll go tell Alex. He's going to run home and get the movies." I turned and went back into the kitchen where Alex was washing the dishes. "We are good to go. Vince is going to join us if it's okay with you."

Alex dropped the plate he was holding and turned to look at me. "That's fine." But by the tightness in his voice, I knew it was not fine. "The more the merrier."

"Alex, are you sure it's okay? I thought we were just going to veg out and since the den is where Vince works he could veg with us." I felt bad inviting more people to his party, but I wanted a buffer too. He did not seem to understand that we were just friends.

"It'll be fine; I'll run to go get the movies now." He dried his hands with a dishtowel and moved toward the door. "I'll be back in twenty minutes or so."

"Perfect." I was excited to spend the day doing nothing for a change. "Alex, thanks for being so great. You didn't have to do the dishes."

"It's all good; you're not going to be doing them for a while. I thought I would help. I'll be back in a flash."

After Alex left, I went back into the den. Vince had picked everything up, and was dusting the television off. "Do you need any help in here?"

"Nope," Vince turned and smiled. "We will be ready

to go as soon as Alex gets back. Why don't you sit down and get comfortable? I will get icepacks for your hands."

"I'm going to put some lounge pants on, get a blanket then I'll sit down," I said, heading to my room. "I haven't cuddled up in a blanket to watch TV in months."

It took longer than I thought to change clothes. When I came out with the blanket from the foot of my bed under my arm Alex was back. He was standing toe to toe with Vince. They were both mad about something.

"Wasn't last night's fight enough for you two?" I asked, continuing on my path to the couch pretending the two of them fighting was no big deal.

"We were just trying to decide what movie to start with." Vince came to me with an icepack in each hand. "Alex wanted to watch 'Bram Stoker's Dracula', and I voted for 'Queen of the Dammed'."

"Are they all vampire movies?" I giggled at the choices they made.

"Yes," Alex sounded embarrassed. "Trying to get in with the locals you know?"

"Nothing wrong with that." I wondered how I could make everyone happy. "How about 'Twilight'?"

They both groaned. "Really?" Vince asked. While Alex said "chick flick," under his breath.

"Okay, let's watch 'Buffy the Vampire Slayer'. Hot girls kicking ass for you two and hot guys for me."

They both agreed and we settled in to watch movies for the day. Vince sat on one side of me while Alex sat on the other. The sofa reclined so it was kind of like being in a really big bed with two guys. Which was fine while we were watching Buffy but when we switched to Bram's I could not do it. I got up to go to the bathroom and when

I came back, I moved to the stand-alone love seat and sat by myself.

We ate junk food and drank beer; it was good for the pain and swelling, right? We talked and laughed through all the movies. Half way through Queen of the Damned, I fell asleep. I had read the book in high school and had seen the movie. I did not miss much.

My dreams were blank until I heard Vince's thoughts. *What does she see in him? He is scrawny; he does not have a pleasant face. I could kick his ass in less than a minute. Is it because he is human?*

I poked my way into Vince's head; I did not need Alex hearing this. *He's a friend Vince. I'm not attracted to him at all. It's nice to have someone I can spend time with in the sun. Someone who isn't involved with all the vampire drama.* I opened my eyes, locked them with Vince and left his mind.

*You heard me?* He thought and I nodded my head. *I'm sorry, it is just that...*" He got up and went into his room without finishing his thought.

Alex watched him go. "What was that about?" He sat up a little straighter in the chair.

"I have no idea." I smiled at him and turned to watch the end of the movie.

After the movie was over I walked Alex to the door, I had to get ready for my meeting with Helen and he had work to do. "That was fun. We'll have to do it again sometime."

"Yeah, definitely." He looked like he wanted to say something else but he stopped himself. "I'll see you tomorrow right?"

"I don't see why not." I opened the door for him.

"Have a good night."

"You too," he said, passing by me on the way out the door.

Vince made me dinner, a sandwich; it was easy to eat one handed. He sat with me while I ate. He wanted to ask me something, but he was carefully guarding it.

"Vince, come on. I can tell you want to say something. What is it?" I finished my first half of the sandwich and picked up the second half.

"I think Alex is in love with you," he said quietly.

"Really?" I thought about it while I ate the rest of my sandwich. He was always ready to do whatever I wanted. He came up with the idea of the movie day, and he was not thrilled when I invited Vince to join us. "I think you're right." I put down my sandwich and drank some water. "What should I do?" I felt bad for the guy.

"You do not feel the same?" Vince asked, wanting to verify the mind-to-mind conversation we had earlier.

"How many times do I have to tell you? He's a friend. I have no feelings for him beyond friendship."

"I am just making sure." He scooted his chair back and stood up. "I do not know what you need to tell him, but maybe Theron can get rid of him. He has been here for a long time."

"That's not the way to solve the problem. I need to talk to him, and make him understand I'm never going to feel like that about him."

"Can I ask you why?"

"Because he's not my type, I like a little more meat on the bones. I'm not in to guys I can bench press." I was getting pissy because he kept bugging me about it. "There's something about him I don't think I could ever trust."

Vince smiled at my comment. "I can work with that," he said, leaving the room.

"Men," I muttered to myself going to the sink and carefully washing the dishes. Why did Vince even care? Last night when he brushed the hair from my eyes he wanted more, I could feel it, but then he shut his feelings off. I understood he was my protector and bodyguard, but why not be my lover at the same time? Wait; did I even want him as a lover?

I dried my hands off and went out to the terrace to watch the waves crash on the beach. Vince drove me insane when he was in Sensei mode, cold and heartless always pushing me harder than the day before. Then he would go all soft massaging me, and he would try to connect with me. He treated me like his equal not his student, slave, or queen in those moments. They were my favorite times to spend with him.

He was nothing like Miguel. He did not want anything for himself; he only wanted me to be at my best. It dawned on me then; I had not thought of Miguel in weeks, maybe Vince was helping me leave everything that happened in San Sebastian behind. I would never forgive Miguel, but at least I could be at peace with what happened. I never would have met Vince if it had not been for Miguel and Lolita.

My feelings for Vince went beyond friendship, I finally admitted to myself. I smiled, at least I felt like I would be able to love again someday. I looked to the west and the rapidly setting sun behind thick purple and pink tinted clouds, it was beautiful. I turned, thinking I needed to make sure Vince had everything ready for Helen's visit when there was a loud boom from nearby.

268

# CHAPTER 31

Instinctively I hit the deck, literally my belly on the wood deck of the terrace; I put my hands over the back of my head to protect it. I heard Vince shouting something, but my ears were ringing from the gunshot and he was too far away. The gun went off again and the wood next to me splintered. I had to move. I belly crawled to the door as the wood around me was peppered with gunfire. I was trying to find the courage to crouch and open the door to go inside when the door opened and without thinking about it, I shimmied into the kitchen. Vince slammed the door behind me yelling something I could not make out.

"Is it safe for me to get up?" I asked in what I thought was a normal voice.

*Yes, there is no need to yell.* I finally heard Vince in my head.

"I'm not yelling you're mumbling," I said over the ringing in my ears. I got up and moved away from the windows. "Was someone shooting at me?"

*Yes, that is why you cannot hear right now. Are you ok?*

"Yes, I'm not bleeding, am I?"

*No, I would be able to smell it if you were. What happened? What were you doing out side?*

"Just thinking, watching the waves and the sunset. Do you

know where the shots were coming from?" The house phone, my cell phone, and Vince's cell phone all started ringing. I pulled my phone out from my bra, I did not have any pockets to put it in. "Hello?"

"Katie are you alright?" Alex asked it sounded like he was running.

"I'm fine, what are you doing?" I wanted to look out the window to see if he was on his way here. "Don't come here someone was shooting at me."

"I know I heard the shots I'm trying to track them."

"Be careful, I don't want you to get hurt or dead because of me." I went over to Vince and mouthed to him that Alex was trying to catch the shooter. He nodded his head.

"I will this is what I do. I'll let you know what I find." The call disconnected, and I looked around the room. Vince motioned me to follow him while he talked to Theron.

"I don't care what you think. We need to find whoever is doing this and stop them," Vince said into his phone as I followed him down the hall to the basement door. "Do whatever you think is necessary. I will not let an enemy of mine be the undoing of the prophecy." He hung up the phone and opened the door.

"Do you think hiding down there is safe? We could get stuck with no way out," I said, looking down at the dark staircase.

"Where do you think we should go?" Vince was irritated.

"The sun is almost down. If it's a vampire after me they can come anyway they want. I don't know what to do, but I would bet waiting in a dark tunnel would be easier than storming the house."

Vince blew a breath out loudly. "Good thinking, but I am at a loss for what to do. Is there no where on this planet safe for you?"

"I don't know. Is there anywhere we can defend ourselves with an escape route if we need one?"

"There is nowhere in the house. The dojo is going to be the safest place. The glass is bullet proof and all the weapons are up there."

"Sounds good." I turned and ran up the stairs to the dojo. I stopped and listened with my vamp sense when I reached the closed door.

"What are you waiting for?" Vince asked, pushing me forward.

"I'm making sure no one's in there." Not feeling anyone but Vince I opened the door and went inside.

"Sorry, I do not mean to be short with you." He followed behind me closing the door and walking over to the weapons wall. He looked over his options and started to load up. He slung a katana in its scabbard across his back, then started picking up various items and stashing them on his body. I went to the corner of the room and sat down, bent my knees, and brought them to my chest. I wrapped my arms around my legs and buried my head in the space between my torso and my knees. It was taking everything I had not to freak out.

"Katie, are you alright?" Vince sounded close and I pulled my head up to look at him.

"I'm trying to hold it together. I've never been shot at before. I'm trying to come to grips with it." I laid my head back down and took deep breaths.

"You did exactly what you were supposed to do. I am proud of you," Vince said placing, his hands on my head to reassure me.

"Thanks," I said indifferently.

"Wait." He held his pointed finger in front of his lips when I looked up. *Someone is on the stairs. Take these and go into the bathroom.* He pulled two six-inch knives from his back pocket. *Hide in the shower. If they get through me, stab them.*

I nodded, got to my feet as quietly as I could and slid my feet across the floor to the massage room. The door was half-open, and I was able to squeeze inside without moving the door. I skirted the table in the middle of the room, and went into the bathroom to hide behind the shower curtain. I wanted to curl into a ball and hide from the world, but I had to be tough for Vince. I pushed my back against the wall to wait and listen.

What was I going to do if they took out Vince? He was everything I had. There was no way I could survive without him right now. This world of vampires was still too new to me. There was too much to learn. I trusted Theron and Helen, but not like I trusted Vince, he was the only one I could depend on. I hoped he kicked the crap out of whoever was trying to kill me.

I heard the door open and felt another vampire enter the dojo. I braced myself to listen to a fight, but there was nothing but some murmuring.

*You can come out now. Helen is here.*

I let out a breath I did not realize I was holding, and went back to the dojo. "Did they find them?" I asked, moving into the room cautiously.

"I was just telling Vince that I was on my way here using the tunnels when Theron called to see where I was. I got here as quickly as I could. I'm glad they're a crappy shot."

"Me too." She was excited, but it was in anticipation

of a fight not because she had been trying to kill me.

*What is wrong?* Vince gave me a sideways glance. I shook my head.

Someone came pounding up the stairs, and Vince pulled me behind him so he was between the door and me.

"It's not a vampire." My vamp sense was telling me there were only two close by. "It must be Alex."

"How can you be sure?" Helen asked, pulling her eyebrows together in confusion.

"We will explain everything later," Vince said, not taking his eyes from the door.

"It's me Alex, don't kill me."

"Come on in Alex," I yelled over Vince's shoulder.

He opened the door and looked inside. "Everyone okay?"

"Yes," Vince said, taking a step toward him. "Where were you when the shots were fired?"

"I was at my house watching television. Why? Do you think I want to kill Katie? Are you out of your mind?"

"Do you have any proof you were there?" Vince asked, flipping the knife in his hand as if deliberating about whether to use it on Alex or not.

"If I wanted her dead she would be dead." Alex's voice had gone cold.

"How so?" Helen asked, not wanting to be left out.

"I go running and swimming with her every day. I could stab her and leave her for dead at the back of the property. I could drown her in the sea. I wasn't me because I don't miss. It's my job not to miss. This was a vampire. I chased them as far as I could, but they jumped the fence and I could not get over it."

"Show me where the vampire jumped the fence and I will continue tracking them." Helen moved toward the door gesturing for

Alex to go with her.

"Be careful." I watched them leave the room. I wanted to move to the windows and look outside but it was not safe. "What do we do now?"

"We wait for them here. How is your knuckle?" Vince picked up my hand gently and lifted it up to inspect the purple mass.

"It still hurts." I looked into his eyes and willed him to kiss me. Instead, he dropped my hand moved to look out the windows. I sat down on the floor and closed my eyes with nothing left to do but wait.

Helen and Alex were not back until hours later, at least it felt like hours, but I could not be sure since there wasn't a clock in the dojo. The only way I had to measure time was how many times Vince paced back.

"Did you catch them?" Vince asked when they entered the dojo empty handed. "Or at least figure out who it was?"

"No, they were long gone by the time I crossed the fence," Helen said, looking defeated.

"I should have been quicker to get here," was all Alex said before sitting down next to me. "Are you sure you're alright?"

"I'm fine. Thanks for trying to get whoever it was. What are we going to do now?" I looked toward Helen and Vince who were having a quiet conversation.

"Theron is taking attendance as we speak, he should be able to figure out who did this, then we will see. In the meantime, let's go back down stairs and continue with our evening as planned," Vince said, looking to Alex. "You can go back home. Thank you for your help." Vince looked like it took everything he had to say the words. He did not want to like Alex.

"Sure, I may hang around outside make sure no one comes back to try and get another shot off."

"If you wish, but do not feel you have to." Vince went to the door of the dojo indicating we could leave.

"It's all good. I want to keep Katie safe too." Alex jumped to his feet then offered me a hand up.

"Thanks." I gave him my good hand and he pulled me up.

"I'll make sure you are safe," he said, before turning and leaving the dojo.

Helen blinked in surprise and Vince rolled his eyes. "Let's get this over with."

Downstairs in the den I took a seat on the loveseat while Helen sat on the couch with Vince.

"How is your hand tonight?"

"It hurts like a mother." I lifted it up to show her the swollen mass. "I think it's better than it was this morning though."

"It's going to take some time to heal. We'll have to work around it when we start jujitsu." I could feel her thinking hard about how she was going to have to change things around.

"We wanted to talk to you tonight about why we are doing this." Vince leaned forward resting his forearms on his thighs and lacing his fingers together. "Have you ever heard of Asteria's Prophecy?"

Helen drew her eyebrows together thinking. "I think I've heard Theron talk about it a few times why?"

"Katie is 'The One' who was prophesized." Vince sat back on the seat and let the information soak in.

"How can you be sure?" Helen asked, looking from me to Vince then back at me. "No offense, but there is nothing outwardly

275

special about you. You are almost as fast as a vampire, but I'm sure it comes with being his slave."

I jumped up from my seat. "I'm no one's slave damn it," I almost shouted.

"Katie, calm down," Vince said sternly.

"Is she not?" Helen asked, raising her eyebrows in question.

"No, Miguel tried to make her his slave, but she broke the bond twice."

"I've never heard of anyone breaking a slave bond. How did you do it?"

I looked at Vince for approval when he nodded I began. "My mom showed me how in my dreams. I picture my brain, find what doesn't belong there and pull it out. It's a painful process."

"I believe you're not a slave, but I find it hard to believe you are 'The One'. I don't even know if I believe in the prophecy."

"Why don't you show her the tattoo?" Vince glanced my way.

"I can't get the shirt on my own." I stood up trying to get a hold of the fabric of my t-shirt but it hurt too much.

"Here I will help." He stood behind me and pulled up the shirt.

"That is an interesting tattoo." Helen moved closer to get a better look. "Where else have I seen this design?" she asked, trying to remember.

"Theron has a drawing of it in his office. I gave it to him many years ago."

*Why is it important?* I heard Helen ask herself.

"Because the original is in the temple of Asteria on

Delos, along with the prophecy." I answered her question.

"Is that why you can read my thoughts?" She looked uncomfortable about me getting into her mind.

"It is part of the prophecy." Vince continued getting up, switching the television on. It was linked to his laptop and he started the same presentation I had watched a few weeks before.

When it was over Vince turned the television off and turned to Helen. "We are keeping this on a need to know basis. Do not be angry with Theron for not telling you about it. We are only telling those who can be trusted. We already have one enemy on the island; we do not want to court anymore." Vince sat back down on the sofa. "What questions do you have?"

"I am Greek, but I think you need to remember myths are just stories. If there was a prophecy it was probably made by some mad woman high on drugs." Helen got up and walked around the room. "It's astonishing how many of us believe in it, we're living in the twenty-first century. The myths are just myths. What proof do we have that any of this is true?"

"Only the tattoo on Katie's side and she can read our minds."

"Where did you get the idea for the tattoo?" Helen looked at me inquiringly.

"It was a sketch my birth mother drew over and over again in one of her sketch books." I was starting to feel defensive.

"Did your mother ever visit Greece?" Helen asked, getting to the bottom of her thoughts.

"Yes, she met my father in Athens." I looked down at my hands, was she right? "But in my dreams my mother is Asteria."

"You have dreams about your mother and she is the Goddess? Vince how can you believe this?" Helen asked, standing with her arms crossed over her chest.

"Helen, when we went to Delos. Katie had never been there.

277

She led us directly to Asteria's temple. There was no way she could have done it without her dreams. It is labeled as the museum on the maps, not a temple, since humans could care less about a Titan's temple." Vince was getting angry.

"Look, Helen I don't care if you believe in the prophecy or not, but I would like you to train me in whatever martial arts you know." I needed this woman's help, I did not need her believe me.

"Will you promise to stay out of my head?" She looked doubtful.

"I do, but you have to understand, when you think loudly." I stopped talking to look at Vince. "Is that a good way to put it?"

"Yes, Helen when you think loudly or project your thoughts, Katie will hear you." Vince finished for me.

"Okay, I'll do it." Helen sat back down. "But can we not talk about the prophecy anymore?"

"Of course. What would you like to discuss?"

"How are you planning to take Lolita out?"

"First we have to find her." Vince sounded frustrated. "She has been moving around every few days. We are always one step behind her."

"Theron had told me as much." Helen tucked a stray hair behind her ear. "What you are going to do when you find her."

"I'm going to kill the bitch. She already tried to kill me once. I want her dead."

"Is that why you want me to train you?"

"Yes, I want to be able to protect myself and kill Lolita." I tried to make a fist with my hand.

"What makes you think you will be able to take down

a vampire who is so old? Other, older, vampires have tried and failed." Helen looked skeptical.

"You have seen how fast she is as a human." Vince got up to pace. "Can you imagine how fast she will be as a vampire?"

"But who is going to change her? No one is going to want to give up their life and spend eternity in Tartarus to make her queen. Even if they don't believe in the prophecy it would be a huge risk," Helen countered.

"We have not figured it out yet. We are hoping we won't have to. If we work together we should be able to take Lolita down without changing Katie." Vince did not sound like it was a plan he believed in though.

"Please Helen, I want your help."

"I don't see the harm in training you. But I hope you can come up with a better plan to kill Lolita." Helen smiled. "We will start as soon as your hand heals." She got up and walked toward the door. "I'll have the mats delivered tomorrow. If your hand is better, try to get a run and a swim in tomorrow but don't hurt yourself."

"Thank you, Helen, have a good evening," Theron said, watching her open the front door. "Be careful, whoever it is may be watching the house.

"I will. See you tomorrow."

Vince's phone started to vibrate in his pocket as soon as the front door closed. He looked at the caller ID before answering it. "Tell me you know who is trying to kill Katie."

I moved to stand closer to Vince hoping to hear the other end of the conversation with no luck. "Who? Katrina? I do not remember anyone by that name." He paced back and forth looking at the ground and almost running into me. "Well, at least we know who we are looking for. You will make sure she cannot leave Crete?" Theron said something on the other end of the line. "Good," Vince finished, ended the call, and stared at me.

"You know who it is?" I asked, moving away from him and back to the couch.

"I do not remember her, but from what Theron said, she was a donor when I was here last. George said she was obsessed with me before he changed her."

"What are we going to do? Do you think she knows who I am and will go to Lolita?"

"Theron is making sure no one leaves the island tonight. He is calling the weather service to tell them about a storm, which will make leaving the island a death wish. We can only pray she does not steal a boat and leave."

"What if she does? What will we do? Do we need to leave?" I was starting to shake again. I was not ready to deal with Lolita yet. If Katrina told her about the woman with Vince she would put it together quickly and I would be dead.

"Theron searched the house she shares with George, she left with nothing. All of her papers, wallet and credit cards were left behind. She was not planning to leave the island. Theron already froze her bank accounts and internet logins. She has nothing. I do not think we need to leave or worry about her getting in touch with Lolita. I doubt she even knows who Lolita is."

"Are you sure we'll be safe here?" I could not stop the dread running through my mind.

"I did not say that. She has lived here for decades. She knows all the ways in and out of the compound. We need to catch her, but in the meantime you will be guarded around the clock."

"Do you have a bullet proof vest I can wear while I'm running and swimming?" All she would have to do is find a shady spot and she could take pot shots at me all day.

"You have better, a human shield." Vince smiled to himself.

"You mean Alex? Why would I want to put him in that kind of danger?"

"He is an assassin. He knows how to take care of you. He would love to be your hero. Just watch."

Vince called Alex inside, and explained what was going on.

"Why don't you just stop training until we catch her?" Alex asked. "Can't you see Katie's tired of it?"

"Katie do you wish to stop training?" Vince sounded confident in my answer.

"I don't want anyone to get hurt because of me." I wanted to continue my training. It was paying off, but I would stop if it meant everyone I cared about would be safe.

"That is not what I asked."

"Yes, but only if you can guarantee me no one will get hurt because of me."

"That chick can't hit the broad side of a barn. She takes one shot at you and I'll be able to catch her if it's during the day. If it's at night I have no doubt mighty Vince will take care of it."

"It's decided then. If your hand feels better tomorrow, you will continue your training with Alex."

"I love my macho men," I mumbled. "I'm going to bed. Maybe when I wake up it all be a bad dream."


My mother was standing across from me at the mouth of a cave. "Mom, how are you?" I was finally getting used to her manipulating my dreams.

"Good daughter, come with me." She turned and walked into the cave leaving me to follow.

The walls were a shiny almost polished stone; there were lit

281

torches all around the room. An angry roar from deeper in the cave startled me making me jump. "What was that?"

"The final test of your training." She turned away from me looking down the dark opening. "It is not yet time."

"Good, I need to let my hand heal." I looked down at it. This was a dream; it should not to hurt, right?

"Let me see." She turned back to face me and took my hand in both of hers. "You did this in the fight last night?" She inspected it from all sides.

"Yes, more accurately after the fight." Remembering the pain shooting through my hand when I punched Ben on the chin.

"Did you win?" She did not stop the inspection of my hand.

"Yes."

"Congratulations." She sounded proud. She encased my hand in hers and squeezed it hard.

I let out a strangled cry from the pain as it burned, but just like last time, she healed me. I took my hand back and brought it up to my face. It was perfect, even the bruising was gone. I made a fist and closed it all the way with no pain. "Thank you."

"Now you can continue your training." She looked behind her. "Your next test will try and break you. You must not let it. Be strong my dear one," she said and was gone.

The monster roared again and I ran to the exit. I was not ready to meet the monster yet.

When I woke up the next morning, I looked down at my hand, it was still bruised but the swelling and the pain were gone. I could make a fist and stretch my hand out completely. I smiled; sometimes it was nice having a goddess for a mother.

I went out to the kitchen and showed Vince, who had made me another wonderful breakfast, and he was floored.

"I do not understand how you were able to heal this in your sleep." He turned my hand over in his almost caressing it.

"Mom," was my only explanation. I did not tell him about the rest of the dream. I did not want him to freak out about what was coming. I did not know if I would really have to fight off a monster or if it represented something else. I really wanted it to. "Has anyone seen or heard from Katrina?"

"No, it is likely she has a safe house outside of the compound and has gone into hiding. At least for today. Are you ready to continue your training?"

I blew out a breath. I could stop if I wanted to. If I stopped to keep everyone safe, it would feel like I was running away from my problems and not meeting them head on. If I was the future queen of the vampires, I could not let some little vampire stop me from doing what I needed to do. If people were willing to help me stay safe, I would take it. "Yes." I got up and went to change into my running clothes ready to take on the world.

Alex was waiting for me when I came out of my bedroom. "Ready?" I asked, bending over to tie my shoes.

"If you're sure you want to do this, then I have your back."

"Let's get it over with, then," I said, opening the kitchen door for him.

I jumped at every new sound while we ran, but of course, nothing happened. It was a clear day without the tiniest cloud making an appearance. No clouds also made it hot; I was down to my shorts and sports bra before we were half way down the beach.

"Katie, hold up a minute," Alex said, stopping beside me.

"What is it? Do you see something?" I crouched low in case someone tried to shoot me.

"I need you to put your tank top back on." He put his hand on his hips.

"Why? It's too hot to run with it on," I said, looking down at my sweaty skin.

"It's . . ." he trailed off then straightened his shoulders and pulled them back. "It's distracting. I need to keep my eye out for hostiles and when you run with your shirt off I can't make myself look around."

I looked down at myself, it was a high intensity sports bra but I guess I could see where he was coming from. "Sorry I'm such a distraction." I pulled my tank top out of my shorts and pulled it over my head.

The rest of the day passed without any sign of Katrina, which was good and bad. Good, because she did not interrupt my training, bad, because she was still out there.

# CHAPTER 32

Everything went back to normal after that, I ran in the morning and swam in the afternoon with Alex then trained with Vince and Helen in the evening. A week went by with nothing interesting happening. We all relaxed a hair, although I was sure either Vince, Helen, or Theron patrolled outside the house every night while I slept just to make sure I was not attacked while sleeping.

The jujitsu training kicked my butt; I had never worked so hard in my life. I treated both Helen and Vince as Sensei, since Vince attended every practice to help and be my partner.

We also started training in the tunnels, which scared the crap out of me. Vince would lead me somewhere in the middle of them, and I would have to find my way out with no light to help me. They said it would help train my other senses to compensate for my lack of night vision. Once I was able to find my way through the tunnels with ease, they started sneaking up on me everywhere. In the tunnels, in the dojo, all over the house. I learned to always be aware of my vamp-sense no matter what I was doing. Before long, I was subconsciously always feeling for vampires. It was not long before the only one who could sneak up on me was Alex. He loved it, he made me jump all the time, but after a few weeks, he too could not sneak up on me.

After a month of jujitsu, Theron joined in and we practiced

with weapons. I was best with the katana, which surprised everyone; they thought I would be too weak to wield it. Theron said I was a natural. I think he was a little jealous of my ease in using it.

After a month of weapons, with three Senseis, we alternated what I trained for every night. Some nights would be hand-to-hand karate, some would be only weapons, and others would be jujitsu. Occasionally we would spar with all three. I found those sessions the most useful. I could use all three together in a real fight.

We did not talk about why I was training, only that I needed to train. Theron and Helen were easier going then Vince was, but I still did more pushups than I thought possible. After my first month on the island, I noticed a difference in my body. It was hard everywhere. My muscles were lean, and were clearly defined under my skin. My stomach had never been so close to a six-pack and I was pretty sure you could bounce a quarter off my ass. My clothes were hanging off me.

Two months in Vince gave me a day off to go to town and buy new clothes, but this time I was not allowed to go on my own. Alex accompanied me, in full bodyguard mode, he checked out every store I went in and stayed close by.

My hair was almost to my shoulders, it looked like a seventies shag cut. It was driving me up the wall. I found a hair salon, and after Alex made sure it was safe, I had it cut in a bob. I had not really paid any attention to it, until I was forced to stare at it in the mirror. The color had changed. Instead of a dark brown almost black throughout, I now had streaks of cooper running through it from the sun.

Vince did a double take when I arrived back at home.

"You got your hair cut."

"Yes, do you like it? It was driving me up the wall with all the different lengths."

"It suits you quite well," he said before going back to his research. There had been no news of Lolita or Katrina in months. It worried everyone. It was as if they dropped off the face of the earth. We hoped they were not together wherever they were.

Alex did not like how hard I was becoming; he thought women should be a little bit soft. I was happy I was turning him off for a change, but he seemed to grow more agitated the more we were together. Finally, one day after our swim I confronted him about it.

"What's your problem Alex? There is a point to all this. You know that right?"

"I hate seeing Theron and Vince mold you into something you're not." He sat down in the sand.

"They're not molding me into something I'm not, Alex." I walked a few steps away then back. "I'm doing this because I want to be able to take care of myself. I want to be prepared for whatever comes my way. I don't want to depend on anyone."

"I know where you are coming from." Alex picked up a handful of sand and let it slide through his fingers. "That's how I've lived my entire life." He paused collecting his thoughts. "I was brought up knowing no one would ever have my back, the only one who was going to look out for me, was me. I know what it turned me into, and I don't want you to turn into the monster I am."

I sat down in the sand next to him. "You're not a monster." I turned my head trying to make eye contact with him and failing. "I know there are people who will protect me and fight for me. I know people care about me." I bumped his shoulder. "But what if the big bad goes through all of them, and I'm the only one left who can protect me? I want to be able to say I gave it everything I had. I used all of the resources available to make myself strong enough not to go down without a hell of a fight."

"I see what you mean." He bumped my shoulder back. "I wish you could leave it all behind and not have to be the person you are becoming."

"I wish that too sometimes." Burning started from behind my eyes when I thought about how much my life had changed in the past few months. "There's no going back. She knows who I am. She's not going to stop until she kills me or makes me her slave."

"Who are you talking about?" He turned to look at me. "All this time you never told me who your enemy is."

"Lolita." I wished I could tell him more but I would not.

"Why does she want you dead?"

"It's a long story and it's safer if you don't know." I did not want him to be hurt if he found out. "Let's just say she already tried to kill me once and if it wasn't for Vince, we would not be sitting here talking."

"I'll let it go for now, but I want to know what you are up against. I want to help." He stood up and dusted the sand off his wet shorts.

"Thanks." I offered him my hand. "You can help me right now with a hand up."

"I see how you are." He grabbed my hand, yanked me hard enough my feet left the ground and I slammed into him. He took a step back bracing himself for the impact when I ran into him, and he put his arms around me to keep from falling.

"Wow, that was a little hard don't you think?" I laughed, trying to wiggle away.

"No, it was just perfect," he said, before kissing me. I kissed him back before I realized what I was doing and it was something I did not want to do.

"Alex, stop." I pulled my mouth away from his and pushed away from him.

"Why?" He tried to move back in for more. "Come on you have to feel the chemistry between us."

"How many times, in how many ways can I tell you? You are my friend. I think you're a good guy. I like hanging out with you, watching movies, and running and swimming, but I'm not attracted to you." I felt like scum. How do you let someone down easy?

He looked at me with despair in his eyes for a moment. I took a step toward him and he backed up a step raising his arms in front of him. "Just stay back." He paused for a second. "I can't believe I was going to give everything up for you. I thought I loved you. I've never loved anyone in my entire life. You were the closest thing. I thought you liked me too. Why else would you want to hang out so much?"

"Alex, I told you from the beginning, I was taking a break from men. I wasn't looking for anything but friendship. I hung out with you because you're my friend and that's what friends do." I felt tears begin to burn behind my eyes again.

Not listening to me, he went on. "I know you and Vince are fucking, just admit he's why you're not into me." He turned to look out at the ocean.

"Vince and I are not having a sexual relationship. How many times have I told you this?" I crossed my arms over my chest.

"But you wish you were." He mimicked my pose.

His words stopped me. Did I wish it? Sometime yes and sometimes no. How could I be honest with Alex when I could not be honest with myself? "Sometimes, but like I said I'm taking a break from men." It was as close to the truth as I was going to get.

"I'm tired of wasting my time with you." He turned and headed toward his house.

"Alex," I yelled after him. "Please, I thought you were my only real friend."

He did not answer, just waved his arm in the air like he was shooing me away.

I watched him until he turned up the walkway to his house. With tears streaming down my cheeks, I went back up to the house. Vince was probably wondering where I was, but I did not want to see him. I went in through the kitchen yelled that I was home then went into my room for a long shower.

There was nothing I could do or could have done differently to change what happened. In all reality, I was not surprised it happened, but it did not mean it did not hurt. The only choice I had was to deal with the loss and move on, but I wished it did not hurt so much.

# CHAPTER 33

Lolita blinked up at the moon light and breathed in the fresh air of Paris. It was nice to get out of the catacombs for a change. She had been so busy creating her army she had not ventured out in months. She had a few old ones who would come to her aid when she was ready but she wanted some cannon fodder as well.

Tonight was her night to hunt and feast before the next stage of her plan went into effect. It was the height of tourist season and the streets were crowded with people looking for a memorable night in Paris.

She walked along the streets aimlessly smelling people as they walked by; she was looking for someone special. Someone she could indulge in. Someone pure. A group of young adults passed her, most likely on a school trip. There was one in the group who was exactly what she was looking for. She turned and followed them quietly, joining them as they moved down the street. When one of them looked at her in surprise, she locked onto their gaze and made them forget she was there.

When Lolita reached the virgin, she took the girls hand startling her into looking directly at her. She took hold of her mind in an instant, and they slowly began to lag behind the others. In a few minutes, they were far enough behind to duck into an alley without anyone noticing they were gone.

"What are we doing?" the girl asked, realizing they were no longer following her friends.

"We are having a date," Lolita answered pushing the girl against the grimy wall and kissing her hard on the mouth.

"I don't think I like girls like that," the girl said in a faraway voice.

"You will never know until you try it." Lolita pulled back and met the girl's eyes again. "Now shut the fuck up and enjoy this."

Lolita bent her head to the girl's neck and began to lick and suck at it, bringing the blood to the surface of the skin. The girl moaned in response. "That is more like it," Lolita mumbled in between nips and sucks.

The girl began to undulate into Lolita, and she smiled, perfect. Lolita slid her fangs into the girl's neck delicately, only allowing a small amount of the warm, pure blood to ooze into her mouth. The girl moaned again and began to grind against Lolita's leg. Lolita sucked, forcing more blood into her mouth before swallowing and grinding her pelvis into the girl. The pressure built and finally the girl moaned her orgasm out into the night. Before the endorphins dissipated, Lolita pulled her fangs out of the girl and latched onto a pulsing artery. The blood poured into her mouth almost faster than she could swallow. When it slowed to a trickle, Lolita released the girl and let her slide down the wall.

Lolita took a few steps away and pulled her compact out of a pocket. She opened it and checked her face to make sure there were no splatters. Without a hair out of place, she pocketed her compact and went back to her office.

Playtime was over, it was time to find Katie and be done with her. Weeks of hearing nothing had quickly turned into months of nothing. She wanted to end the girl herself, but time was ticking by and there was no news of her whereabouts. She did not have time to track her anymore, every day she went unfound was another chance for her to be turned, and Lolita could not allow it to happen. She brought up the email she did not want to send, and sent it. Katie had to die, it no longer mattered who did the deed as long as it was done.

# CHAPTER 34

"I need you to come up to the house," Theron said down the phone line. "Something has come up."

"You found Katrina? I will as soon as Katie is out of the water." He looked at his watch. "I will be there in fifteen minutes."

"No, I haven't but we need to soon. Hurry, it's important." The line went dead.

Vince wondered what was going on. He wanted to leave for the mansion right then, but making sure Katie made it back to shore safely was more important. Not that there was anything he could do if something happened to her, but if something did, he would take great pleasure in punishing Alex for not protecting her.

He could not believe how much her body had changed. She was hard now. She still had her curves but her soft spots were gone. Even her breasts looked firmer and perter. Part of him missed the soft on her; it was what made a woman. When she walked in a few days ago with her haircut and styled she looked like the queen she would be come. He had not realized how badly she needed a haircut. It was becoming harder and harder for him to keep his feelings locked up while they trained. Every day it seemed she did something that made him want to kiss her.

He told himself when her training was complete he would

explain to her how badly he wanted her. If she rejected him, he would step back and be the protector he was meant to be. It was not what he wanted, but he would do anything for her.

Katie made her way to the shore with Alex, the scumbag, following her, his were eyes glued to her ass. The man infuriated Vince. Alex was so blatant with his flirtations toward her. Vince had to talk himself out of having Alex for dinner constantly. Katie still did not see Alex for who he was.

With Katie safe on the beach Vince ran to Theron's wondering what was going on. Why did Theron want him up at the house at this time of day?

Theron met him at the mouth of the tunnel. "What took you so long?"

"I told you I wanted to make sure Katie made it back to the shore before I left."

"We have a problem." Theron turned and headed for his office not waiting for Vince to catch up.

"You said that already. Are you going to tell me what the problem is?"

"When we get to my office." Theron pointed to his ears. Meaning it was something he did not want anyone else to hear.

Anxiety rocked through Vince. If there was something going on that Theron did not want other vampires to hear then it must be pretty bad. Vince followed Theron to his office and closed the door behind him. Theron went to his computer screen behind the desk and turned it for Vince to see.

He read the email. Not believing it, he read it again. "We always thought she would go this route if she could not find Katie on her own."

"Yes, but did you look at the dollar amount? It is more than any hit I have seen unless they are on the CIA's most wanted list. This is what governments offer for terrorists or world leaders."

"Only your people know she is here. How well do you trust your people?"

"Under normal circumstances implicitly, but when you are talking about this much money it would test the most loyal of my people. It's enough to buy a small country. Do you think Lolita actually has that much to spend?"

"I do not know, but I would not put it past her. She has always been devious in her endeavors. She might be promising a large payday only to kill the one who brings Katie in. I think it is time to move."

"Where will you go?" Theron sat down in the chair and leaned back with his hands behind his head.

"I do not know. I will start looking when I get back to the house."

"What about her training? She is ready for the test."

"No, she is not." Vince crossed his arms over his chest. He thought she had a long way to go before she was ready. He doubted she would ever be ready. Theron trained for two years before he took his test.

"Why not?" Theron leaned forward in his chair and laced his fingers together.

"Think about who she is, who she will become. She needs to be better than you, me, and Helen put together. Maybe then she will be ready."

"She's not your typical student. I don't know how much more I can teach her. Helen said the same. Katie feels like she's not good enough, but it's only because she has us as comparison. We have taught her everything we know; time and real-world experience is the only way she will grow stronger." Theron pushed back from his chair and stood up.

"I want to give her the time she needs to become better."

"Vince, until she is turned, she's at her peak and we both know it. Let's set up the test for this week. It should give you enough time to figure out where you are going to go next."

Vince went to the window and looked out. They had been in Crete for too long. He trusted Theron and Helen, but there were others who would be called to the money Lolita was offering. Katie was better than he gave her credit for. If she were a typical human, he would have been blown away by her progress. She was not as fast as an old vampire but she was faster than any human he had ever seen, including himself while he was human.

"Set it up. We will tell her about the test tonight but not about the bounty on her head."

"Understood, I can't wait to watch her kick some ass."

"I will see you in the dojo." Vince left the office to return home and start working on new traveling papers for them.

# CHAPTER 35

When I entered the dojo later that night, my spirits were low and my mind was not on my work. It showed, I did at least two hundred pushups. When we were done for the night Vince, Helen, and Theron knelt in front of me not looking happy.

"Katie, I do not know what is going on in your head right now, but your effort was unacceptable tonight." Vince shook his head.

"Do you have anything to say for yourself?" Helen asked.

"I'm sorry, Senseis, I had a rough afternoon. I will not let it happen again."

"Everyone has a bad day once in a while." Theron sounded more serious than he ever had before. "However, when your life is on the line you can't allow outside influences to affect your fighting."

"Yes, Sensei." I lowered my head to look my legs.

"Your final test will be in two days' time." Vince scowled. "There will be no more formal training. Use this time to think about everything you have learned and seek us out with any questions you have."

"Yes, Sensei I will." I bowed to them.

"You may leave now." Vince got up and walked to the open windows.

"Thank you, Sensei." I got up and left the room. They had no idea what I went through with Alex, but I doubt it would have mattered if they did. I needed to focus, no matter what was going on around me, when I was fighting, I needed to be in the present. I had to forget about everything else going on in my life, and concentrate on the fight.

I went into my room and took a shower trying to wash away the loss I felt over Alex. I could never love him, but he was special to me in a way no one here was. He took me for who I was, not what I could do or who I would become. I laid in bed for a long time that night trying to sleep, and unable to believe Alex hated me.

When I woke up the next morning I felt like crap, like I had just broken up with my boyfriend, even though Alex was just a friend. He was the first friend I had made with no strings attached since I left home.

The sting of his words the day before still hurt. He and I would have never worked out. I had this whole prophecy thing going, I did not want to drag a human into it, plus I never really saw him that way. I prayed I would be able to keep him as a friend, even if it was a distant one.

I made myself get up and get dressed. I had a few days off but I wanted to get in a light workout. I went into the kitchen and found it empty. Vince was nowhere to be seen. For the first time since I arrived breakfast was not waiting for me. Vince must be really mad about my performance last night, I thought to myself.

I made some eggs, toast and coffee then ate at the table by myself wondering if I had pissed off everyone I knew the day before. I went by the den before I went for my run and found it empty as well. Vince must have gone to Theron's already.

It was nice to run by myself for a change; it gave me time to think. I should not feel bad about not returning Alex's affection. It would not be fair to him if I gave in just to make him feel better; it would only prolong the pain when I had to end it. I thought about what he said about me and Vince. I admitted I was attracted to Vince, but he was odd. Sometimes he was very caring and considerate. I was sure he had wanted to kiss me a few times. Then, like the flip of a switch, he was all business. He kept his distance and wanted his orders followed to the letter. I was worried if I fixated on him I would become the girl who let her man boss her around and isolate her, like I did with Mark and Miguel.

Mark has been verbally and emotionally abusive to me. He separated me from my friends and to some extent my family. Vince separated me from them too, but there was no way around it. If I had kept my name and went home to my family, Lolita would have found me, killed me, and likely my parents as well. Vince did not need to manipulate me to make me believe she would.

If I wanted to walk away at any moment, Vince would let me. I did not think he would be happy about it, but he would let me go. The idea had me feeling better. What kind of bugged me was how he took care of me. It was nice, do not get me wrong, he always made sure I had a healthy meal and took care of myself, but I could have done some of it myself.

I lost my train of thought when I ran by Alex's house. He was on the patio watching me. I slowed down and waved at him wishing we could still be friends, but he turned away, went back inside, and slammed the door behind him. I would give him some more time. Maybe after he cooled down we could talk, I thought as I continued my run. I listened to music after that and tried not to over think everything else going on.

# CHAPTER 36

The house was eerily quiet when I got home. I could feel a vampire close by, but it was not Vince.

"Hello?" I called out as I walked down the hall checking the rooms as I passed.

There was no answer, and the rooms were quiet. I stopped in front of the door for the basement. My vamp sense told me a vampire was down there.

"Hello?" I called through the door. I tapped on their metal shield; it was not Theron or Helen. I flicked my imaginary finger at the shield and it fell.

*I have to kill her. It is the only way Vince will notice me. With her out of the way he will be mine, just like we should be,* Katrina thought.

I backed up a step then turned and ran for the dojo. I needed weapons. *Katrina is in the basement,* I thought to Vince as I ran up the stairs. He was far away; there was no way he was going to get here in time.

*Get out of the house. She will not be able to follow you there. I am on my way,* Vince yelled at me.

*Too late, I went up the dojo to get a sword.* I took the katana off the wall then located Katrina's mind. She had heard me outside

303

the door to the basement and was looking for me on the first floor.

*Stay where you are and keep your head down. Theron and I will be there shortly to deal with her.* Vince sounded worried like I might not be able to handle her on my own. I agreed with him, I was not ready to fight a vampire with no one to watch my back.

"I can smell you, little slave," a voice called out from the bottom of the stairs. "Come out so we can play." It was not the voice of a sane person. I had no idea where she had been for the past two months, but it did not sound like it had been easy on her. I heard footsteps on the stairs, she was slowly moving up them.

*Vince, get your ass here. She is coming up the stairs to the dojo.* I moved as quietly as I could to the edge of the door and raised my katana ready to strike.

*She blocked the tunnel,* Vince thought. *We are in the process of clearing it. For the time being you are on your own. I'm sorry, I failed you.*

I took a deep breath; this is what I had trained for. I could do this right? I thought to myself as the door started to slide slowly back and I pulled my arm behind me.

I watched her feet, as first one then the other stepped into the room. I swung my katana around hitting her in the chest, but no blood came pouring out. She bent over and I pulled my sword back. Fuck, I thought to myself, I forgot to take the sheath off. A lot of good a sheathed katana was going to do against a vampire.

I moved to run to the other side of the room but Katrina recovered and a fist came out of nowhere hitting me square in the nose. I flew through the air and landed on my back in the middle of the room with blood pouring out of my nose. I thought I heard a snap and prayed it was not broken.

"You think you have a chance without Vince here little slave?" Katrina asked, slowly walking toward me.

"He gave you the power to beat Ben, but it isn't something you have on your own. You must know this." I watched her slowly walking around me in a large circle.

I needed a plan fast. If I could get to the switch for the windows, I could fry her in the sun but it was noon. The sun would be overhead, we would be in the shade and she would be fine. My sword was on the other side of the room along with the rest of the weapons. I needed to stall her, give Vince and Theron time to get here. "What did I ever do to you?"

"I was like you once. A blood donor, waiting for the right vampire to come along and change me. When Vince chose me as his donor, I knew we were meant to be together forever. It was magical; he made me feel so important. He was such a gentle lover, always checking to make sure I was not in pain. The night I spent with him was the best night of my life. I knew he loved me, but he had to go before he could tell me," she said with a wistful expression in her eyes.

"How long ago did this happen?" I asked, trying to keep my voice strong.

"It has been fifty or sixty years. I begged George to change me a few years after Vince left. I didn't want get old waiting for Vince to claim me. Theron gave George permission to change me a few years later. I have done nothing since then but prepare for Vince to come back for me."

She was standing over me and I had no idea what I was going to do. I let out a moan and pretended I could not get up. "Oh, poor baby can't get up?" She brought her leg back to kick me when my arm shot out; I grabbed her leg and pulled it forward throwing her off

305

balance. She hopped on the other foot trying to stay up right before falling on her ass. I brought my knees up, arched my back and jumped to my feet facing her.

"You just don't know when to give up do you? Vince is mine; it is time for you to die." She jumped to her feet and came at me with her fangs out. She was not playing anymore.

The sight of her fangs froze me in place and my mind was filled with the image of Lolita biting into my neck. I shook myself out of my stupor and I tried to duck under her embrace when she reached me, but I had nowhere to go. Her hands latched onto my shoulders and she tried to move her mouth to my neck. I placed my hands on her chest and locked my elbows. I did not want her fangs anywhere near me. She was done talking. The only sounds coming from her were growls and slurping, as she smelled the blood from my nose. She pushed me back against the wall. When my back met it, I kicked her in the crotch. She screamed but did not let go.

My arms were getting tired. I did not know how long I was going to be able to keep her from my neck. *Vince, please I'm losing.* I began to bend my elbows, unable to keep them straight any longer.

Vince and Theron streaked into the room and tore Katrina off me. I heard a bang on the other side of the room; it must have been Katrina hitting the weapons wall. I let my back slide down the wall, bent my knees and rested my head on them when my butt hit the ground.

"Katie, are you alright?" Theron was crouching down in front of me trying to get me to look at him. "Did she bite you?"

"No," I sobbed, not even trying to hold back the tears. I failed, if it had not been for Vince and Theron I would be dead. How was I ever going to beat Lolita when I could not beat a little vampire?

"Where did the blood come from? Are you still bleeding?" I heard Theron sit down on the floor and touch me knee.

I jerked back, was he going to go into blood lust? "Don't touch me." I screamed, pushed away from him, and slid down the wall. I needed to get out of there. I stood up, my legs felt like jelly, but I could walk and I wanted to get out of there.

Vince was on the other side of room; he had tied up Katrina and was speaking too low for me to hear. He glanced up as I moved slowly toward the door. "Are you hurt?" he asked taking in my blood covered my face and chest.

"No, just a bloody nose. Please stay back I don't want you to go into blood lust." I sounded calmer then I felt. Running would not be a good idea, predators loved to chase their prey.

"Why would I go into blood lust?" Vince looked confused as he stood up and made a slow move in my direction. "I would never hurt you."

"Just stay where you are. I'm going to take a shower, then we can talk," I said when I got to the door. I bowed, exited, and closed the door.

I ran down the stairs into my room and locked the door behind me. I went into the bathroom and locked that door too. I turned on the shower then looked in the mirror. A zombie stared back at me. My hair was matted; my face and the front of my shirt were covered in dried flaking blood. My shirt was shredded; it must have happened when Vince pulled Katerina's off me. I pulled the shirt off, finding three long oozing scratches on my shoulder to match the tears in the shirt. I threw it and the rest of my clothes into the trashcan and got in the shower.

When I was clean and dry I looked at my nose in the mirror.

It was swollen and red but it looked straight. I touched it gingerly and hissed in pain. Dark bruises had blossomed under my eyes. Just what I always wanted two black eyes for the price of one. I got dressed and went to the kitchen for ice.

Vince was waiting for me when I walked in. I was not ready to talk yet so I ignored him, went to the freezer, and took out an icepack. I went into the den and laid down on the couch. I gently put the icepack on my nose and closed my eyes.

"Will you talk to me?" Vince asked, picking up my feet and sitting down before resting my legs on his.

I groaned. "What would you like to talk about?" I asked, trying not to move my face too much. Every muscle twitch shot pain through my nose. "The fact that I got my ass kicked by a young vampire? Or the fact that I will never be able to beat Lolita as I am?"

"Have you thought about why you failed?" He sounded just as defeated as I felt.

"I froze," I said, thinking back to when she let her fangs descend. "When I saw her fangs. She wanted to drain me and I froze."

"Then your failing is my fault." Vince took one of my feet in his hands and began rubbing it.

"Why is it your fault her fangs scared the shit out of me?" I groaned. Vince gave the best foot massages.

"I did not train you to deal with fangs. I trained you to fight as a human, not a vampire." Self-loathing was pouring off him.

"I should've known I would have to deal with fangs. You all have them. I froze because of what Lolita did to me in the club, not because you trained me wrong. Stop feeling

308

sorry for yourself. I'm the only one allowed to do that."

"Oh really?" Vince asked, tickling my foot.

"Hey, I'm injured here." I laughed and kicked at him. He let my foot fall and picked up the other one.

"Are you going to let me look at it? I want to make sure it is not broken."

"Yes I'll let you look at it but not until you are done with my feet." I was relaxing slowly. I was still afraid of what would happen the next time I had to deal with someone coming after my blood. If I froze when I met Lolita, I would be dead in a heartbeat. "How am I going to overcome this?"

Vince let out a breath. "I wish I had an answer for you, but everyone has to deal with their phobias in their own way. You will figure something out or you will die." He squeezed my foot for emphasis. "Fangs are not a very useful weapon. You have to get too close to your target for them to do any good. They are more of a last chance weapon."

I thought about it. In a fight they were useless unless you could get close enough to your opponent to bite them, and even then, your opponent would have to be incapacitated enough not to be able to keep them at arm's length. "You're right. They suck as a weapon."

"Remember that tomorrow night, when you are facing a vampire."

"Can you tell me what I can expect?" I asked, unready to face another fight yet.

"It will be an obstacle course of sorts. Each obstacle will require you to use one or all of your skills. You will be fighting vampires. Your goal will be to incapacitate each one, then move on to the next one"

"What if I don't get past one of them?" I thought of my performance against Katrina and those damn fangs. How was I going to get over them by tomorrow night?

"Then you fail," Vince said blandly. "You will pass; I have no doubt about your ability or your self-preservation instinct."

"Thanks," I said with a shaky smile. "What can you suggest for prep work today and tomorrow?"

"You went for a run, and got in a fight." He dug his fingers into the spot under the ball of my foot. "You should meditate on your fang problem; think about not freezing when you see them. Remember they are a useless weapon in a fight."

"Thanks. I don't want to dishonor you, Helen, or Theron. You've all been a huge help."

"You will be fine," he said, dropping my foot in his lap. "Let's take a look at your nose."

I swung my feet around, sat up and pulled the icepack off my face. Vince moved closer, placed his fingers on each side of my nose and slowly moved it back and forth. I held my breath to keep from crying out in pain. Satisfied he moved his hand to my jaw and pulled it up so I would meet his eyes.

"Is it broken?" I asked, blinking back the tears that only come when you get hit in the nose.

"Yes, but it does not need to be reset." He rubbed his thumb back and forth gently against my jaw. "I will get you a piece of tape to keep it in place. He let go of my jaw, and left the room leaving my jaw cold from the loss of his touch. I slumped down into the couch; he was so gentle when he wanted to be.

He came back and knelt in between my legs holding a piece of tape. "Hold still." He arranged the tape over my nose and pressed down sending a wave of pain through it. "That will keep everything straight. If you are lucky you will not even get a bump on your nose like mine." He ran his pointer finger down his nose showing me where he had broken it likely centuries ago.

"Thanks for fixing me up," I said while he got up and moved to the seat next to me. "I wanted to apologize again for my performance last night."

"Apology accepted. What happened yesterday?" He leaned back on the couch and looked at me.

"Alex and I got into a fight." I shifted to look at him in the face.

"A lover's spat, is that why I did not see him running with you this morning?" Vince lifted an eyebrow.

"We are not lovers," I yelled, slapping my leg for emphasis. "He wishes we were." I managed a calmer voice.

"Temper," Vince said with a small grin on his face. "So he made a move and you rejected him, hence the fight."

"He kissed me, and I told him I only saw him as a friend. Then he accused me of fucking you." I regretted bringing that part up, but it was too late. "I told him I was taking a break from men in general, but I would never feel that way toward him. He got pretty upset and stomped off."

"I am sorry your friendship is over." Vince lied.

"Vince, don't lie to me." I pushed his shoulder to try to move him, he did not budge. "You know I can tell. I know you don't like Alex, but he was a friend when I needed one with no strings attached."

"You are right, I do not like him, but I am sorry he messed with your head enough to screw up your last night of training." He held his hands up in an 'I don't mean you any harm' motion. "What do you mean a friend with no strings attached?"

"He liked me for me. He didn't know about the prophecy or

Lolita or any of the drama surrounding me." I was trying to find a way to explain it without hurting Vince's feelings.

"Are you saying I am only here because of the prophecy?" he asked in an angry voice. "That I am only helping you because I want to be near you, because of the power you will wield once you become a vampire?"

"No, I don't think it's the only reason. Can you tell me with absolute honesty that if it hadn't been for the prophecy you would have done all this to protect me, simply because Lolita wanted to kill me?"

He was quiet for a moment and his eyes went from me to his shoes then back to me. "The prophecy is what brought us together. In the beginning, yes, I thought helping you would guarantee me a position in your retinue. But now, I am helping you because I know you. You have a warrior's honor, a heart that wants to see the best in everyone you meet, a determination to win at whatever you do, and a sense of humor that makes me laugh even if it is not always on the outside. Katie, I have not had a friend like you since I turned Theron."

His words made my anger slide away, and I found myself holding back tears. I did not realize how much his opinion mattered to me. He did not declare his undying love, but it was nice to know he liked me for me, not only because I was 'The One'.

Before I knew what I was doing, I moved to him and wrapped my arms around him in a hug. "Thanks Vince, you have no idea how much your friendship means to me." He stiffened for a moment, then softened and hugged me back.

"Right back at you, sweetheart." He pulled back and stood up.

"Wait, what happened to Katrina?"

"Theron moved her to the dungeon. He is going to hold a trial tonight. It is likely she will be meeting the sun tomorrow. Do you want to go?"

I thought about it, she had tried to enslave me and when it did not work, kill me. Did she need to die? Maybe, but did I want to watch it happen? I did not think I was ready for that yet. "No, I think I can skip it. I wish she would just get over you. It seems like a dumb thing to die for."

Vince moved to stand toe to toe with me. "She tried to kill you, Katie. How could you say she should live?" His nostrils flared in anger.

"That is not what I meant. Why go to such great lengths over a guy who hasn't given her the time of day? It seems like a waste to me."

"Did she tell you why she did all this?"

"Kind of, she said you used her as a donor, it sounds like you spent the night or the day with her. She thought you were both in love. When you left without saying goodbye she decided to wait for you."

"I remember her now; it was many years ago, before I stopped having sex with donors. We had a good time, but I did not mean to lead her to believe it was more than a one-night thing."

"Well you must have some mad skills in the bedroom, if she was ready to kill to get you back." I giggled on the outside but I was jealous on the inside.

If Vince could have blushed, he would have based on the feelings I was getting from him. "At least the threat has been taken care of. I almost killed her in the dojo, but I must follow the rules Theron made. She gets a trial, then she will die. I will enjoy watching her fry from the house. No one gets to kill you Katie, not while I am around to stop them." He moved toward me as if he wanted to hug but he changed his mind and quickly pulled away.

"Thanks?" I said, more as a question than in gratitude. I had never seen him speak so fiercely.

"You are welcome," he said in a calmer voice. "There have been a few developments in terms of Lolita. I need to go back over to Theron's to strategize and figure out where we are going to go next."

My blood pressure spiked at his words. "Does she know where we are? Do we need to leave?"

"Not yet, but I fear we have been here too long. The night after your test we will be leaving."

"Where are we going to go?"

"I am still working on it. I want to go somewhere you will be safe where we can come up with a plan to end her, but it is easier said than done. There are too many factions. I do not know who she has recruited. I can trust no one."

"Do you think I am ready to face her?" I asked, standing up with him.

"We will find out tomorrow night. Do not worry about her now, worry about your test," he said, walking down the hall toward the tunnel.

I made myself some food while worrying about Lolita and my new problem with fangs. Vince said to meditate and figure out how I was going to get over my phobia of fangs. I went up to the dojo to meditate and found a disaster. My blood was all over the place and half the weapons had fallen to the floor. Vince did not let me do very much around the house. He was always cooking and cleaning, doing my laundry. I could do this for him.

I went back down stairs, got a bunch of cleaning

supplies, went back to the dojo, and started cleaning it up. It ended up being just as good as meditating. I spent my time thinking about how useless fangs were, and as I cleaned up my own blood, I realized fangs were the least of my concern when it came to fighting vampires. They were faster, quieter, and stronger. Their fangs were nothing compared to their other skills.

# CHAPTER 37

I did not dream of my mother that night. It was odd, she normally showed up before something big happened. Maybe it was a good sign; maybe I would pass the test without any problems. At the same time, she said I was going to have to battle a monster before long. I wondered if it would be part of the test or if the monster was Lolita. As much as I wanted to put off the fight it was inevitable. I wanted to be as strong as my body would let me be, but part of me just wanted to get it over with. I wanted to get on with my life.

When I went into the kitchen Vince had breakfast waiting for me. I took my plate into the dining room and found him working on his laptop at the table.

"Good morning," I said, setting my plate down and taking a seat.

"Good morning." Vince looked up from his laptop, cringed at me and went back to staring at the screen. "Did you sleep well?"

"I look that bad huh? But I did sleep well, no dreams." I took a bite of eggs. "Thank you for making me breakfast."

"You do not look bad, but it is my fault you have two black eyes. I am sorry."

"It wasn't your fault you had a deranged stalker, look at Miguel, we aren't that different."

He looked up at me with his eyebrows high. He let a little smile pass his lips. "I guess you are right. We really know to pick them."

"That we do Sensei, that we do." I giggled, I am not sure why but it felt good to laugh about how messed up our lives were. "Did Katrina fry?"

"Yes, she screamed like a little girl the whole time." Vince smiled to himself without looking up.

I cringed. "At least we have one less thing to worry about now."

"Yes, I should not have to worry about anyone taking pot shots at you for a while."

"What are you working on?" Since it was unlike him to work at the table.

"I am still trying to figure out where we should go next."

"Have you narrowed it down yet?"

"No," he looked down at his screen again, "it needs to be a secure place, where we will be able to monitor who comes and goes. I would prefer a place with a moderate climate, and any vampires in the area need to be on our side. That is where I am having problems. I know many vampires, but none like I know Theron. He is the reason why we came here; he is the only one I could trust with your life."

"Well I'm sure we will be able to figure something out." I was not ready to think about leaving. Crete had become a home to me. I loved it.

"What is your plan for today?" He looked up from his computer again.

"I was going to go for a short jog, but I think I'll do laps in the pool instead."

"Good idea. Less impact, but it will loosen up your muscles. I will stay close by just to make sure you are good. We are leaving here at sunset to go to the location of your test."

"It's not going to be here?" I was surprised, and maybe I would to get to see a bit of the island.

"It is on the property, but kitty-corner to where we are now. It is a surprise."

"Okay, I'm going to go change and get my laps done," I said, getting up and taking my plate back into the kitchen.

I swam laps for an hour then I let the sun dry my skin. I was worried. I did not want to fail everyone. I was afraid Lolita would show up at any moment, and try to take me or kill me. I tried to relax and take a nap, but my brain would not stop coming up with what ifs.

Vince called me in for a late lunch. He said I would be ready for tonight with a light snack before we left. We did not have much to say while I ate. He was still working on his computer and I was hungry after swimming and spending most of the day in the sun. It was nice to have a comfortable silence with him; there were not very many people I could have that with.

When I was done eating, I did the dishes then went into my room to clean it up and get organized. Vince said we would be leaving the island soon. He was trying to be causal about it, but I could feel his anxiety. There was something going on he did not want to tell me. I checked my go bag, most of the clothing in it no longer fit. I dumped everything out, put new clothes in it, made sure my computer, phone and travel wallet were stowed. If the shit hit the fan all I would have to do was grab my bag, and I would have something to start with if we had to leave in a hurry.

The sun began to set when I finished and I realized I needed to get ready to go. I dressed in my gi and soft-soled shoes, left my room and went into the den where I found Helen and Theron sitting on the couch.

I bowed to each of them, in kind, to acknowledge them, "Senseis." They returned my bows from their seats.

"Vince will be here in a moment; he is taking care of last minute details. Are you ready for this?" He put one leg over the other and wrapped his hands around his knee.

"Yes," I said, standing with my arms loose at my sides. "I don't really know what to expect so I'm trying to stay positive."

Helen smiled. "You're going to be fine." She turned her head when she heard Vince's bedroom door open.

Theron got to his feet and turned. I had not realized until then, they were all wearing gis. I bowed to Vince. "Am I going to have to fight all of you?" There was no way I could beat them.

"We will explain everything when we get there." Vince motioned toward the front door. "Let's get going."

He led us out to the golf cart where he sat in the driver's seat; Theron took the front passenger seat. I sat behind Vince and Helen behind Theron.

"How are you feeling after your run-in with Katrina?" Helen asked as I stared at the dark landscape.

"Paranoid I'm not ready. I should've been able to beat her easily, but I let fear get in the way, and I got my ass kicked. Thank god for Vince and Theron, otherwise I wouldn't be here."

"The only thing stopping you from completing this test is yourself," Helen said. It reminded me of something Yoda would say. I had to remember, fangs were the last thing I needed to worry about.

"Thanks, for the vote of confidence." I liked Helen

but she was an odd duck. She still did not believe in the prophecy but hated Lolita almost as much as I did. I wished she would tell me why.

We rode in silence for what felt like forever. I had run along the path we were on many times in the past months, but when I did not know where I was going, it was hard for me to judge where I was. Finally, I saw torches ahead of us. It looked like they were outside of an odd door in the side of the hill. I remembered running past it and always thought it was just a storm shelter or utility room.

Vince stopped the golf cart just outside of the ring of torches and got out. Theron and Helen followed close behind him. I slowly got out and looked around. There was not much to see beyond the torch light. The ground was covered in brown, water deprived grass, a few inches tall. The hillside with the door had nothing growing on it.

Vince, Helen, and Theron stood with their hands behind their backs in front the torches. I got out and stood outside of them somehow knowing a ceremony of some kind was about to take place.

"Katie, do you wish to complete your training this night?" Vince asked in a loud and stern voice.

"Yes, Sensei." I bowed to him.

"Very well, once you enter you will not be permitted to leave until you have completed the Minotaur's Labyrinth and the challenges awaiting you." Theron waved at the door behind him.

"Yes, Sensei." I bowed hoping the Minotaur was dead like the myth said.

"You will receive the necessary weapons as the need arises. There will be no blood shed tonight. You will be told when you have completed each challenge. This is full contact with light contact to the head," Helen said.

"Do you understand the rules?" Vince asked.

"Yes, Sensei."

"You may enter when you are ready," Theron said.

I walked through the door, turned, and bowed again. They bowed in return. Theron stepped forward. "Have you heard of Minotaur's Labyrinth?"

"Yes, Sensei, King Minos trapped the Minotaur in the labyrinth and Theseus killed him." I was trying to remember my mythology class. "I believe King Minos's daughter gave Theseus a spool of string, he unraveled it as he moved through the labyrinth allowing him to find his way back out after he killed the Minotaur."

"Your goal is to reach the center of the labyrinth. You will find your challenges along the way," Helen said.

"Do you have any questions?" Vince asked.

"No, Sensei." I felt my nerves kick up a notch. This was going to be like being left in the tunnels to find my way out, only this time I would have to fight someone on the other side.

*Breathe with me,* Vince thought noticing my anxiety. *You will be fine.*

I matched my breathing with his and nodded. "You may begin whenever you are ready," Theron said.

I approached the door and put the plan I came up with into action. I found each and every vampire mind in the labyrinth. I did not want to enter their minds yet; I just wanted to know where they were. I was going to use them to lead me through the maze.

Once I had them all including Vince, Theron and Helen I went through the door into the labyrinth. It was dark and smelled of mildew, but it did not smell rotten. The walls were a rough brick that looked like they had been installed into the dirt long ago. The floor was hard packed soil. There

322

were three directions I could take, left, right or center. There were two vampires pretty close and to the left. I took the left hallway, moving toward them. I walked quietly keeping track of the closest vampire, thinking he would be the first one I would come across.

I was wrong; he was on the other side of the wall I was walking along. My first attack came quickly and from behind. One second she was a long way behind me, and the next she was right behind me. Damn she was fast. I ducked just in time to miss a punch aimed at my head. I swept my leg out behind me, still crouching, and tripped her. Torches along the walls sprung to light, and I had to close my eyes for a second to allow them to adjust to the light after being in the dark for so long. As soon as I heard her hit the ground I turned in fighting stance and looked at my first opponent.

She was tall and thin, with long blond hair pulled back in a low ponytail. She was wearing a black gi and belt. I vaguely remembered seeing her at the party after the fight with Ben.

She jumped to her feet quicker than I could have. *Bring it on bitch*, she thought which was nice, it made it easy to create a door into her mind allowing me to anticipate her moves.

She launched into a dizzying array of punches and kicks. Without thinking, I blocked and countered when there was an opportunity, but I was not sure what I was doing. I saw a fist coming at me and blocked, then saw a foot coming at the side of my head, blocked. I countered with a punch to her face, it was probably harder than it should have been, but she was coming after me so quickly I could barely block her. I had no time to think about pulling my punches. Finally, I found my pace with her and I threw a roundhouse kick meant for her ribs.

Her arm swept out and grabbed my ankle after I made contact. She twisted my foot out and using her for leverage, I jumped and flipped in the same direction as she turned my ankle forcing her to let go. I landed with one knee on the ground; she saw an opportunity and charged me. As she moved to stomp on my shoulder, I tucked and rolled under her, grabbing her planted foot as I went. She tried to kick it loose but her other foot was still in the air, and she fell to the ground on her back. She was up quicker than she went down. I jumped to my feet, turned, and met her in midair sweeping my leg out and connecting with hers. She dropped to the ground; I straddled her, and cocked my arm to punch her in the face.

"You pass," she gasped going limp on the ground.

I smiled and offered her a hand to help her up. "Good fight." I pulled her up.

"You too, you're better than I thought." She took my outstretched hand and used it to help her stand up. She released my hand, stood at attention, and bowed to me. I straightened and bowed back to her. "Good luck." She turned walked toward the exit.

"Thanks." I took a second to catch my breath before continuing down the hall. It had been a quicker fight then I thought it would be, but I was not done yet. There were at least four more vampires waiting for me. I found the next vampire's mind and walked toward him.

I hoped the torches would guide me for the rest of the test but when I came to the first turn in the hall, I was in the dark again.

As I walked to my next opponent, I felt the other vampire following me. It was not Theron, Vince, or Helen, maybe they had another vampire watching the test to make sure I did not cheat, but I did not have time to worry about him. I rounded a corner and saw a faint light ahead.

The light brightened as the corridor opened up to a

good size room with torch light all around it. Instead of a dirt floor, this room was wall-to-wall mats. I had a feeling my jujitsu was going to come in handy with this fighter. Instead of sneaking up on me, he was kneeling in the middle of the room with his eyes closed. He was bald and looked to be of Asian descent. I approached him slowly while I tried to gain access to his mind. He was completely closed off.

I stopped when I was about three feet from him. I bowed and took my fighting stance. He opened his eyes and bowed his head at me. I stood waiting for him to get up or make a move of some kind. When he did neither I relaxed a touch and asked him. "Are you my next challenge?"

"Yes, I am." He smiled, his mind still closed to me.

"Would you like to begin?" I asked, wondering what he was playing at.

"We already have begun." He was still kneeling calm and unmolested.

"What do I need to do to accomplish test?" Maybe I would not have to physically fight him; maybe the test was to gain access to his closed mind.

"Same as the rest." A small smile formed on his lips. "You must beat me."

"Very well." I knelt before him and found my breathing. I wanted to close my eyes and concentrate, but I did not trust him. There was nothing to guarantee me that he would not rush me and take me out quicker than I could defend myself.

I stared into his eyes and found my way into the outer layer of his mind. He had the strongest shield I had ever felt. It was going to be hard to find my way in.

I matched my breathing to his and let my eyes bore into him. In my mind, I began to punch his wall over and over again, in time with my breathing. I hit it as hard as I could every time. After a few minutes, I was winded and sweat was pouring down his face, but I did not stop.

Finally, the wall cracked, it was a small crack but it was enough to give me the will to continue punching his wall. It was working, but I needed more power. Mentally, I pulled my leg around in a roundhouse kick and the wall shattered. I was in.

I felt his mind make its move a second before he launched his body at me. I was able to dodge and then to wrap my legs around his waist. I locked my ankles around each other and squeezed. I was thankful for all of the running I had been doing. I needed every ounce of strength my thigh muscles could give me to keep the pressure on.

He tried to roll out of the position, but only allowed me to roll with him and move my legs around his ribs. We struggled on the ground rolling around until he figured out he could not win and tapped out. I released him and we stood up then bowed to each other. "It was an honor to fight you," I said, backing away on unsteady legs and a tired mind.

"Good luck in your next fight." He bowed back to me then knelt on the mat.

"Thank you." I moved out of the room and down the next corridor.

When I was out of sight of the chamber, I stopped and leaned against the wall. My legs were shaking and my head was killing me. He put Vince to shame when it came to mental walls. I found my breath, stretched my legs out, zeroed in on the next vampire and started walking toward her.

I walked as quietly as I could. I was not trying to be sneaky, vampires had good hearing, but I was trying to listen for anyone who might sneak up behind me. As I came around a corner a lone torch was lit and on the ground under it was the katana, I trained with, lying on a piece of silk. I knelt, took it with both hands and bowed to it. I pulled the scabbard back and saw training plastic running along the edge of the sword. I would not have to worry about drawing blood.

I pushed the scabbard back over the blade and carefully stood up still holding it with two hands. I pushed the scabbard into my belt on the left side of my body and continued down the passage. There was a vampire not very far away, and I began to bang at her mental shield. I was not screwing around anymore.

I walked around the last corner, and I pulled my katana out just in time to block a blow aimed at my neck. I spun around the torch lit room to face my attacker. It was a tall woman with short bright pink hair wearing the traditional kendo garb.

She swung her blade out to me, I blocked, our swords now locked against each other as we both tried to gain ground. Getting dizzy from our around and around dance, I pushed off her and found my stance. My scabbard was in my left hand held low to block an attack, while my katana was in my right hand held high behind my right shoulder. She held her sword in the same manner.

I moved toward her and she took a step back. I did it again and she again took a step back. She was frightened. I could feel it in her mind. She liked to play defense. I was going to have to make this happen instead of reacting as I had been doing all night.

Moving in quickly I swiped up and down in a quick combination and she blocked every blow. Using my scabbard, I hit her in the midsection while I span away from her. She was surprised I used it as a weapon and not as a shield.

I chased her again using a different combination; I did not think about it I just did it. I could not find an opening to take her down though. She only seemed to want to use defensive moves, and she was good. Since she did not attack me, I could not find a way to get around her blocks. We moved apart again and circled each other; I found my breath and rummaged around in her mind.

*This is awesome,* she thought to herself. *Helen said she was good, but she isn't that good if I am still standing here. I don't understand why they are doing this for a human anyway. She will never be as good as a vampire. Damn my stomach hurts from that hit.*

Her stomach hurting gave me an idea. I began my next attack going for her arms and legs forcing her to twist around more in order to block my blows. It was working, she was tiring. After constantly attacking her for what felt like hours, I caught her blade with mine, I twirled the blades around until she was forced to let go. Her sword raced across the dirt floor and came to a stop yards away.

She gasped and swept her leg out trying to take me to the ground. I jumped it and came down with my sword at her throat.

"You pass," she said and slid to the floor. As I watched her fall, I saw blood on the front of her tunic, and the point of a knife sticking out of it.

I jumped back, looking around the dimly lit room and pulled my sword up. "Who's there?"

Ben walked out the archway where I had entered. "She was weak," he said, kicking the body of the vampire, and stopping in front of me. "You are going to come with me now."

I dove into his mind, he really wanted to kill me, but he would get more money if he brought me to her alive. I

328

jumped out of his mind; he wanted to take me to Lolita.

Keeping my eyes on him, I backed up while trying to find Vince with my mind. I needed help and soon. Ben laughed. "No one is going to come to help you, Katie," he hissed out my name like it was a dirty word. "You can save yourself a lot of pain right now by just coming with me. Lolita isn't going to hurt you. She is just going to make you her slave and turn you."

"Why won't they come?" Fear for my friends poured through me, but I could not let fear get in my way. I had to find my center. I found my breath, calmed down and lowered my heart rate. I beat him once I could beat him again.

"Because I made sure they are busy." He walked around in a circle. "Plus do you think they really care about you? You are just a piece of ass to them nothing more."

"Whatever you say Ben." I would not let his words get to me. I amped up my vamp sense and found their minds. They were alright for the moment but they felt off. It was time to get rid of Ben once and for all. I dropped my scabbard, wrapped both hands around my katana and held it behind my right shoulder.

"Your safety plastic is still on. Do think you will be able to bleed me before I bleed you?" he asked around hysterical laughter.

"Why don't we find out?" I asked, ready for this to be done.

He shifted back and forth on his feet, pulled out another knife; it was about eight inches long and an inch wide. He stood stock still for a moment, then ran toward me in a blur. I blocked his blow with my blade and watched out of the corner of my eye as part of the training plastic went flying across the room. He pushed against me trying to knock me back; I brought my foot up and kicked him in the groin.

He groaned; fell to the ground and his knife skittered across the floor. This was not a sparring match; this was life or death. I was going to fight dirty, I wanted to live and I was not going with him.

I went for the knife, but he grabbed my ankle and I fell hard to my knees. Scrambling, I kicked back at him and managed to hit him in the face, forcing him let go of me. I swiped the knife from the ground and got to my feet.

He was up and waiting for me with blood pouring from his nose, and he laughed again. When did he turn into a monster?

"Looks like I got first blood," I said, circling him. "Does she know I'm here?" I wanted to get as much information out of him as I could before I killed him. No one who wanted to kidnap me and take me to Lolita had a right to live.

"No, if she knew, she would be here herself to claim you, then I wouldn't get the reward." He ran his arm across his face in an effort to remove the blood. "I need the money. I want to ruin Theron and Vince, the bastards."

I felt him preparing to attack me again. It felt odd to have a sword in one hand and a knife in the other. I had not trained for this situation, but I could take him. I had before; I just needed to wait for an opening.

I moved closer to the vampire Ben stabbed, she should not be dead, the wound was not to her heart, and she still had her head. Maybe she would help me if I needed it. Ben saw me glance at her and laughed. "She's going to be out for hours, Katie. Why don't you just give up already? It's been a long night. You have already fought three of us, you must be tired. Let me take care of you."

"Are you trying to mind fuck me, Ben?" I laughed. "You didn't do your research before you came after me, did you?"

"Stop fighting it, I'll make all the pain go away." I felt him trying to control me again.

Tired of listening to him I charged, I faked with my katana and drove the knife into his stomach and pulled it up his torso, trying to gut him. I felt the gush of blood and other viscera I did not want to name splash the front of my gi before he slammed his fist into my face and I went flying backward. I hit the ground and I lost the grip on my weapons. Blood began to gush from my nose for the second day in a row.

I watched him fall to his knees while trying to keep innards inside his body. Blood loss must have made him weak; he did not stand back up but started to crawl toward me, using one hand to hold his guts in place while the other dragged him forward. He stopped on his way to pick up his knife and put it between his teeth. I looked at my katana; there was no way I was going to get there before he was on me with the knife.

Reading his mind, he no longer cared about the money. He wanted me to die; he wanted to suck me dry. I humiliated him once; he could not let it happen again. I could not take my eyes off his fangs. My breathing was too fast. I tried to calm down, but it was taking too long, I needed to be able to move if I was going to live.

Ben knelt on the ground in front of me while I tried to breathe; his fangs were out and covered in his own blood. He leaned over slowly, moving toward my throat. Blood and other things dripped on my skin as he moved in for the bite that would end my life.

I tried to push him away as I did the day before with Katrina. I forced myself to close my eyes and breathe. They were just fangs, fangs coming right at me for a killing bite but just fangs. What fangs could turn me into scared me, but there was so much I could do

331

before they reached me.

*Stop!* I shouted into his mind. He grabbed his ears and rocked backward. I kept screaming into his mind until I was able to crawl to my katana. My breathing was still ragged as I wrapped my hand around my sword, forced myself to my feet and walked over to where he was huddled on the ground. I stopped screaming and he put his hands on the ground to steady himself.

"How did you do that?" He lunged for my foot, but I got to his hand first with my katana. Even with the training plastic on the edge, I was able to sever his hand from his arm. He screamed in pain bowing his head before me. I raised the katana over my head and brought it down on his neck. The blade made it part way through before it stopped. Damn safety strip, I thought to myself. Ignoring his screams of agony, I tried to yank my sword out of his neck but it was stuck in between two vertebrae. I put one foot on his shoulder and yanked my blade free from his neck.

I took a few steps away from him and started peeling the safety strip off the blade like nothing interesting was going on. When I flicked the last bit from my fingers, I looked back at Ben. It was one of the most nauseating things I have ever seen. A vampire pulling himself across a dirt floor with his guts trailing behind him and his head bouncing around unnaturally. One hand was digging into the dirt trying to find pull its body forward while the stump on the other arm flailed around trying to find purchase. Grossed out I walked to Ben, and raised my katana above my head. "Go to Tartarus, Ben." I brought my sword down on his neck. This time the katana did its job and Ben's head separated from his body. Just to be on the safe side, I picked his head up by the hair and threw it to the other side of the room.

I hurried over to the female vampire who had been stabbed and put my hands on her face. I entered her mind and found her. She was in a healing sleep and was already growing hungry. Glad she would be alright I stood up and wondering where everyone was.

I stuck the knives in my belt, picked up Ben's head by its hair and continued down the corridor. I had no idea if I had any more tests to face but I did not care. I was done with this, the labyrinth, the fighting, the training, I needed a break.

I closed my eyes and reached out to find the other vampires in the labyrinth. I only found my Senseis; the rest of them must have left after our matches were over. *Vince, I need you Ben was here,* I thought but received no reply. *Theron, Helen, please guys I'm pretty sure Ben was not part of the test.* There was still no reply. I left the torch lit room and made my way toward the vampires who trained me. I held my katana in one hand and Ben's head dangled by his hair in the other. It took a long time. They must have been in the center of the labyrinth because I ran into multiple dead ends and had to turn around. I was tiring and ready to give up when I saw a light at the end of the corridor I was in. Finding energy from who knows where I jogged into the room.

Vince, Theron, and Helen were chained to a wall nearly fifteen feet off the ground. Their hands were secured above their heads, and their feet were attached lower on the wall, but still higher than I could reach. Their heads were lolled to the side, their eyes were closed and their faces were slack.

It did not look like they were hurt and, I did not see any signs of a fight. There were no bruises or blood. It looked like they had been drugged.

"Senseis." I yelled out loud and in their minds. They jerked but there was no other movement. I jumped into Vince's mind. It was sluggish and blissful.

Helen was the closest to me, but I could not reach the shackles on her feet. I followed the chain around the room with my eyes, there had to be a way to lower them down. I found a lever on the far side of the room. I pulled it and they all dropped to the ground so quickly I was worried they may have broken some bones.

I ran over to them and undid their shackles one by one. They did not seem to care I just dropped them to the ground from fifteen feet in the air.

"Vince?" I said out loud and in his head. "Wake up, I need your help."

*Katie? Where are you?* He sounded far away. *Where am I?*

*I think you, Theron and Helen were drugged by Ben. You have to wake up; we need to get out of here.*

*I need to sleep a little bit more then we will leave.*

*That's not going to work,* I thought slapping him hard across the face. *Snap out of it.* I laid my hands against his face. I looked into his mind and saw the drug coursing through his body. How was I going to get rid of it? Vince mentioned Mom had burned the drug out of him in Madrid.

"Mom, I could use a little help here," I said, willing her to hear me. I imagined my hands heating up until they burned a bright white. I took Vince's hand and he jerked at the heat, but as I watched, the drug evaporated from his blood. I moved my hands up one arm, then the other. When the tainted blood was gone, I moved on to his legs making sure none of the drug was left.

His screaming began as soon as I touched his torso. The last was his head, there seemed to be more drug tainted blood there than the other areas. By the time I finished he was whimpering in pain.

With the drugs gone, I pulled my hand back from his head. "Vince, I really need you to wake up now."

He blinked and jumped to his feet. "Why did you do that to me?"

"Because while you and your friends were getting high I was fighting for my life."

He blinked and took in the state of my gi. It was no longer stark white. It was more of a burnt umber with blood and gore covering it and my skin.

He looked at me for a moment as if he did not recognize me then finally focused. "Katie, are you okay?" He looked over to Theron and Helen who were still on the floor drugged up.

"It was Ben, I'm okay. I have a few bruises but that's all. Ben stabbed the vampire I was sparring with. I'm sorry I don't know her name. She has pink hair? I think she'll survive. He didn't stab her in the heart." I was rambling and sat down hard on the ground. "Should I do the same thing to Helen and Theron?"

Vince nodded his head and looked down at them. "But they may hate you for it. I have not experienced pain that intense since I was human, but I do not see another way. We need to move as soon as possible and those drugs were meant to last a week by the feel of it."

I went to Theron and began the same process. Theron took a swing at me when I was done, luckily, his aim was off and he missed. Vince held him back and made him stay calm while I did the same to Helen. When she came out of it, she spit in my face. I felt their pain; they had a right to be pissed.

"What happened to you guys?" I asked, wiping the spit off my face and moving back to sit cross-legged on the floor.

335

"It is hard to remember." Vince was shaking his head like he was still feeling a little cloudy. "We walked into this room and the lights went out. I felt something prick my neck and I was gone."

"That's all I remember too. It was quite a high, but not the place for it." Theron looked over to Helen to see if she remembered anything else.

"It was a well-planned attack. Sorry I spit on you, Katie."

"I felt your pain, no need to apologize. I'm just glad you didn't do anything else."

"What happened to you, Katie?" Theron asked, finally taking in my blood-covered appearance.

I explained everything: passing all of my tests only to have a real fight with Ben.

"Where's Ben?" Theron looked like he was ready to murder him.

"His head is over there." I pointed to the spot where I dropped it. "The rest of him is in the last chamber I sparred in." Theron tore off down the corridor. "This is all Lolita's fault; she took a hit out on me," I said, before passing out.

# CHAPTER 38

Miguel was in his own personal hell. He was living in a cave of all places; no one back in San Sebastian would believe it without seeing it. The king of the town, who lived for opulence, was living in a cave all because of a human. When he first arrived at the island he thought of it as an off the grid adventure. He did not think he would be there very long, he figured Vince would come to him for help tracking down Lolita. No one understood how her mind worked like he did.

The weeks had turned into months, with no word from anyone on the island. He was tired of spending night after night seeing the island where 'The One' was living and not be able to see her.

With nothing else to do, he spent his days roaming the caverns waiting for adventurous humans to explore the cave. When they arrived he would eat, and they would leave with no idea what had happened to them except that there was something not quite right about the cave.

At night, he would roam the shore making sure everything was alright on the island across the way. In his mind, it was part of his penance for what he did to Katie. In reality, he was wasting his time. Vince had her over there doing who knew what, with who knew who. All he wanted to do was tell her he was sorry and beg her for forgiveness.

If he was honest with himself, he was bored. He had nothing to do but wait. He could leave if he wanted, he was not trapped and his city was in the middle of rebuilding after the fire he set. They needed him, but 'The One" kept him where he was.

One night in late summer, a group of men showed up in RIB boats and camped on Miguel's favorite beach, the one with the best view of Theron's beach. He wanted to kill them for taking away his spot, but he thought better of it. They were up to something and he was going to find out what.

He snuck to the edge of the beach, hid in the shrubs, and tried to figure out what their mission was. Were they going after Theron, Katie or no one he knew? All they would say was the target and the payoff would be big enough to retire on. It sounded like something Lolita would do if she were desperate enough. He had to keep Katie safe, even if they were not after anyone at Theron's he needed to warn them. Katie had to be protected. Decision made, he left the camp and climbed to the top of the mountain dominating the island. He dialed Theron's number, the only one for anyone on the island he had. It went straight to voicemail; he was not surprised. Theron was not happy with Miguel so close to Katie. It did not matter how many times he told Theron he just wanted to apologize to her.

"Theron, this is Miguel. There is a group of mercenaries camped out on the beach directly across from you. I don't know who they are after, but they were talking about a target and a payday big enough to retire on. It's likely they know Katie is there and they are going to come in guns

338

blazing to get her. Please call me." He hit the end button on his phone and sat down to wait, hoping Theron would call him back before the sun came up.

# CHAPTER 39

I was still in the labyrinth, but it was different now. The stone walls looked newer; the edges had not yet worn down with time. I looked around, the torches were still lit but they smelled different than they had a few moments ago. I was alone; I looked down to see I was covered in wet, sticky blood.

The blood of my enemy, I had killed him. I smiled, brought my hand to my lips, and licked the still dripping blood. It tasted like blood, but better. It was still coppery and rich; maybe it tasted better because it was the blood of my enemy.

"You did well, daughter," I heard my mother say and I turned around to find her covered in blood. She lifted her hand to her mouth and licked it as I had. "I approve of your sacrifice. He was a worthless power-hungry idiot."

"Was he the monster you warned me about?" I asked, thinking of our last meeting.

"Yes, one of them." She looked at her arm as if she was considering licking it clean as a cat bathes itself after a kill. "You still have many monsters to slay before you will rule."

"Great. Well, at least I can fight now."

"Be well my daughter; do not give up on hope." I sank to the floor and closed my eyes. Everything went black.

I woke in my bed the next morning with all of the curtains closed. I looked around the dimly light room to find Vince sitting in a chair next to the bed. "Hi," I said, my voice rough with sleep. "Did I pass the final test?"

"That is all you have to say?" He was pissed. "You kill your first vampire, one of Theron's, tell us he was trying to kidnap you to take you to Lolita, all while covered in blood. Then you pass out and the first thing you want to know is if you passed some dumb ass test I made up a few hundred years ago?" He took a breath and laughed long and hard.

"Well, I know what happened before I passed out, and I can probably guess what happened after I passed out." I checked under the covers to see what I had on, nothing, of course.

"Really? Enlighten me, what do you think happened after you passed out."

"Let me see . . ." I tucked the sheet securely around my breasts, and sat up so I could rest my back against the headboard. "You freaked out for a few minutes until you knew I'd be okay. Theron came back into the chamber confirming Ben was dead, beheaded, and most of his entrails were hanging out. Hopefully he told you the vampire with the pink hair would be fine.

"Then you scooped me up and left the labyrinth talking about the hit on me. Then you brought me back here, cleaned me up because you like bathing unconscious chicks and put me in bed. Then you sat here and wrung your hands worrying about me until I woke up." I grinned even though it hurt from where Ben punched me. "How did I do?"

"You were right for the most part. The pink haired

vampire will be fine; her name is Susan, by the way. Helen actually cleaned you up and put you in bed, she would not let me. I did not sit here the whole time. We found out a few days ago about the hit. I did not tell you because I wanted you to finish your training. You passed, and I am proud of how you handled Ben."

"That was the only person, vampire I've ever killed, why am I feeling no remorse?" I asked, remembering licking my hand in my dream and cringing.

"It was a he die or you die situation. Would you change what happened, now that it is done?" Vince asked, folding his hands together and placing them on his lap.

"No," I said quickly. "The bastard wanted to take me to Lolita, and I knew what would happen if she got her hands on me."

"Then there is no reason for regret." He looked at his watch. "Are you ready to get up or would you like to sleep some more? It is early."

"Wait, I can't believe you didn't tell me about the hit." I had to back up. He knew about the hit? I thought I could trust him, now he was neglecting to tell me things that directly affected me.

"What would it have changed? You would have freaked out and probably failed the test." Vince's hands balled into fists.

"Didn't you just say the test was dumb?" I countered, looking around the room for my robe. I did not want to fight with Vince naked.

"Do you think it was dumb? If I had told you when I found out you would have run and never gained the confidence you needed to kill Ben."

He was right, it might have been dumb on some level, but it got me over my fang phobia. Hell, I had killed one who wanted to kill me. "No, it wasn't dumb, but still, what if I couldn't burn the drugs out of you? I would just be hanging out waiting for the drug to wear off while there could be vampires on their way here to take me while you were out. Will you please hand me my robe?"

Vince ran his fingers through his hair; he let out a frustrated breath before standing and going to the closet to get my robe. "I agree; I should have told you in case something happened to me." He threw me my robe and turned his back to me.

"Okay then." I got out of bed slowly, my whole body protesting the movement. I pulled the robe on and tied the sash. "I'll be right back." I went into the bathroom and closed the door. I used the toilet, brushed my teeth, and brushed my hair before opening the door to see Vince sitting in the chair waiting for me.

"I am sorry," he said, burying his face in his hands. "I am trying to do everything right and it feels like all I am doing is pushing you away."

I sat down on the bed in front of him. "You try to push me away but Vince, I'm still here. Not just for the training, I'm here because of you." I took his hands in mine and pulled them away from his face, forcing him to look at me.

"Your formal training is complete," he said, as if it was just dawning on him.

"Great, now what?" I asked, not understanding what he was saying.

"This." He took his hands from mine and rested them on either side of my face and pulled me in.

My eyes widened for a second, was he really going to kiss me? I quickly closed them and let out a sigh when his lips touched mine. Electricity surged through my body, my arms went around his back and I deepened the kiss. His mouth opened and his tongue prodded my lips requesting entrance. I opened them and met his tongue with my own. His hands moved from my face down my neck to my shoulders then snaked their way around my ribs.

Kissing Vince was like being kissed for the first time. There was so much love in his thoughts and emotions it brought tears to my eyes. I pulled away. "It was me?" My voice was rough from tightness in my throat.

"Was what you?" he asked, in a soothing voice, using his thumb to wipe away a tear that snuck out from my eye.

"The love, I felt from you in my dream? You feel that way for me?"

"Who else could ever compare to you?" He kissed my cheek then his mouth moved down my neck kissing as he went.

"Why did it take you so long to make a move?" A shiver went through me and I pushed him back. "No biting."

"I would never dream of biting you, but to answer your question." He paused to moved back in and continue his kisses. "There are rules to training. If we would have become involved during your training you would not have been as good as you are now." He moved down to the 'V' my robe created on my chest kissing every piece of bare skin he could reach. "It would have been a distraction for both of us."

"You? Distracted?" I asked, running my hands through his hair. It was just like I had dreamed it would be, thick and soft. "I don't believe it's possible."

He pulled away from my chest. "You will see, and soon, how distracting you can be. I hope you are ready for this." He moved to the other side of my neck and kissed his way back up finding my lips.

I let myself fall backward on the bed and brought him down on top of me. I would love to have him distracted in bed for a week at

345

least. His hand moved up my side to brush the side of my breast and I moaned.

*Did Vince forget to tell you that you have company?* Helen's thought broke through my mind.

I sat up straight pushing Vince off me. "What's wrong?" He looked deflated.

"I'm beginning to understand how easily you can become distracted. Why didn't you tell me Helen and Theron were here?" I blushed, knowing they heard everything.

"I forgot." Vince got up from the bed looking embarrassed. "Can we continue this later?"

"Bet your ass we will." I moved to him and gave him one last kiss before going to my closet to get dressed.

"I will leave you to get changed."

"Vince?" I asked as he turned to go, but stopped and turned back to me.

"Yes?"

"Thank you for sitting with me and not outside the door."

"You are welcome," he replied and a small smile played on his lips as he closed the door behind him.

When I entered the kitchen Vince was at the stove cooking me breakfast again. "You must like cooking, since you are always making me food." I sidled up next to him. "It smells great."

"I do enjoy cooking, get your coffee and go to the dining room. Theron and Helen are waiting for you in there." He gave my hip a tap with his hip.

"Yes, Sensei," I said, getting a coffee mug out of a cabinet and filling it up. I walked into the dining room and found Theron and Helen both working on their computers.

"Good morning," I said, taking my usual seat.

"Aren't you chipper?" Helen glanced up from her laptop for a moment.

"I guess so." I think I blushed from my toes to the ends of my hair. "Hum, sorry you had to hear that."

"It's about damn time," Theron said, laughing. "I was getting tired of the secret glances you were always giving each other when you thought no one was looking."

"I agree." Helen looked up smiling. "You two were like two teenagers with crushes on each other, but you were too shy to do anything about it."

"Can we please stop talking about this now?" I put my head down on the table and wrapped my arms around it. I did not think I had ever been more embarrassed.

"Fine, we can stop talking about the love birds and figure out what we are going to do now," Theron said looking up. "How much time do you need to pack?"

"I have an emergency bag already packed," I said, happy I double checked it the day before, "and to get everything else, less than an hour."

"Good, we're going to move you to the mansion until we figure out where we are going to go," Theron said as Vince walked in with a plate in his hands.

"I'll start packing as soon as I am done eating." I picked up my fork as soon as Vince put the plate down in front of me. "What did you find out about the hit?"

"If you are brought in alive it's enough money to buy a small country. If they bring you in dead it's enough to buy an island and live like a king," Theron said in a dry voice. "That's good motivation for most mercenaries and hitmen. Were you able to get any information out of Ben before you killed him?" He did not sound happy about me killing his third in command.

"I'm not sorry I killed him, but it was him or me and I'm always going to vote for me in that situation." I hated feeling like I needed to defend my actions. "I asked him if he had been in contact with Lolita, if she knew where I was. He said, no, if she knew I was here she would be here."

"He was always a greedy man," Theron said, turning back to his computer. "I'm not angry you killed him. I'm upset because one of my own betrayed me and mine."

"What are we going to do after we move up to the mansion?" I asked, looking at Vince who was sitting next to me. He put his hand on my thigh and gave it a reassuring squeeze. I almost jumped; it was going to take a while to get use to him touching me so intimately.

"We are going to have to draw Lolita out since we cannot find her or where she plans to be next." He did not sound very happy about the plan. "We are all tired of hiding. It is time for action now that your formal training is complete."

"I agree." Smiling at the thought of meeting Lolita in battle. Beating her would not be easy, and I might not make it out alive, but this woman was making my life hell. It was time for her to pay for what she did.

"We need to talk about one more thing about before we go any further," Helen said, closing her laptop screen, and waiting for everyone to pay attention to her. "You passed all of your tests last night. You have done your Senseis proud, and we would like to present you with this." She pulled a velvet box from under the table.

"Wow, thank you." I took the box in both hands as Helen presented it to me. "I appreciate all the time and effort you gave me." I opened the box and found a thick braided gold necklace with a quail pendant snaked through it. The quail was gold except for the tiny diamond where the eye was, its claws were out and its beak was open like it was in the middle of a fight. I took it out of the box and held it up to the light. "This is beautiful." I undid the clasp and put it around my neck. "Thank you so much."

"You earned it," Vince said, smiling and tapping my thigh with his hand.

"This means so much to me." I looked down at it resting against my chest. "I'll cherish it."

"And here is your katana back," Theron said, handing it to me with two hands. "While your formal training is done, remember, your training is never really complete. Every experience you have in the future will be an opportunity to learn and increase your skills."

"I do, thank you. I never want to go anywhere without it again." I took it with both hands and bowed.

"That's not a bad idea." Theron laughed. "We need to get back to my house. When you're done packing you can put everything in the golf cart outside and meet us up there?"

"Sure, Vince, are you all packed?" I looked over at him.

"Nearly." He did not look happy about moving up to the mansion. "I just have a few more things. I will leave my bags by the front door before I leave."

"Okay, I should be up there in an hour or two," I said, taking the last bite of food.

Theron and Helen got up to leave. "We'll see you in a little while then. There is no time for any hanky-panky hurry up." He said looking over to Helen and laughing while walking to the basement door.

"What an ass. I am going to go finish packing," Vince said, taking my plate from me and giving me a quick kiss.

"Hey, I was going to do that and the dishes before I went to pack." I got up, following him into the kitchen.

"I will handle this. I want you up at the mansion as soon as you can." He put the plate in the sink and turned the water on. "Go pack".

"Thanks, Vince." I headed to my room to pack everything up.

# CHAPTER 40

An hour later with everything packed in the golf cart I made one last pass through the house to make sure we had not forgotten anything. I took one last look at the beach and the awesome view we had from the terrace. I looked down the beach toward Alex's house wondering if he was still there, and if he would ever want to see me again. He had been a good friend to me when I needed one.

I looked out at the sea and smiled. I loved living by the water, I hoped wherever we went next would be near it. I squinted, there was something bobbing in the waves. Maybe it was just trash, but it looked like it was moving toward the shore. It was black and round, and there was more than one. It looked like there were six or seven of them. One popped out of water more than the rest, then went back down. Was it a seal? I had never seen one around before. It popped up again and I made out a snorkel and a mask. We were about to be under attack.

I pulled my phone out of my pocket to call Vince but there was no service. They jammed the cell tower? Who were these guys?

Panic raced through me. I needed to tell Vince what was going on. I slapped my palm against my forehead. I knew how to let them know what was going on. I started running toward the front door trying to find Theron, Vince, or Helen with my mind. I was still searching for them when I opened the front door, jumped in the golf cart and took off toward the mansion. Finally, I found Vince and went through the door in his mind.

*Vince, I think we are about to be attacked. I just saw at least six guys in combat gear coming toward the beach from the sea,* I thought to him putting the pedal to the metal.

*Where are you?* He thought to me.

*On my way to the mansion. I have everything with me.* I said navigating the curves as quickly as I could without the bags flying off.

*Hurry, leave the bags if you have to.* He must have been consulting with Theron and Helen.

Worried, I drove along the path leading to Theron's wondering if we were going to make it out of there. Going to the mansion seemed like a bad idea. I stopped outside the front door and something whistled through the air before an explosion rocked the ground beneath me. *Vince what's going on? I'm here.* I watched as the house that had become my home was engulfed in flames. They blew up my house, those bastards.

*Someone is going after the hit on you,* Vince thought it felt like he was fighting with someone. *Go to the garage, grab a car, and run, get off the island I'll catch up to you as quickly as I can. Be careful.*

I wanted to stay and fight but the sound of gunfire had me moving. *You be careful too,* I thought back to him while getting back into the golf cart and speeding toward the garage. I still could feel all vampires on the grounds, they were doing their jobs, protecting their land, their anger was getting in the way of their fighting abilities though.

I stopped outside the garage, grabbed my emergency

bag, and ran inside. I found the keys to the BMW and jumped in. I opened the garage door keeping my senses honed on my vampire family, I had lost a few on the drive over, but I could not let myself think about what that meant. I pulled out of the garage and drove for the gate as fast as I could manage the car. Behind me, there was another explosion. I turned my head to see the mansion engulfed in a fireball. Then they were gone, all the vampires who had been with me while on Crete were gone from my mind. There was a black hole in my mind where they had been and if I did not stop it from growing it would swallow me, and I would give up on everything I had been working for. I had to stop it. Stop thinking about everyone I had just lost. I would give myself time to grieve once I was safe.

I held back my tears as I drove through the gate and more explosions went off behind me. I was on my own and I needed a plan. Vince said to run, it was a start, but where would I go? I needed to get off the island as soon as possible. I pulled over under the cover of a tree and pulled my phone out. I dropped it as it began to ring, scaring the crap out of me.

I fumbled with it and managed to answer it before it went to voicemail. "Who is this?"

"Who do you think it is?" Alex asked with a tight low voice I had not heard from him before.

"It was you wasn't it? Why the fuck would you do this Alex? Theron helped you. You were my friend." I held back my tears and programmed the port in Heraklion into the GPS while I talked. I needed to get off the island. There would be too much security at the airport. A ferry was going to be my best bet.

"Do you know how much money is on your head? Enough for me and all my men to give this up for good. I couldn't pass it up, especially since I got to take out the man who stole you from me."

"No wonder you have never had a home. When you treat

people like this, you don't deserve one. Vince did not steal me from you. I was never yours. All I wanted was to be your friend, but not anymore."

"You can't run from me. I'll find you. There is no one left to help you. We killed them all, and they died screaming as the mansion exploded. What are you going to do now?"

"I will get you back for this Alex. I promise, you will pay for what you have done." My tone was colder than I had ever spoken. I wanted to kill him more than I wanted to kill Lolita.

"I'm right here, come and get me. We will see who the better fighter is once and for all." He was goading me. He was trying to play on my anger and grief. I could not let him win, but today was not the day to take him on.

"Fuck off, Alex," I said, hitting end on the phone. I did not want to believe they were dead. I called Vince's number, and it went straight to voice mail.

"I hope you're ok. I'm alive. I'm running. I don't know where I'm going, but it will be far away from here. I'm ditching this phone. You'll be able to find me when you can. Take care Vince. I . . . I love you." I hit the end button on my phone, got out of the car and put the phone under the rear tire, so I would run over it when I left.

I drove wiping the tears from my eyes as I went; I needed to hide from Alex now too. How was I going to do that? I needed a disguise. I passed a big box store, paused for a second then turned around and parked as close to the front door as I could. I ran inside trying to keep my head down. I went to the beauty section and picked up a few things. I paid for them, then went into the bathroom and got to work.

When I left the store forty-five minutes later, the

bruises under my eyes were covered with makeup and bug-eyed sunglasses, and my hair was now bottle blond covered with a wide brimmed hat. I did not think it would be enough but it was better than nothing. I got back on the road reminding myself not to cry or I would have to reapply my makeup. I did not let myself think of anything other than getting off the island free and not as Alex's prisoner.

I parked the car in the ferry parking lot and locked the keys inside. I bought a ticket on the next ferry leaving for Athens, and started pacing. If I sat down I would think about everything I had lost, and I could not do that yet. I was not safe yet.

Why was I was running away from the bad guys again? This was just like a few months ago at the airport, running for my life. Shit had to change. At least I was not the same frightened little girl in the airport now. I was tough, and I could fight, but I was still running away. I could not fight the bombs that likely destroyed the people I loved though. Alex and his buddies were prepared for more than hand-to-hand combat; they were going to take me or kill me. I had done the right thing, but it did not mean I was happy about it.

I closed my eyes remembering Vince's lips on mine; the black hole was starting to open up again in my mind and opened my eyes to stop the thought. I could not think about him yet.

The horn on the ferry blew indicating it was time to board. With all of my possessions I ran. At least I had more than I did last time I ran, I thought to myself as I found a seat on the top deck where I would be in the shade.

Where did I want to go? I could go anywhere in the world with the credit card Vince gave me, but wait. Who was going to pay that bill now? How long would the card work if the bill was not paid. I had no idea how Vince took care of that stuff. I would have to pull out as much cash as I could from my ATM card and save it for when the credit card stopped working. I would use the credit card for everything else I could until then. I was going to need a job. Work visas were not easy to obtain in most countries. I would have to figure something out.

I was getting sidetracked; I needed to move around for a while. The horn blew indicating we were finally leaving. I looked over at the dock and saw a few people waiting for their loved ones to leave the island. I scanned them quickly without recognizing anyone, but then again, I did not know very many humans.

I sniffled holding back the tears. I was not safe yet; I could not let myself fall apart yet. I had to hold on a little bit longer. When I was off this island and somewhere Alex could not find me, I would let myself fall apart. I would think of Vince and what had almost been.

The dock-lines had been cast and we were moving away from the dock when I saw a Land Rover come to a stretching halt next to the pier. I took a few steps back when I saw Alex jump out of the jeep and run toward the ferry. He was wearing a black wetsuit, but based on the tear on the arm, he did not walk away from the fight unharmed.

I wanted to yell at him, but I could not, he did not know I was on board. If he saw me, he could take an airplane and meet the ferry at the dock in Athens with no problem. I was stuck on the boat until we hit land again. All I could do was pray he did not know I was there.

As we pulled away from the dock, I relaxed a fraction. I was safe for the next seven hours. I wanted to take a deep breath, but I was afraid I would lose what little control I had on my emotions and the black hole would open and swallow me. I had to keep busy. I needed to come up with a plan to stay safe.

I wanted everyone to pay for what they had done to me. Miguel and Lolita for forcing me to run away from the life I had, and Alex for killing everyone who helped me create my new life. I could lure them to me, I did not know if I could beat them both, but I would not go down without a fight.

I went back to my seat, pulled my computer out, logged on to the boat's Wi-Fi and got to work. I brought up my social media website and stared at the log in. All I would have to do is log in and update my status with my current location. They would meet me at the dock and we could end this. I closed my eyes and remembered what Vince said about letting anger influence a fight.

I closed the website and found the research I had done months ago when I found out Miguel had found us. I could not draw them out until my anger had passed. I needed to get away from everything reminding me of Vince and try to find a new normal.

The Bahamas, it had everything I wanted. The island I was looking at was too small for a vampire population and it was not very touristy. I found a house to rent and sent an inquiry to the owners.

I set up my plane tickets; I had about forty-eight hours until I needed to be at the airport. I set up a hotel room near a shopping center so I could buy new clothes, again. Everything on the island was going to be expensive, and I did not want to spend money on something I could have gotten in Greece for a third of the price.

Now if I could just make sure Alex did not follow me. Did he even know what my traveling name was? I thought back no, I was always Katie to him and I never told him my last name. If I could get off the boat without him beating me there or spotting me I would be home free.

All I had left to do was wait until the ferry came into Athens and not think about everything I lost. I closed my eyes and found my breath. I would be safe and alone soon, then I could fall apart. I forced myself to meditate. I drifted in and out of sleep for the rest of the trip.

I changed my clothes before we pulled into the port in Athens in case Alex had seen me from the dock. I was glad to get off the ferry but I was terrified by who may be waiting for me in Athens. I had no choice but to get off the boat, the longer I lingered the better chance of Alex finding me.

I walked with purpose through people milling around the dock waiting for people to disembark until I found a group of American tourists. I fell into step with them, pretending I was with their group. Alex and his men would be looking for a woman traveling alone not in a group.

There were a bunch of people holding up signs and one holding a photograph. I watched as he looked at the photograph and then look around. As our group approached him, I pretended to look for something in my bag until we were past him. Then I casually looked over my shoulder and zeroed in on the photograph he held. It was of me, in my favorite shorts and tank top; I was smiling at the camera even though I was covered with sweat. Alex took it after our run the day before our fight.

Rage surged through me, I wanted to turn around and punch the man until he gave me the photo back. I took a breath and forced myself to walk to the taxi stand. I climbed into the first cab in the line and I told him where to take me while trying to forget about the photo the man had.

I looked out the window as we traveled through Athens to my hotel and smiled. It was not a happy smile; it was a smile of perseverance. I made it out alive once again. Vince, I let myself think of him, Theron, and Helen were likely dead. They lost their lives saving me. It was not fair.

Vince and I had really just begun and now he was gone. I was not sure I knew how to go on without him, but I would try. I needed time to regroup. Then, I would figure out how to take care of Lolita. I did not care about becoming queen, hell I did not really want to be. All I wanted was to end the life of the woman who kept taking away everything I loved.

Dear Reader,

Thank you for reading, <u>Trained by Vampires</u>. I hope you enjoyed this phase of Katie's journey into the world of vampires.

If you liked this story, please tell a friend and leave a review on **Amazon** or **Goodreads**.

Look for the next book in the series in early 2018.

Happy reading!

Joy.

Visit Joy's website at: **www.joymosby.com** or follow her on social media: **https://www.facebook.com/joymosby81625**
Twitter: **@joy_mosby**

# ACKNOWLEDGEMENTS

I could not have accomplished this book if it was not for the love and support of my husband, who is all too familiar with the phrase, 'All book all the time'. Thank you for putting up with me during this process.

Leah, thank you for taking time out of your day to edit my books. Your support and ideas help me more than you will ever know. Thank you for listening to me babble nonstop about it.

Amy, thank you for keeping me going, and writing the best notes in the margins. Your positive influence makes me not give up.

Mom, thank you for getting my book out there to your friends. You are my one-person marketing team. Thank you for your support.

Dad, the video you posted on Facebook is about the funniest thing I have ever seen you do. Thank you!

# ABOUT THE AUTHOR

I love to write about the Heroines Journey in the paranormal universe, because writing about everyday life is boring for me (hence I am horrible at blogging). I love taking a character who thinks she is weak and show her how strong she really is.

I live on forty acres in Northwest Colorado with two dogs (Ajax and Achilles), a few barn cats (Two-Face, Skeletor, and Silvester) and my amazing husband. I love not having any neighbors, being outside in the summer and inside in the winter. I have traveled to many places in the world, but I have many more places to visit before I am done.

When I am not staring at the monitor writing, I am staring at my Kindle reading, or spending time with my husband and animals.

Check out my website: Joymosby.com to find out about new releases and join my mailing list. I am not very good at updating it but bear with me I am working on it.